SATAN'S
FAN CLUB

MARK KIRKBRIDE

PRAISE FOR SATAN'S FAN CLUB

"Mark Kirkbride's debut novel, *Satan's Fan Club*, explores territories only an experienced novelist would dare attempt. Utilizing a unique pair of protagonists, twins Louise and James, we ride along with them on their trip to 'hell' in this well-executed cross-genre thrill-ride. Equal parts horror, thriller, and dark fantasy, *Satan's Fan Club* brags the writing skills and storytelling adeptness of a seasoned novelist, with the freshness of a strong new voice. I would urge any fan of cross-genre fiction to pick up a copy of this fine debut novel."

—Michael Laimo, author of *Deep in the Darkness* and *Dead Souls*

"Mark Kirkbride's voice is refreshing, original and poetic as he tells the tale about twins named James and Louise. *Satan's Fan Club* is tight, dark and wonderfully disturbing—and a treat for fans of dark fiction. A macabre celebration of imagination and some good old-fashioned horror."

—Sandy DeLuca, author of *Messages from the Dead* and *Hell's Door*

"A smart, well-written, and eerie foray into the realm of psychological terror, Kirkbride's novel will prove a joy for readers who wish to luxuriate in uniquely poetic language pitched starkly against a backdrop of unmitigated horror. Recommended!"

—Ronald Malfi, author of *Floating Staircase*

"*Satan's Fan Club* is a powerful psychological crime chiller where fear stalks every page. Yet Mark Kirkbride is fearless in his portrayal of obsession and treachery. The darkest parts of the human heart. Definitely a writer to watch."

—Sally Spedding, author of *Cold Remains* and *Malediction*

For Patricia

PROLOGUE

M usic thump-thump-thumped. Smoke eddied and churned, tinged first with yellow, then blue, then green. And James put a hand up to his brow as the man fixed him with red eyes. *This can't be happening. It just can't… Because it already has.*

"Don't you ever feel like throwing off society's shackles, its straitjacket, and running amok?" The man's dry tongue flicked around even dryer-looking lips as light speared grandiose darkness off to the side and his eyes flashed. "Of course you do. You're human. And aren't you tired of that voice in your head, the one that's been drilled into you by endless repetition, always telling you to do the right thing? Wouldn't you like to start thinking for yourself?" Another tongue-flick, as animal people stirred in the colored shadows. "Of course you would. That's why I'm offering you the chance to join a secret society where you can explore these ideas further, debate them at your leisure. I call it Satan's Fan Club. Wanna join?"

James nodded. *Have I fallen off the back of my own mind? I'm stuck in a kink of time.*

"I had a feeling you would. There's just one catch." The man smiled. "Yeah, I know. There's always a catch. You have to commit a crime, tailored to you. That's how you prove your worth. And this crime is the realization of your darkest urges. So you should enjoy it. You'll never have experienced freedom like it. That, I guarantee. But don't think it's going to be easy. Remember, I'm asking you to do the very worst that you can do. Still wanna join?"

Leaning back against the painted brickwork of the wall, James pressed his palms against it, stuck his fingertips into its rough grooves and ran them along it. *They say the mad live in a world of dreams, or nightmares. I just need to find the way out.*

But the gewgaw world distracted him again. A giant bar of light scanned the entire ceiling, as the man turned to leave.

James heard his own voice: "You haven't said what the entrance requirement is."

"You've got to kill them," the man shouted over his shoulder.

Now where in the purgatory of memory—back to the start, or on from here? And apart from pleading puffs of madness or *folie à deux*, what could he usefully say in his own defense?

The Devil told me to do it.

CHAPTER 1

The curtains breathe, in and out. The window behind them is open. And while darkness drapes the room, light, gaining ascendancy outside, imbues the gently swaying lengths of material with color.

The complicated twitter of birds comes from all around.

James knows that he has to act now, before anyone stirs.

He leans over and, reaching under the bed, pulls out the meat cleaver he's hidden there, gets out of bed and cuts and slashes his way through the cobwebby light over to the door.

Stepping out into a drift of darkness, he creaks along the corridor towards the half-light of the landing, which he crosses with the blade swishing at his side, before plunging back into darkness.

When he arrives outside the room he wants, he enters.

The interior is, like his room, different shades of grey. But in the quarter-light he can just make out the seal-like humps the sleeping man and woman form in the double bed.

Fingers tightening on the cleaver, he approaches the side of the mattress.

Although there's something trustingly childlike about the protracted regularity of the couple's breathing, there can be no reprieve. He lifts the blade high—as high as his arms will reach—then swings it down.

Instantly awake, the pair scream, but their cries have no effect on him. He repeats the action, over and over. And every stroke tears into one or the other of them.

Escape attempts are easily intercepted, as they give him something to aim at.

Chop. Chop. Chop.

He's really getting into it now. Depending on the angle of the blade, with each reverse arc of the cleaver a dark spray whips the headboard, the wall, the ceiling. The man's pajamas and the woman's nightdress are damp. The bed likewise. That is sopping. Because, visible through the slashed covers, the bone-deep wounds that crisscross the couple's bodies pump blood.

Some of the flaps of skin resulting from glancing blows are like gills, breathing.

Yet even as the cries die away, he carries on.

Chop.

Chop.

Chop.

———

An hour later—back in bed—the thunk of a car boot burst the iridescent bubble of sleep. One by one, strands of birdsong unpicked themselves from the silence. But this was at the outer limit of consciousness. James' mind was still furred with drowsiness. And he was trying to find a way back into his dream when a blade plunged past his inner vision, causing his eyes to start open.

It was then he remembered the blood-drenched bed.

Fully conscious—hyperconscious—now, he tore the bedclothes from his face. *Oh, God, I didn't... Did I?*

Had he dreamt it, or had he done it? He didn't know.

Yet his insides liquefied. Because he'd fantasized about doing it, and he'd been given to bouts of sleepwalking most of his seventeen years. What if sleep had removed his inhibitions? Was his night-self haunting his place of residence again, unleashing his unconscious on the world?

He looked at his hands, but it didn't help—if he was capable of killing in his sleep, he was more than capable of getting cleaned up afterwards. It wouldn't even be the first murder committed in such a state.

James needed to know, one way or the other. He swung his legs out of bed, slid his feet into his slippers and headed for the door. He made his way along the corridor, emerged from the sharp-angled shadows and flitted through spokes of light.

He then trampled more remnants of night until he came to the right room.

Bloody hell, what am I doing? I've lost it, either way.

Even as he paused in the hallway, his heart attempted to box its way out of his body. He shook in time to the blows. He wanted to turn back—only that would mean the hell of not knowing. So he pushed open the door and crept in.

The room was still. And though the day was bright, the light coming from behind and around the thick curtains didn't amount to much. He couldn't make out anything very clearly. Were the rumpled bedclothes blood-soaked or not? He couldn't tell. Two bodies lay side by side. Was sleep imitating death or death sleep? It was impossible to say.

The only breathing he could hear as he moved deeper into the room was his own.

Fuck, fuck, fuck...

Stopping at the top of the bed, he could make out a high forehead, thick black eyebrows, closed eyelids, cheeks and a nose. The chin was beard-fuzzy.

Was there a gash in the neck or not? He couldn't see.

He spotted a scar down the left temple. It ran around the eye socket and across the cheek. And while it looked to him in this light, or lack of it, like an old scar that had healed, there hadn't been a scar there before. It could only be a new one.

His breathing started running away with itself.

Please, God, no...

He was leaning in for a closer look when the shut eyes opened.

"Agh!" went the mouth.

"Christ." James sprang back.

A moment later he realized that this was good. He hadn't done it. The line down the side of the older man's face was probably just from a crease in the pillow case.

"James?" The deep voice was slow, sleep-thick. "What are you doing?"

James' cheeks radiated heat, because he could hardly tell the truth—*I was just checking I hadn't murdered you.* He had to think of something else.

"I thought I heard something," he replied, hurrying out of there before he got entangled in a net of questions.

Yet even when he was alone and back in his room, he still shook to every smack of his heart. Because although he'd merely dreamt the double murder, he couldn't ignore the implications.

It told him just how much he hated his parents.

6

CHAPTER 2

In her birch-veneer kitchen, Valerie Glavier smoothed her dark green apron and adjusted the matching Alice band in her brown shoulder-length hair. Her eyes ran over the black ceramic tiles of the floor, searching for specks of dust in the early evening light.

She jumped and put a hand to her bucking heart. "Dear, oh dear..."

Her husband Alistair smiled. "All right if I come in?"

He ducked through the archway into the vaguely steamy kitchen.

"You all right, love?" he asked.

She could feel her blood-rouged cheeks burning. "I'm just a little edgy, that's all."

Alistair deposited his slim, black leather briefcase on the kitchen table and placed a hand on her shoulder. "Why? What's up?"

"They've found another body. This side of London."

"I know. I heard about it on the car radio." He put his arm around her, squeezed her to him. "It's not here, though. It's Fulham. And last time it was Paddington, wasn't it? Which is even further away."

"It's near enough."

"Well, as the crow flies, maybe, but not given how many people there are in the area in between." Then, after a pause, "You've got to stop worrying so much about everything."

The "everything" caused her cheeks to burn again. "I'm not worried for myself. I'm worried for the girls."

She was conscious of Alistair following her with his eyes as she stepped away.

The pot gurgled, the lid got restless and a cluster of bubbles peeped out.

His beard brushed her shoulder as he stepped forward to raise and lower one side of the lid as if it were hinged on the other side. A foul-smelling steam genie mushroomed out and up to the ceiling—gave it a lick, before fading.

"Mmm, boiled face cloths. My favorite."

This was a glimpse of the shy, tender playfulness that had won her heart twenty-three years before. She'd fallen for that and his inner vibrancy and kaleidoscopic mind.

They'd met at a gathering of the local evangelical church one freezing, December evening. He'd walked her home on streets paved with silver. They'd been transfigured by frost glistening under the alchemy of moonlight.

Roused by laughter from the back yard, Valerie turned around to switch the gas off and for a moment got a Bunsen burner-like whiff of it. The face cloths were new. She'd only been boiling them so the color wouldn't run in the wash. She removed the lid and left it off to allow them to cool.

"I wasn't sure when you'd be back," she said, once she was facing Alistair again.

"I had to check on the shelter."

He'd set up a hostel for the homeless, recovering drug addicts, alcoholics; anyone in need of getting off the streets or out of temptation's way.

"Honestly, you'll wear yourself out."

She turned and watched—as if from far away and zooming in to bridge the chasm—as a teenager with straight brown hair and an oval face with large brooding brown eyes and a compact mouth came through from the hallway. He had on a tennis T-shirt, jeans, and sneakers, and carried a racket under his right arm. His eyes turned their dark light on them as he slogged across the kitchen floor. Then he passed out of the back door.

A few seconds later it happened all over again. The same elliptical face looked up with the same chocolaty eyes, yet belonged to a girl in a pastel cotton dress. With a swing of her tennis racket and a flick of her long hair, she likewise exited out of the back door.

It wasn't long before the *chock, chock* of a tennis ball started up in the yard.

"Have you seen the scissors?" Alistair was going through the drawers. "I need to get in that parcel and I can't find them."

Valerie pointed to the second drawer down. "In there."

Hearing *click-click* on the tiled floor, she spun around.

A young woman in a tight black top, black liquid-looking leggings and long black boots stood in the doorway.

"Oh, hello, Riika," said Valerie.

Riika had a face of almost glacial purity. She had a sculptured nose, razor-sharp cheek bones, long blonde hair and eyes as pale as an Arctic husky's.

"I go out," she announced, in a Finnish accent.

Riika was their *au pair*, primarily acting as nanny to Harriet. She had been working for them for two months now and performed her duties diligently, if without distinction. Then in her own time she became this other person, a frequenter of pubs, a creature of the clubs, rarely getting in before one in the morning.

"You must come and go as you please," Valerie instructed the younger woman. "This is your house now, as much as ours."

"Thank you, Mrs. Glavier. I go out this way and say goodbye to Harriet."

The *au pair* flounced out of the back door, sending a waft of ylang-ylang their way.

"Night, Riika. And be careful."

Valerie turned to her husband. The upward cant of his chin made him look as though he were peering from under a peaked cap.

"What's the matter?" she said.

"I think you know."

"She's good with Harriet. She really is." Valerie paused for a moment as a mechanical lawn mower clattered, back and forth, outside. "Only you can't see it."

"Whatever do you mean?"

"It's not so much what she does. You just don't like her." Valerie had noticed it right from the start. He'd left all dealings with the new *au pair* to her. She wasn't sure if he'd ever spoken to Riika.

"Don't be ridiculous. I don't even know the girl."

"Well, maybe you should get to know her, before you start judging her."

"Don't you think I'd like to know who this person is we've let into our house, into our lives? Of course I would. I mean, for goodness' sake, she looks after Harriet. The point is, it's not possible. She just glides across the surface of things."

"We never got to know Gundula properly, remember? And you never had a problem with her."

"There was nothing wrong with Gundula. She was just a bit quiet, that's all. While this girl…" Alistair stared out through the doorway, with his head tilted to one side. "I wouldn't put anything past her." He turned back. "Didn't you see what she was wearing?"

"What she does in her own time is nothing to do with us."

"It is while she calls this home. Because this is a Christian household, and she sets a bad example for the children."

"What are you talking about? She only dresses like that to go out."

"She is an unnecessary distraction."

"Who on earth for?"

"James."

"Oh, rubbish. James is a sensible boy."

"Maybe, but she's got sloppy morals. Mark my words."

Valerie tutted her disapproval.

For her, Christianity meant being tolerant towards everyone, even those who failed to live up to her ideals. Her husband, on the other hand, insisted that being a Christian meant making sure that the Lord's Commandments were upheld. So no wonder they could never agree.

"Let's just let the matter drop, shall we?" she said.

"All right. Please just remember that you wanted her here, not me."

"I don't think you're likely to let me forget."

With something like a vacuum forming in her head it was an effort to focus. So she went back to her boiled face cloths.

When Alistair left the room, she gazed out through the hazy folds of the net curtain. She was concerned about Riika's dress sense too.

Though, in her case, it was for the *au pair's* sake. Because of what had happened, not that far away.

11

———————————

"I'm brilliant at spinning on my points," Harriet told Riika, as they stood to one side of the lawn in the long back yard with high hedges, tall trees and a brick wall at the bottom. "Mrs. Prentice says my pirouettes are the best in the class."

The *au pair* nodded and smiled.

Mirrors set into the rear of The End House dazzled Harriet. The eye of the sinking sun stared back from each one. Yet it wasn't just the windows the sun transformed. Its low, buttery rays gave the stone a painted appearance. Only the mini castle wall along the top of the building harbored darkness.

Resettling her glasses on her nose, Harriet looked up at Riika. She was short for eight and the *au pair* was tall for nineteen.

Riika followed James and Louise's tennis game, so she did as well. And despite their difference in height, their heads turned together left... right... left... right...

The twins *thwocked* a bright yellow ball back and forth over the washing line.

They reached; they ran.

Louise smiled.

They grunted; they groaned.

James scowled.

They sliced and tapped.

Louise laughed.

They lobbed and smashed.

James super-scowled.

And still the rally went on.

Coming up the lawn, pushing the mower, was Harriet's friend Verge. The gardener was ten times her age, with posture so bad that his head didn't sit on top of his shoulders; it stuck out of his chest.

Although he took one step back for every two steps forward, he made steady progress. By the time he came to the edge of the makeshift tennis court, the hay-feverish scent of cut grass tickled her nostrils.

"James, Louise," she called. The ball jostled a bush. "You're going to have to stop for a bit."

While Verge went off to empty the grass collection box, her brother and sister raised the washing line, retrieved the ball and joined her and Riika on the mown side of the lawn.

In the border behind them, a bee thrummed in a flower pouch.

In the trees above them, magpies chattered like harsh football rattles, while smaller birds chirped and cheeped and peeped and tweeted. One of the latter would occasionally pass low overhead with a soft flap of wings like the shake of a salt-cellar.

Ponytail tapping first one side of her back, then the other, Harriet skipped over to a small tree frothy with white blossom. She gave the skinny trunk a knock and the branches shuddered—letting loose a shower of petals like silken confetti.

This time she called, "James, Riika."

Her brother and the *au pair* came over and she got them to face outwards and link arms. Then she sneaked around the back, got hold of the trunk and pushed, pulled, pushed, pulled. Pale petals twirled and fell. She'd just started humming *Here Comes the Bride* when James broke free, threw down his racket and strode off.

"Hey, where's he going?" she said.

Birdsong unravels all around her and she is left staring at a tense droplet, hanging from a leaf.

It has dribbled along the mid-rib to the point, bending its temporary platform. As soon as it falls, the leaf springs back into place. And in this fashion many tiny drops drip from the leaves of the tall trees—slip from leaf to leaf, to the ground.

A splash in the face had woken her.

For a while she watches droplets falling, horizontally.

Everything is on its side, because she is. But she can see through the trunks of the trees that, apart from black fingers of cloud with red tips, the sky has cleared again. To the right— above her, in this orientation—the last shreds of cloud blaze pink and yellow and gold because of the presence, low down, of the setting sun.

Voices float in the distance.

"Help," she wants to cry, "Over here," yet all she can produce are gurgles of blood.

She's lying in the small wood near the center of the park that's just a few streets away from home. She's cold, because it's wet. Inside a wood is largely dry during a downpour, but it continues raining long after the real rain has stopped. The soil squidges to mud between her fingers, releasing unpleasant boggy odors.

She had taken her run much later than usual because of a phone call from Sean, her boyfriend, and had got caught in a shower half-way round. When, with something like a hiss of release, the rain had gone up a gear, she'd taken shelter in the wood. Despite, or perhaps because of, the slap of rain against the leaves, all had seemed peaceful.

Until she'd heard what she'd taken to be wildlife scuffling in the undergrowth. Before she had a chance to turn around, she'd found herself being hauled, backwards, deeper into the wood. Her arms had been pinned by stronger arms than hers, a hand had covered her mouth to gag her and stale aftershave had enveloped her. Heart thrashing, she'd struggled and fought back—kicked with her sneakers, but her attacker had swung her around and slammed her into a tree.

A woody knock makes her jump. *He's come back.* Her heart thuds and she has to strain to hear over it. Yet all that follows is the groan of a branch. Just as the air had been clarified by the rain, so this scare brings everything into sharper focus.

He must have assumed she was dead to leave in the first place. It wouldn't have taken much to finish her off if he'd known she wasn't. As numbness wears off and flashes of pain give way to something more palpable, she knows she needs to get help, urgently.

She doesn't even have her watch, let alone a phone. Keys are the most she's willing to carry on a run. With her tracksuit bottoms still around her ankles, and pushing back sticky black earth with her elbows, she propels herself towards the dwindling light.

She shivers. *How can it be getting dark so quickly?*

Ahead, green has drained from the park. The delicate filigree of the trees is like black lace.

The sun has gone down, already. The stratified sky is mauve, orange, yellow and a lucent blue. She consoles herself with the thought that even if it's nighttime on the Earth, it's still daytime in the sky.

Until she sees a star and, peering around, discovers that half the firmament has turned black. Stars are coming out above and behind her, winking through the trees.

Darkness is closing the lid on the day. And still she drags herself towards the receding light.

The rain's applause had long since petered out. Night had rotated into place. And James no sooner leaned back against the wall of his room than he slid down it.

When his bottom hit the floor, he put his arms around his knees, shuffled his feet to the side and pressed his temple hard against the wall.

It proved a welcome distraction from putrid desires that, once again, he'd struggled, and failed, to keep quarantined inside him.

My nights are spilling out into my days.

He was getting to his feet to look for something more effective to take his mind off today's lapse when he thought of reading. That always relaxed him.

All he could find in his room, though, were *Lord of the Flies, 1980, Border Crossing, Hannibal Rising, 1983, Crash, American Psycho* and a couple of Chuck Palahniuks—all of which he'd read. So he headed downstairs to hunt for his copy of *Q Magazine*, and found it in the lounge.

He breathed in a clean, heady smell—furniture polish, probably. As the main room was nice and quiet, with all the lights on in the wider lower part and nobody about, he sat down in one of the armchairs to read his magazine. It was like degaussing his brain.

He was mid-way through a review of a book on a songwriting duo he'd liked, before they'd split up, when the door opened and he looked up to see Louise, followed by Riika.

He looked down again, straight away. He was still aware of the girls, but at the edges of his vision. One pair of legs made straight for the sofa while the other crossed right in front of him.

The latter, a milk-white pair, lingered a moment on the Persian rug as she took something down from the mantelpiece. He didn't know what because his sight was only detailed as high as the bump of vein at the back of her knee.

As her perfume reached his nostrils, he tried to appear absorbed in his reading matter. He discovered that customary, silent breathing was beyond him.

When the one rejoined the other, both girls fell back, *whump… whump*, onto the sofa.

Thankfully, as a couple of glances their way revealed, neither of them paid any attention to him.

Riika sat back with legs crossed. Top leg gently kicking. She opened a magazine and they studied it together. They pointed and giggled, giggled and pointed. The piece they pored over was called *The Opposite Species—Love Them or Loathe Them?* So Riika let slip. When they finished that one, they found another. Riika read the title aloud: *10 Ways to Tell What Men Are Thinking*.

James' heart thumped as hard as if he were coming to the end of a 10K run. He even had a stitch. What if the tips really did enable them to see right inside the male mind? His was full of degenerate images.

Knowing that such intimate access was impossible didn't help much. Trying to breathe quietly—through his nose—ended up sounding more like snorting, and he was rocked by the detonations of his heart.

Although he knew that leaving would, temporarily, draw attention to himself, he couldn't stand it any longer. He jumped up and dashed towards the door.

He shouldn't have stayed in the lounge in the first place, because it was ridiculous trying to behave like a normal human being when he manifestly wasn't.

Other teenagers only had their grades to worry about.

He paused out in the hallway.

Why can't I be like them, and have natural, healthy inclinations? What kind of monster am I?

Sooner or later, something in him was bound to give under the strain.

He just wasn't sure what.

When he awoke the following morning, he put his legs out of bed and felt for his slippers.

They weren't there. Yet that was where he usually left them.

Rubbing his eyes, he looked around. His slippers were halfway across the room. His dressing gown lay near them instead of hanging from the hook on the door.

Putting these small deviations from habitual practice down to his present abstracted state, he gathered his school uniform together for his turn in the bathroom.

Fifteen minutes later, he swung around the post at the foot of the stairs, which had a pineapple-sized carving of an acorn on top, trudged half way up the cream and white hallway and turned left into the dining room.

"…known anything like this." This was his mother's voice, strangely modulated, as though starting to fray. "I just heard about it on the radio. It happened last night, yet they only found her body this morning."

Mum sat with her back to the door; Louise likewise. Dad was at right angles to them.

James made his way around the long oak table, clothless and cluttered with racks of toast, the butter dish, jars of honey, marmalade and jam. He sat down behind a convenient wall of cereal packets.

"It happened in Amberly Park and they say she crawled half way across it in the dark," Mum went on. "It was too late when they found her, of course. Though they say it's amazing she managed to cover any distance at all given her injuries. Imagine the—"

Dad pressed a finger to his lips.

James followed his eyes.

Wearing her school uniform and the round spectacles with gold frames that were a permanent fixture, Harriet entered.

As soon as she'd sat down at the table, the eight-year-old shook herself out some Shreddies and splashed milk over them.

Taking a long time to butter a slice of toast, James turned back to Mum.

From the movements of her eyes, darting around, glancing at things that weren't there, he could tell that her mind was brimming over with all the information she'd intended to relate. Her gaze latched on to him.

"You've been sleepwalking. Wasn't he, Louise?"

His twin looked up from her cereal. She obviously resented being roused from her own reflections to be put on the spot like this because they had to wait half a minute or more for her mumbled, "Yes."

"And you were talking to yourself," Mum continued. "I couldn't hear what about, but it was ages before you went back to bed. And even then you were still muttering something."

Remembering his dressing gown and slippers, James groaned. He cursed himself for failing to realize that, given he'd always been prone to night-walking, this was the form the breakdown would take.

"Can I watch next time?" asked his younger sister.

"No, you can't," said Dad, picking his teacup up off its saucer. "Eat your breakfast."

That normally docile rear appendage to Harriet's head, her ponytail, came alive briefly as her head jerked around. "Why not?"

China clicked against china as Dad replaced his teacup. "Because you can't."

Harriet got down from her chair and stamped her foot. "Why?"

"Because I don't want some sleepwalking conga every night, that's why."

Turning and marching out of the room, Harriet bumped into Riika in the doorway. The *au pair* almost dropped the jug of orange juice she was carrying.

James excused himself.

Valerie put her tea down, listened to Harriet clomp up the stairs—funny how children's footsteps were heavier than adults—and watched James make his way around the table and back the other way over to the door.

His shuffling steps were like a re-enactment of the very phenomenon they'd been discussing.

Memories of the zombie teenager of the night before became overlaid with older memories; of a child in red slippers and Superman pajamas lost in sleep's maze in their old apartment. She'd had to follow him around to help avert accidents and to try to guide him gently back to bed.

He'd seemed happy enough during the day, though, so she hadn't been that worried. Especially once her husband had informed her that sleepwalking wasn't uncommon among children; that ten per cent are prone to it.

This time was different. James wasn't a child anymore. She could no longer take comfort in statistics. Also, he didn't seem at all happy. And adolescence alone couldn't account for such sullenness and torpidity.

She'd have suspected drugs, only there was no evidence of drugs—apart from her own, all of which were legal—in the entire house.

She knew. She'd rummaged.

So while it was obvious something troubled him, she had no idea what. All she could do was hope that one of these nights he'd act out his malaise in his sleepwalking, or mumble it in his sleep-speech.

———————

Getting his folders and textbooks together in his room, and picking up his pens and memory stick, James ran through a mental checklist of ways to outwit his sleep-self.

Set his alarm clock to wake him every hour…

Lock his door…

Remove the belt cord from his dressing gown and tie one end around his ankle and the other to a caster at the foot of his bed…

But any trap he knew how to set, his unconscious would know how to wriggle out of. And if it was so powerful that it could commandeer his body, get him out of bed and send him roving all over the house without him even knowing about it, it could give him away. So no wonder his stomach bubbled and glugged. The feelings he managed to suppress most of the time during the day could easily burst forth at night, and he wouldn't even know what he'd blabbed or done until the consequences were already cataclysmic.

CHAPTER 3

"There will be terrible times in the last days. People will be lovers of themselves, lovers of money. They'll be boastful, proud, abusive, disobedient to their parents, ungrateful, unholy, without love..."

James fidgeted in his fifth row seat, with Louise on one side, his mother on the other, and Harriet on the far side of her. They were in a hall half a mile down the road from The End House, referred to, by the attendees, as "The White Chapel." One wall consisted entirely of glass. Otherwise, the building was white inside and out, with wide, white pillars.

The preacher, all flashing eyes and wind-milling arms, electrified the congregation. But James was less impressed. He was familiar with all the tricks. His parents were members of a charismatic Christian sect—or "cult" as he referred to it—called the Doomsday Church, and his father was the man in the pulpit.

"What are the signs to look out for?" asked Dad. "How will we know when we are about to be saved?"

I didn't ask to be born again.

"Well, when moral anarchy is loosed upon the world, that's when you'll know that you're walking in the last days. And do you see it? Do you see the signs?"

Hell, I didn't ask to be born the first time.

"Yes, of course you do. Because they're everywhere. It's happening already, I tell you. The moral fabric's being torn asunder."

The veil of hypocrisy, you mean.

"Children are bringing up children."

Good for them.

"Alcohol consumption's at record levels, even—no—especially in the young. I mean, Saturday night in any town or city center is like the land of the drunk. Drugs are freely available. And no one's even bothered anymore."

Yeah, ban fun, why don't you?

"Because if we encourage rudeness and ruthlessness on Darwinian game shows at one end of the spectrum, we shouldn't be surprised if criminality gains a certain cachet at the other. And the police have a hard enough job without those who break the law being virtually feted."

James yawned as the voice droned on.

"That's why I applaud the Metropolitan Police's new initiative: Operation Serpent."

James slid down his pew.

"Yes, it mainly removes the visible element, the lackeys and the gofers, but as long as crime is normalized on our street corners, we'll continue to suffer the consequences. Take this serial killer."

James sat up.

"He's as much a product of the society we live in as a curse upon it, because society's almost like a training ground for serial killers. Which I suppose, in a way, implicates us all."

Yeah, it's not my fault I turned out the way I have.

"Yet 'the cowardly, the unbelieving, the vile, the murderers, the sexually immoral, those who practice magic arts, the idolaters and all liars—they will be consigned to the fiery lake of burning sulfur.'"

James shook his head.

He had been giving religious belief a lot of thought lately and had decided that if God existed, He'd never allow all the badness there was in the world—including, of course, his. This realization had crystallized into a raging conviction: *God doesn't exist.*

While he hadn't mentioned this to Dad—because, all being well, he'd be at university before the year was out—he was becoming increasingly tempted.

He might even do it today.

Doomsdayers eagerly awaited the Day of Judgment, because when the reveille came on that glorious morning, they would be called by the Lord to join Him. But only if they'd spurned vice in all their earthly transactions and followed the precepts of the Church—which provided the only guaranteed path to salvation.

Apparently, everyone was in debt because of the actions of one man and woman, and those outside the Church weren't even managing to pay off the interest. The human race was like a giant pyramid scheme, built to collapse. Apples didn't enter into it. Adam and Eve's real transgression was giving in to lust. Original sin was sex.

Or, to put it another way, sex was original sin.

Yet life was predicated on sex. So, by such logic, life itself was noxious. Life was a sexually transmitted disease.

James sighed.

He had always found Sunday mornings irksome. This one he detested. He couldn't just leave, though. He was surrounded. So he compromised. He'd stay, but never again would he put himself in a position where he had to passively imbibe crackpot homilies. This would be his last.

Trying to blot out preacher and parishioners alike, he looked around at the sharp shafts of sunlight slanting in through the window, illuminating millions of dust motes floating in the high ceiling-space.

Strange to think that these micro-blizzards were always present, just invisible most of the time. He watched the dust particles swirl, in slow motion, in and out of the cheerful yellowy beams. Stared at them until the death-shadow of a passing plane made him flinch. It was almost as if God had blinked.

His heart knocked; Dad shouted in the jet's sound-wake.

Then James remembered that he'd smuggled in an MP3 player in the pocket of his jacket. And quickly, checking that no one was watching, he inserted the earphones and switched it on.

He selected the thunking monolithic *Religion II* by Public Image Limited, which he'd only recently discovered. The scorching blasphemy of its sentiments made the hairs stand up on the back of his neck. When God's cheerleaders started warbling in the background, he put the volume up. But he was late turning it down when the hymn finished, and several members of the congregation peered around at him.

He only switched it off, though, when he saw the big Bible being closed—which signified "end of sermon."

Everyone immediately rushed to congratulate his father or hail friends in the congregation.

Then, at last, it was time to leave. Thinking that the worst was over, James slumped in his seat when he saw that they were being followed—by the police. To be exact, the black Bentley behind them contained an off-duty Detective Chief

Superintendent and his wife. They were recent converts to the Doomsday Church. His parents had obviously invited the couple over for lunch. They led the way in their silver Mercedes-Benz.

Twelve minutes later, both vehicles pulled up outside The End House, the only property to be perpendicularly situated on Linden Close. It was unusually secluded even for this affluent enclave of suburbia, with just the one way onto the site.

James followed the others through the wrought iron garden gate. The huge, oak front door at the opposite end of the concrete pathway hung open. Ignoring sweet scents from the flower garden, he strode towards it—picking up speed. The façade expanded to fill his field of vision. The path ran out. The doorway loomed.

After drinks in the lounge, everyone took their seat at the dining room table. Everyone except for Riika, who had the day off, and Harriet, who—over by the window—waved to Verge.

The gardener was planting bulbs in the border that ran down the side of the property.

"Harriet," called Dad. "Come and sit down."

Mum carved and served the joint of lamb and everyone helped themselves to roast potatoes, mashed carrots and swede, home-made mint sauce and gravy spiked with Merlot.

Dad clasped his hands in prayer.

Everyone bowed their heads and shut their eyes.

Or nearly everyone.

James couldn't take his eyes off his father's face. Where had that big toothpasty smile come from? Dad delivered the grace deadpan, then there it was again.

"Please, tuck in," he said. "And help yourself to more wine when you're ready."

"Good idea," said the Detective Chief Superintendent, refilling his glass. He then stabbed and sawed along with the others and up-ended that important first mouthful.

He joined in the chorus of appreciative mmms and ahhs.

James wasn't eating. He was waiting for the dinner guest's Christmas cracker moustache to fall off. *It can't be real, surely?* The man's hair was white. His moustache was black.

Detective Chief Superintendent Deverick Mace and his wife Charmaine were card-carrying Christians. The former's intolerance when it came to moral issues was well-publicized. James had already christened him "The Moral Policeman."

The Moral Policeman was also grand wizard of the local Masonic Lodge. James wondered whether that was the real reason for the lunch invitation—his father wanted to join. The bonhomie of the host merely served to strengthen this suspicion.

James didn't care if his parents belonged to a cult or had mooseheads around to lunch. He just didn't see why they had to involve him. It wasn't as if they ever sought his opinion. He couldn't even imagine them doing that. They denied him the opportunity to speak and then interpreted his silence as endorsement. But when their beliefs were the relief side of the mold and his the hollow reverse, reticence was hardly a natural response. It required meticulous self-control.

He'd survived the sermon. Was this the longed-for and well-deserved respite: a tableful of chit-chat? He couldn't blot this out. Of every word he was totally, torturously, conscious.

"The worst thing is that it doesn't show any sign of stopping," Mum said. "That's three now and all this side of town, so they must be linked."

"I shouldn't really be discussing it…" The Moral Policeman hurriedly chewed, and swallowed. "But yes, it's common enough knowledge now—we're looking for a single killer in connection with all three crimes."

James needed some wine, but Dad didn't approve of Louise and him drinking.

Then again, he'd already helped himself to the bottle that had been used for the gravy—which accounted for the sloshing in his head.

"Any leads yet?" asked his father.

"It's an ongoing investigation."

Mother sighed. "Those poor young women. They had their whole lives ahead of them. It's too distressing for words."

Charmaine, an immaculately-dressed woman in her fifties, with close-set eyes and a pointy chin, nodded tragically.

James heard creaks in his cranium as the headachy storm brewing there got ready to break.

"How's Friends of the Friendless doing?" asked the Moral Policeman.

Friends of the Friendless was the open-to-anyone refuge Father had founded. The Detective Chief Superintendent had presented him with some silverware for this achievement. That was how the two men had met.

"Very well," replied Dad. "I've scaled back my involvement now it's up and running, but I looked in the other day and the latest success story left last week to take up a post in the Midlands. It's very rewarding seeing someone they literally found in the gutter land on her feet. And yet that sort of thing happens, well, if not every week then certainly every month. It's the Lord's work, truly."

"Imagine the sycophancy in heaven." James delivered his debut remark with mock nonchalance, and even executed a pantomime yawn.

Knives and forks fell silent, all conversation ceased and everyone turned and looked at him.

Charmaine had been staring at him and his sister all along. A lot of people were fascinated by the way they only seemed to be distinguishable by their sex. She didn't even bother to hide her interest.

"I beg your pardon?" said Dad. "Was that a contribution to the conversation?"

"If you're trying to score points in heaven," James went on, "you're going about it the wrong way. Because correct me if I'm wrong but don't good deeds cease to count as soon as you tell anyone about them?"

Dad shot back in his chair. "And you think that's what I'm trying to do? "Score points," as you so crudely put it?"

James shrugged his shoulders.

He wasn't interested in polite debate. He was just lobbing hand-grenades.

His mother fiddled with her crucifix. "More lamb, anyone?"

Amid polite refusals, eating and drinking recommenced.

"I must just tell you," Mum chattered on, "Alistair's success story visited old Mrs. Davis every day she was in hospital. Absolutely nothing in it for her, yet took the old dear flowers and everything. After the life that girl's led... The funniest thing is, though, she doesn't even believe in God. I asked her one day and she came straight out with it. What do you think of that?"

James set his knife and fork down. "That's typical of believers, forever equating morals with religion. What about all the good atheists? What about the bad believers?"

His ideas came from reading long into the lonely night.

"You almost make it sound as if you're not a believer," said Dad.

"Well, I wasn't going to tell you just yet," —James gave an infinitesimal nod in the direction of the Moral Policeman and his wife—"but I don't think I'll be going to church again."

Dad gave him a cold, fish-like stare. "Why not?"

"Because it's against my religion."

"What nonsense are you on about now?"

"I don't want a religion. I'm an atheist."

"You're a *what*?" Dad banged his water glass down, which shook the other glasses and remaining clean cutlery. James couldn't imagine a more extreme reaction than if he'd just told him he was in league with the Devil himself. "You never told me."

"You never asked. It's just, well... He doesn't do a lot, does He? Our Father which art lost in heaven. I mean, if He *did* exist we'd have to sack Him. Or maybe He's a *laissez-faire* God who just likes to watch."

Dad leaned back in his seat. He pressed his knuckles to his forehead as he grunted a sigh.

"How do you explain the eye?" said Deverick Mace. "Or the eye on the butterfly's wing for that matter?"

James turned to the Detective Chief Superintendent. "Evolution. God didn't create us. We created Him, in our image. Because that's Christianity's first lie: that God exists."

Mother had been taking a sip of wine, some of which had got sucked up the back of her nose. She coughed and spluttered like someone who had narrowly escaped drowning.

But James was on a roll. "The second is that there is such a thing as immortality. I mean, just think of all the millions who had faith and went to their graves believing they were going to a better place. Of course, they didn't find out they'd been cheated, so they couldn't even claim their money back."

Charmaine's mouth gaped.

He ploughed on. "You've got to admire the audacity of it. It's the ultimate con trick. That's what religion is. A con trick. It's all just lies parents tell their children."

"Do you really think I'm in the habit of lying to my own children?" asked Dad, eyes bulging, and moving independently—at least, the pupil of one had drifted off to the side.

"Well, you lied to us about Father Christmas. Why not about God as well? Although it's not really your fault, I suppose. Someone lied to you once."

Mum frowned. "No one's lying, love. The Lord does exist."

"Oh, sorry. My mistake."

His mother snapped her head aside and her cheek colored up as if she'd been struck across it.

James sensed the futility of his anti-crusade. Even if he put every argument on the table, his parents still wouldn't acknowledge that he might have a case. It was hopeless. They'd stopped thinking years ago.

"Who would you rather go to a party with..." James poured red wine into his empty water glass and spilt some on the damask table cloth. "Jesus Christ or the Devil?"

Dad clutched his temples.

"At least with Jesus you wouldn't have to buy the wine," replied Louise.

Even though Mum's head dropped, James felt laughter burst from him; that was the sister he knew and loved. They hadn't had much to say to each other lately, but now they shared a smile.

Dad flung them each an excoriating glance.

Charmaine's eyes were feeding on them.

The Moral Policeman leaned back in his chair. "I think the Devil's present at this table."

"Yeah, his car's parked outside," said James.

He'd always known he possessed a mordant sense of humor, a viper wit. Yet for fear of what his parents would do to him, he'd exercised a degree of self-censorship. Now that he had nothing left to lose, he enjoyed deploying it.

"James," said Dad. "I will not have my guests spoken to like that."

"If God exists, He's so useless He might as well not exist."

Dad jerked to his feet. He almost knocked his chair over. "This is your final warning." His voice had a braying quality. "I won't tolerate blasphemy in my house."

"Ah, but blasphemy can only be blasphemy if you believe God exists." James held his hands out, palms upwards. "I don't."

Dad's finger shot out towards him, pointing as the hand shook. "Get to your room," he bellowed.

"If sex is original sin," said James, getting up, "then I suppose I shouldn't be here anyway. Mum, Dad, I'm sorry I was born."

His younger sister sat upright in her chair. "What's "regional slin?""

"Get to your room," yelled Dad, but at Harriet.

She ran screaming from the dining room and thudded up the stairs.

James followed, at a more leisurely pace.

———

Breaking the ensuing silence, Alistair sat down again and half coughed, half laughed. "That boy'd sell his soul to the highest bidder."

About the only way to salvage the situation was to try to make light of it. Yet he knew that what had taken place today was more than just a teenage tantrum or routine family warfare. The sense of finality was unmistakable.

"I think we'd better be on our way," said the Detective Chief Superintendent. "I've got a serious pile of paperwork waiting for me at home."

"What about the sweet?" Valerie's forehead crumpled. "It's caramel soufflé."

"I couldn't eat another thing," replied Charmaine, chin upturned. "It's been lovely. Thank you. We really must be off."

After a round of polite goodbyes, she left the house in a hurry.

Deverick lingered only to collect his wife's blazer.

"I'm so sorry," said Alistair, following him out into the hallway. He'd wanted to impress these people. His chest felt tight, as if he were breathing at high altitude. And he was shaking, but he couldn't let the Detective Chief Superintendent see this. "I don't know what's got into him, I really don't. I'm sure it's just a phase he's going through."

"Yeah, life," said James from half-way up the stairs.

Alistair froze in the middle of the hallway, keeping his reactions in check and scrupulously giving no indication of what was thrashing around inside him—until the moment Deverick stepped out of the front door, when he turned and glared up at his son.

"I'll speak to you later," he growled, before hastening out of the front door and catching up with his friend at the garden gate.

Deverick unlocked the door to the Bentley for his wife. As soon as they were both in, he started the engine.

"I'll wait to hear from you then," called Alistair, hoping that the Detective Chief Superintendent would establish eye contact, give some kind of secret signal.

But it was too late. Deverick reversed out of his parking space.

As soon as he'd given himself enough room, he turned up the close and, hugging the gentle curve of the kerb, bowled along it. A few seconds later he rounded the corner at the top and then he was gone. No nod, no look, nothing.

Neighboring gardens' conifers went all swimmy as Alistair's eyes filled with tears. A few spilled out onto his cheeks and he wiped—swiped—them away.

He spun around to face The End House.

He headed indoors and stopped at the foot of the stairs, where his wife sat with her hands covering her face.

The small, pitiful sounds she made conveyed, better than words ever could, her bafflement and pain. It was only when she looked up and saw him that she started bawling.

He sat down next to her on the second step and put his arm around her. Yet even as he comforted her, he envied the way she could give herself up to emotion, with a total lack of shame.

Finally she began to quiet down.

"Wha-*at* must they thi-*ink* of us?" she said, shaken by thick, hiccupy sobs. "You'll never ge-*et* in the Lodge no-*ow*."

Was it his fault for wanting to be a good parent? Had he been too lenient with the kids? They didn't know how lucky they were.

He was just formulating a suitably palliative reply—while silently cursing the culprit—when his youngest daughter shouted from the landing, "Daddy, Daddy, come quickly. There's a man in my room."

"What?" He twisted around. Harriet was bobbing up and down at the top of the stairs.

He jumped up, streaked up the stairs and burst into his daughter's room.

Panting, he stood in the middle of a boxy pink bedroom. He looked left and right, but couldn't see anyone. This was probably just as well, because he'd have been too puffed to do anything. He'd outrun his capacity for respiration. His breathing needed time to catch up.

He checked under the bed, in the wardrobe, and behind the curtains.

"Ugh." He turned only to be confronted by two sets of demonical eyes. Identical dolls, one in male attire, the other in female, stared at him from a shelf on the wall.

"There's no one here," he said, once his breathing had returned to normal.

Harriet had been padding around in the corridor outside. Now she peeked around the open door. "There was, Daddy."

"Well, there's not now."

Strongly suspecting that his youngest daughter was playing games with him, he left her standing in the corridor while he went to sort out his son.

Still shaking from the fiasco of his lunch invitation, he tried the handle of James' door, and found it locked. "Open this door."

"No."

He depressed the handle again, and let it *chung* back into position. "Open this door, now."

"No. It was you who excommunicated me, remember?"

Determined to ignore any provocation from his son, at least until he could get his hands on him, he leaned his head against the door so that there could be no excuse for shouting.

"Listen, I'll stop your allowance if you don't get out here now."

"If that's the price of honesty, so be it."

"I'm warning you, if you don't come out right away, I'll never forgive you for the things you've said today."

"What? Call yourself a Christian?"

Alistair smacked the door with the flat of his hand. "James, you're going to regret this."

"Oh, hurry up and die."

———————

That night, in bed, James tried to stay awake. He knew that his somnambulism was worse when he was agitated, therefore the chances of him betraying himself in speech or—more catastrophic still—action were greater; and he'd just spent the entire afternoon and evening bouncing off the walls.

"I'm cracking up," he moaned.

For someone who spent most of his time keeping himself in check, he certainly hadn't held back today. He'd rejected two fathers: one earthly, the other heavenly; and while he'd enjoyed attacking Dad, God, and the Church, it hadn't achieved anything. Everyone had ended up more entrenched than they had been at the start.

He wished now that he'd had a weapon handy. If he'd had a knife or, better still, a gun, he could have proved there was no benign deity.

As doubtless everyone suspected, his rant against God had been personally motivated. The problem was, any relief it brought had been strictly transitory. What he needed was a more convenient remedy.

Thankfully, he knew where to look.

He counted the number of times the chain was pulled in the bathroom. Then, when the lights had gone down and the house had fallen silent, he unlocked his door, crept up the corridor and tiptoed down the stairs.

At the bottom, he turned left into the lounge and flicked the switches on the wall as he passed. But he must have missed some because only the wall lights came on. He made a detour and turned on the standard lamp.

He searched the sideboard. Papers, bric-à-brac, jammed its drawers.

The rest of the house wasn't much better. He'd opened his wardrobe a few days before and almost been killed in an avalanche of junk.

"Where the hell are they?"

His mother was marketing manager for a pharmaceutical company and sometimes brought home samples. The company, BraxPelling Pharmaceuticals, was currently developing an antidepressant wonder drug called *Zing!*

If that didn't work, he could still go to his father for confession. If he decided against talking to a deputy of the guilt God, then there was always the secular confession. Dad ran a firm of psychoanalysts.

But it probably wouldn't be possible to escape religion even there. The practice specialized in Christian psychoanalysis. His father claimed to have effected a synthesis of contradictory dogmas.

At last, at the back of the bottom drawer, James found the packet of *Zing!* tablets.

Once he'd opened the tiny green and red box and unfolded the information leaflet, he stood in the circle of yellowish lamplight and read the possible side-effects: "Headaches, nausea, anxiety, insomnia, night sweats, mouth ulcers, black tongue, urticaria, diarrhea, sexual dysfunction and (rarely) anaphylactic shock."

"Fuck it," he said, going back to bed. "I'd rather be depressed."

Minute detonations, maybe caused by the cooling air or perhaps set off in the floorboards by corporeal feet, creak and crack.

Certainly something of greater substance than a shadow, yet blacker than the loose element of night through which it passes, prowls about the house. It floats up and down staircases, glides along empty corridors, turns corners—up and down, round and round, trapped.

Narrowly avoiding the booby-trap of a discarded handbag, the form stops level with a recess in the wall and, arm rising, black on grey-black, reaches for the merest glint of a handle.

The curtains are open and a white moon bathes the room in its pallid light.

She can't sleep. Maybe the light is disturbing her. She sighs. She huffs. Literally every minute or two she executes a half-turn, or quarter-turn. As almost all of these are in the same direction, the white sheet winds around her a little tighter each time.

When the door opens, someone enters. The sheet comes with her as she sits up.

He closes the door and slouches towards her in the back-of-the-mirror moonlight.

What's he doing here?

"Hi…" she says.

He bumps into the bed, stoops, turns, there's a depression of the mattress, one heavy bounce, then he's lying beside her.

This time she doesn't say anything.

He rolls onto his side, facing her. His pulled-up knees come to rest against hers, and she doesn't do anything. In this case inaction is the wisest strategy. Even though his eyes, glistening in the thin, grey light shed by the moon, are open, they are sightless.

She waves a hand in front of them and he doesn't even blink.

"James," she says.

"Wake up."

"Huh? What?"

James almost fell off the bed. He'd been pursuing a woman in his dream, and that woman now shared his pillow.

Recumbent in the ghost-light, she looked like a photograph that was still being developed. From her body heat and scent, he knew she was real. There could only be one possible explanation for why she'd come to him and lay next to him, right up close.

Like a spy in his own home, sometimes he'd glimpsed the look of longing on her face when she'd thought that no one was watching. He'd even heard her night sighs and wondered whose image monopolized her mind, keeping her awake. All that time, it had probably been his. It made what came next much, much easier. It wasn't that he had no feelings. He had the wrong kind.

"Sorry if I've been behaving strangely," he said. "You know, distant and everything. I just didn't know how to deal with what was inside me. But now I can tell you, and it's all right. There's no need to worry. Because I love you."

It was true. She was his soul's star. His heart ignited every time she came into the room, flared with every just-so gesture. Anything she touched became instantly talismanic.

Yet as it was such an unlikely match and one that, if known about, would prove distinctly unpopular with his parents, most of the time he'd denied his emotions, even to himself. Love had been self-immolating.

Now that his secret was out, all his angst seemed over-the-top, unnecessary. Reciprocation changed everything. It virtually reconfigured his senses.

He was about to embrace her, crush her to him, when, glancing over her shoulder, he noticed that a wall had descended to the left of his bed. Jerking upright, he could just make out that his desk had turned into a chest of drawers, that his wardrobe had grown—vertically and laterally—and that the window and door had swapped places. What soundless, infernal machinery could have rearranged his room in this fashion?

His throat constricted.

What's happening? Is this a nightmare?

A sickening ripple of gooseflesh ran the length of his body, reminding him of his hairy origins. This confirmation of his animality made him cringe even more as he contemplated the only possible explanation. She hadn't come to his room.

He had come to hers.

Enveloped in dreams, he'd virtual-reality-walked here.

"Oh, God, God, *God.*" The degeneracy of what he'd done was so great, he knew that, no matter how much time elapsed, he'd never be able to put it behind him. He'd never be able to forgive himself, so he could hardly expect her to.

He rolled onto his front, hid his face in the pillow and wept. How could he have dreamt of desecrating the affinity that exists between twin souls?

It had happened. The thing he had feared most had happened.

He'd awoken in his sister's bed.

CHAPTER 4

Louise raised a hand, luminously pale in the moonlight's whitey darkness. Her brother flinched, like a child expecting a blow to fall.

Instead she ran her fingers across his cheek, then reached out and took his head in her arms, cradling it. She brushed the hair back from his hot, damp, sticky forehead.

She surprised herself. It hadn't even occurred to her to scold him. Then again, why should she? It wasn't just looks they shared. They had similar character traits too. And was she any less willful, any less weak?

Yet what was he doing? He'd sat up and now he got out of bed and turned towards the door. In a few seconds he'd close it behind him. Then tomorrow his visit would seem like a dream. All she had to do to get things back to how they were was not say a word. For a single syllable now would acknowledge the madness, make it real—wake them both up.

Dead man walking, thought James. *Dead man walking.*

It was the end; the end of everything. He'd said how he felt and she hadn't responded—presumably because she didn't want to hurt his feelings. Yet he didn't want her pity. He couldn't stand it. So he was leaving, and he'd never mention his love for her again. Judging by the hot cheeks that he endeavored to keep hidden by fixing his gaze on the door, he didn't know how he'd even be able to look at her again without his face combusting.

His sister said something but he needed to get out, away.

"James," she called.

He paused, with his hand on the doorknob.

"Please. It's all right."

He turned, slowly. "All right?"

Louise sat up. "I feel like I'm the sleepwalker, and I've only just woken up."

While the encroachment of cloud caused the more phantasmagorical fluctuations in the brightness of the moon, the pale rays making it into the room were as playful as underwater light. He saw ripples, bars, parallelograms. Huge pockets of blackness surrounded these shapes, recasting the room in elongated 3-D; and while he could see her from here, he couldn't make out her expression.

He shivered, feverish. "And why's that?"

"I know how you feel."

He swayed, giddy. Did she mean she knew how he felt because she felt that way about someone else, or because she felt that way about him? He steadied himself against the jamb. "You do?"

"Yes. I've been waiting for something too. I just didn't know what until I saw you nearly walk out of that door."

To the drumbeat of his heart, he marched back over to the bed.

For the second time that night, only this time conscious of what he was doing, he lay down beside her. In her bed — unrepulsed. It was like entering a rarefied plane of existence. Even with their parents just at the other end of the corridor, the humdrum world they inhabited by day seemed very far away.

His left hand and her right slid across the wrinkled under-sheet in converging arcs. The pads of their fingers touched, as if in prayer. Then their fingers interlaced. As they turned towards each other, lips brushed against lips.

"Don't say anything," she whispered.

Semi-darkness did the rest.

They stole little butterfly kisses at first. Then mouth sealed mouth and they kissed for what seemed like ages, probing deeper and deeper.

This is wrong, this is wrong, James' conscience screamed.

Yet another voice weighed in with, *Where's the harm? You're not hurting anyone.*

He lifted his hand, helping loosen the sheet that had wound around her like an extra layer of clothing, or the mummy-wrappings of convention. Moving it up towards her breasts, he touched them through her nightdress; tentatively at first, as if they'd explode in his hand. With all the blood in his body driving him on, his touch grew bolder. It wasn't long before he was caressing them, cupping them; first one, then the other. Now he didn't care if what they were doing was immoral. The same hand travelled down her body, coming to rest between her legs.

The uncanny resemblance he saw in her face and yet essential difference he felt between her thighs almost caused him to pass out. With blood booming in his ears, all he could think was, *I'm in love with my sister, I'm in love with my sister.*

Finally they came up for air. Both of them were breathing heavily. He undid his pajama top, removed his pajama bottoms and threw them out of bed. She reached down and, in one swift movement, pulled her nightdress up over her head.

Louise had decided to choose love, whatever the cost. She wasn't going to forgo happiness just to please other people. She'd sell her soul if necessary, for an hour of bliss with her brother.

His hands were on her breasts. Her nipples were bruise-tender. His mouth closed around one of them and she sighed contentedly. He slid across to the other breast and she ran her fingers through his hair. Then his head came level with hers again. As they kissed, she could feel him against her thigh.

He climbed on top of her. She bit her lip as he eased himself inside her. Then he pushed, and it felt as if she'd been stabbed. It was pleasure and pain commingled.

James couldn't believe it. This was his sister. His own sister. His senses were suffused with her—her scent, her softness, her hair in his mouth, her moaning in his ear. As he raised his head off the pillow, her doubly familiar face filled his darkened vision. It was as if he only experienced her in totality for the first time now. They were conjoined, coitally. And yet, it didn't feel unnatural.

They couldn't have stopped even if they'd wanted to. They had gone too far to turn back. Nothing could ever be the same again. They were covered in sweat and panting, as he cleaved to her and she cleaved to him, in sweet friction, skin against skin.

Nothing else mattered except what was happening here, now, on this bed.

CHAPTER 5

The bright, sunny, sharp-shadowed day's warming up nicely. Yet it's a little wind-snappy. Hence the lethargic jerking of the wet washing hung from the line, two items of which, cleaving together, will only slide across each other. They stretch, distend, balloon alarmingly.

Then, suddenly, there's the back door—ajar.

Come on, it seems to say. *Come in.*

The glass in it catches the light. Everything looks fish-tank dark within.

The patio itself is surrounded by perky plants in pots. Flies zip this way and that, and a catkin lies on a flagstone like a dead caterpillar while two butterflies go languidly flapping past with the faint clicking of eyelids opening and closing.

Then it's through the gap. The gloom is disorienting. Yet, squinting at the magnolia walls in the one plane and the caramel carpet in the other, eyesight adjusts to the dim stillness of an unpretentious lounge. Magazines and DVDs on the coffee table, a vase of pink carnations at the center of the dining table, watercolors on the walls and free-standing photographs on the shelves—first of a couple, then of a couple and child and finally some of the child, a girl, alone. It's hearing that's straining, because in addition to water sploshing upstairs, there's a faint rustling coming from the very next room. The house should have only one occupant at this time.

Hence, carefully, creepingly, it's through to the short hallway and the kitchen off to the side with terracotta walls, white cupboards with brass handles, a blond table, silver chairs and slate-colored flooring. The source of the sound turns out to be the net curtain blown in and sucked out of the open window.

A long rubbery squeak from above.

So it's back, out, down the hallway and around; up, up the stairs, slowly, silently, with a surgical-gloved hand gripping the banisters and one leg turned out slightly because of the chill feel of steel against that thigh.

Although the stairs, like the lounge, are dark for early afternoon, the first doorway on the landing is open with light spilling out of it. In fact, it looks as if there's a ball of light hovering near the center of the ceiling. The steady …plink …plink …plink of water dripping on water is amplified; strange.

Moving in closer, the ball fades until all that is left is steam swirling around a bright bulb. To the left, a toilet and sink in profile, like junk sculpture. The slosh and slap of water comes from the recess to the right.

Leaning in, a woman's leg appears: pale, supple and smooth. It's raised above the rim of a bath and for a moment is surrounded by twisting rivulets, yet these slide out of sight like transparent serpents.

Then the leg is lowered, and slender hands slide into view, lightly soaping pink-tipped breasts. The soft skin gives at their touch.

Finally, the woman stops, relaxes, and there's a tiny trigger sound from her throat as, with obvious contentment, she yawns. Which is why he isn't prepared when she moves suddenly. Light hair tumbles around pale, freckled shoulders as she leans, slides and reaches forwards with a smooth, rower-like motion and pulls out the plug.

She's about to get up, turn around, so he reaches in his pocket and lunges.

It isn't long before the water gurgling down the plughole runs red.

Alistair stretched in his seat in his office at home. He was surrounded by shelf upon shelf of books.

Shutting the lid of his laptop, he shoved it aside, leaned back in his brown leather swivel chair and rested his feet on the mahogany desk. He was just about to start making notes for a sermon on Christ's temptation in the wilderness when his mobile phone rang.

His feet crashed to the floor. He'd introduced a new service: psychoanalysis by phone. It represented the ultimate in impartiality, and it meant he could work from home.

Pressing the call key, he put his mobile up to his ear.

"Hello."

Scratchy breathing.

"Hello?"

Cumbersome breathing.

"Alistair Glavier here. How can I help?"

"I've just come from this house—"

"Ah, Godfrey."

The number hadn't come up, and sometimes it was hard distinguishing one microwaved voice from another, yet Alistair was fairly certain he'd identified this rasping voice correctly.

"How've you been?" he asked.

"Not good."

"Why? What's happened?"

"Something terrible."

"Where? At home, at work?"

"In this house I'm trying to tell you about."

"Somebody else's house?"

"Yes."

Alistair sighed as if he had a puncture. This phone client was a scopophiliac, or voyeur, and he always seemed to be more interested in confessing his trespasses than being cured.

"Godfrey, we're supposed to be trying to get you to stop spying on other people, remember? Fighting the feelings that give rise to your unacceptable behavior, killing them and burying them." According to Christian psychoanalysis, repression was only a problem in so far as it was incomplete. It was therefore encouraged. As the ultimate goal of treatment was taming the ego, every effort was made to bolster the superego. "You know the consequences."

"But you've got to hear this. I mean, it's essential that you do…"

As Godfrey chattered on, Alistair mopped his brow and undid an extra button of his shirt. Yet it was no good; he needed some air.

He left the room, crossed the hallway and strolled up through the lounge.

Ahead, the world beyond the costly tinted glass of the sliding door occupied a different medium altogether. It had a subaqueous aspect.

Reaching the door, he was about to give it a sideways yank when he spotted a woman on a pale blue towel in the middle of the aquamarine lawn. She lay on her back, with her feet farthest away, so he effectively looked at her from above. She wore blue wraparound sunglasses, like goggles, but he knew who she was.

It was the *au pair*.

The whole garden threshed gently, as if alive. The breeze teased and tousled Riika's hair, green-tinged from the tinted glass. She rolled onto her front and, reaching behind her back, undid the strings to the top half of her blue bikini.

He couldn't go outside now, so he had to content himself with cooling his forehead against the glass.

A moment later she turned to the left, and he noticed Verge pushing a wheelbarrow piled high with fluttering hedge trimmings.

The old man nodded to them both, in turn, and she looked up to see who the other person was.

Alistair saw her peer at him with underwater eyes, and smile.

He swung around, turning away.

"Bloody Verge," he muttered, retreating up the lounge.

The gardener had come with the house. He'd worked for the previous owner, who'd died within its walls. Alistair and his wife had been happy to stick to the same arrangement. Glance out of any window, though, and there he was.

"Mr. Glavier…"

As if he'd come to the end of a long leash, Alistair jerked to a halt and put the mobile back up to his ear. "Hello, yes? I'm here."

"You haven't told me what you make of what happened in the house."

"Oh, for pity's sake. It's perfectly clear you're making no effort whatsoever." He was supposed to limit his input to gentle jogs towards self-knowledge. Yet where once a compartmentalized mind had enabled him to keep each client's problems separate, contained, now they all just seemed to merge together. "I mean, where do you think it's going to end? Because what happens when looking isn't enough and you want to go inside, be in the picture; touch? Do you think you'll be welcome? No. Of course not."

"But—"

"No, that's it. I'm sorry." He headed back to his office. "You need to stop now before you go too far—assuming, of course, you haven't already."

"What's Verge doing?" asked Louise.

"Watering the roses," answered her brother. "And I don't mean with a watering can."

"Are you serious?"

"Yeah. That's what you get when you employ a garden gnome."

Louise sat on his window seat. Gripping her shoulders, James leaned over her.

She and James were taking it easy on a Sunday morning while their sister and parents were getting ready for church. She hadn't just embraced love and accepted sin. Emboldened by her twin's stand, she'd likewise left the Doomsday Church.

With Riika up and out, they'd soon have the house to themselves.

They probably should have been studying, but they hated school. Although sixth form wasn't anywhere near as unpleasant as earlier years, when they'd been laughed at and taunted on a daily basis, they still got shunned for the cloying stench of piety that clung to the family name.

Louise heard the front door open and shut. Finally free, they bounded over to the bed; rolled around on it, with eager mouths and busy hands.

Old Marilyn Manson posters, which James had put up purely to annoy Mum and Dad, provided relief, of sorts, from the monotonous whiteness of the walls. Neither of them had any interest in their surroundings. The edge of the bed might as well have been the edge of the world as far as they were concerned.

"You've changed," said James, and he was right. When they were children, each had known everything there was to know about the other. They'd been joined at the soul. Now that they were older, they had so much to catch up on. "I feel I have to get to know you all over again. And I want to. Oh, how I want to... Will you let me?"

Still on the bed, they knelt facing each other. Slowly, they started undressing, until all they wore between them was a necklace, a ring and a grin. James contributed the latter. His smile, where the lines of it cut into his face, was diamond-shaped.

Louise contemplated telling him but he distracted her by saying, "There's something I've been dying to do."

Uh-oh.

He made her lie back and roll over. Then he paused.

Her throat tightened, until she felt the wet press of lips in the hollow behind her left knee.

She laughed and flopped over onto her back.

"You've got a delicate blue-green vein back there," he said, straightening up.

The look he gave her was one hot beam of love. It left her light-headed, but with a tingly, energizing sensation, as if champagne bubbles—recalling the one time she'd tried a glass—were fluttering up her nose.

"You sick puppy." She sat up, then knelt opposite him.

They stared at each other in the streaming light.

They'd never seen each other naked in childhood. They hadn't been allowed. Separate bath times had been enforced right from the start. Yet in those days their sex had been irrelevant; now it was impossible to ignore.

Even the contours of their bodies were different. His were angular, hers were all curves. He kept hugging her waist and clicking his tongue, as if amazed at how slim she was. He made her feel as if there was nothing of her. The flatness of his chest contrasted sharply with the roundness of hers. She tweaked one of his nipples and asked, "Why have you got these?"

The sight of his eyebrows looping and unlooping, like restless caterpillars, made her cackle. He obviously hadn't given it any thought before.

"I don't know," he said at last. "God must have had a few nuts and bolts left over."

Louise wasn't laughing anymore.

Why did he have to bring up God? She may have evicted Him from the church of her heart but He was still a potent totem. She was continually stepping between a diabolical Heaven and a holy Hell—all within the compass of her own home.

Twisting slightly, she slumped back onto her right buttock, stretched her legs out and, letting her arms take her weight, slid forwards until she sat on the edge of the bed. "Do you think what we're doing is wrong?"

James walked on his knees down the bed, strode off the end and wheeled around to face her. "I've been thinking about it a lot and, no, I don't. Not when we love each other. I mean, how can love be a crime?"

She smiled weakly. "I hope you're right."

"I know I am, Lou. I know I am. Because if two people love each other, what does it matter if they happen to be related? Yeah, if it's between generations or one of them's underage then of course there's a case for forbidding it. Otherwise, what's the problem? I mean, all right, okay, it's bound to weigh on our minds sometimes because we've been through that glorified sheep-dip, indoctrination. Yet I suspect there's a lot of brothers and sisters out there who give in to feelings they think they shouldn't have. The only difference is they probably let the pressure get to them and try to forget it ever happened. Or maybe on the night before one of them is due to get married the other will ask, 'Do you remember that time we...?' And the husband or bride-to-be will shush the other up with "We were just children." But not us, Lou. We're going to stand by each other. We're going to be strong. I'll take on God Himself if necessary."

It was a bravura performance, showcasing a new, strident militancy. Yet it was as if sickness had suddenly declared itself health, health sickness. Everything was reversed, as in a mirror.

Louise let out a long, quivery sigh.

Her brother obviously failed to grasp that when a transgressor starts trying to justify his actions by making out what is considered bad is actually good, he simply demonstrates his continued enslavement to the moral code he affects to despise.

James even seemed to have forgotten whose house they lived in.

"You won't have to take on God," she said. "We've got Dad."

CHAPTER 6

They couldn't escape the changing of the seasons even at night. One particularly sticky, moonless, summer's night, James and his sister had to lie on top of her bed.

Her head rested against his chest as he held her in his arms. "I don't want these days to ever end," he said.

They'd had their exams, their birthday and finally left school.

"I don't want these nights to end," she replied, through her nose. They'd been struck down by summer flu this last week and she was still getting over it.

He knew what she meant. Days had become nights and nights had become days.

With the lights off, they could discuss anything, ask each other anything.

His head woozed as he turned it too quickly in the hanging heat. "What's it like being you?"

She lifted the suction pad of her ear from his chest and he felt instead her nudging, squelching nose. "I was about to ask you almost the exact same question."

Things like this always happened to them. Although such synchronicity impressed, it rarely surprised; because they were twins—mirror people.

"Come on," he said, "up you get."

"Why? What's happening?"

The sweat that had poured out of them at all points of contact had dried, acting as adhesive; so separation was almost as bracing as ripping off several large plasters at once.

He got out of bed, switched on the Anglepoise lamp, adjusted it, then turned back around.

"What? What is it?" She was sitting on the edge of the bed now.

He knelt in front of her. "We're going to solve the essential mystery of male and female once and for all."

He had the Anglepoise positioned just right.

His sister shuddered and hugged herself.

"You all right, Lou?"

Her breath had a claustrophobic echo. Sounding like a deep-sea diver, she answered from inside her invisible flu-helmet, "Yeah, just cold."

Before he could point out how worrying that sounded on the hottest night of the year so far, she'd darted under the top sheet.

"Lou, what's wrong?"

"Do you ever get the feeling you're being watched?"

"Watched? That's just the policeman of the soul, your superego, flexing his moral muscles." He pulled back the sheet.

"Please, turn the light off."

"It's okay. There's no one here."

"It's not that."

"What then?"

"Suddenly...very...tired."

Tired. *Tired...*

The very word itself was like a charm, a drug, a... *yawn.*

Night after night they'd talked till two or three in the morning and the debt to sleep had grown and grown.

He'd no sooner plunged them back into gloopy darkness and joined her between the sheets than time elided; first seconds, then the minutes...

The mannequins have escaped and the people are all trapped in the shop windows.

That's how it seems, in the heavy, sluggish air, as nondescript silhouette after silhouette flits by in front of the endless succession of brightly-lit shop-fronts. These slide past framing Technicolor, three-dimensional people reaching for a DVD, paying for tomorrow's carton of milk or raising a burger in a bap mouthwards. Here, in the road, dark vehicles appear to spark with electrical currents as random reflections move along chrome finishings and across bonnets, windows, roofs, boots and side panels.

Inside and out—with the windows down, there's little difference—the heat feels like a half-remembered holiday, sounds like a funky seventies disco track, and smells like reeking rubbish.

One yank of the steering wheel and a tire squeals as he peels off down a long, sloping side street.

Here, figures pace, bent-kneed in high heels under the street lamps.

Indicator tick-tick-ticking, he drives round and round the broken-windowed block just around the corner.

Ultra Sheer legs shimmer in the glare of his headlights every time he approaches the fourth corner.

Finally, he pulls up alongside the young woman.

She stoops and peers in, with wide-apart eyes and a pasted on smile. "Buying, or just window-shopping?"

"Get in."

She nods and climbs inside. Switching off the headlights, he turns left.

The car noses into the anonymous night.

A summer storm has blown the heat right off the city. It isn't close anymore, it's cool. Wet pavements are splashed with artificial light. And the constant press of tires leaves partially dry bands on the slick streets.

Speeding to clear a crossroads just as the lights change, he swerves right before the roundabout, up a ramp.

He rides the flyover up, along and down and around, then accelerates to join the dual carriageway.

It isn't long before a flashing blue light catches his attention in the rear-view mirror.

And braking, braking, braking, he pulls over.

His right hand remains on the steering wheel as he brushes a foot-length hair off the front passenger seat with his left.

Fortunately, it's extremely unlikely the officer will ask to see inside the boot.

When James' head slipped through the gap between his and his sister's pillows, it jolted him awake.

He blew a tickly strand of Louise's hair out of his face, straightened his spine and stretched his legs. One of his arms rested in the crook of his sister's waist. The other had gone numb because she was lying on it, but until he'd worked out how to remove the latter without disturbing her, he contented himself with trying to get the blood flowing. He clenched and unclenched his hand. He did it a dozen times in all, and her breathing, which he monitored carefully, remained sleep-slow, snuffle-loud, throughout.

He crept along the corridor nightly now, which was more often than when his somnambulism had been at its height. In the blueness of dawn he always kissed her one last time before stealing back to his own sheets.

He had to wake up before his normal waking up time. He'd trained himself.

All that was unusual about the present occasion was its earliness. What he saw with his eyes open was what he'd seen with them closed: undifferentiated darkness.

He decided not to risk disrupting Louise's sleep. He would wait for her to move of her own accord before reclaiming his arm and leaving on tiptoe.

His sister had a number of preferred positions for sleep and periodically rotated, through forty-five, ninety or one hundred eighty degrees, from one to another, such that in an average night she could get through several revolutions. So, she was bound to roll over sooner or later. He just had to stay awake.

But the heat was baking his brain. When he and his twin started glowing in the dark, melting like butter, they gradually coalesced to form something inchoate, something vaguely marsupial. Every transmogrification followed quite naturally from the one before it, in dream logic.

Having just slipped into her black cotton trousers and blocky, multi-colored, patchwork top, Valerie turned right out of her and Alistair's bedroom and, before she got to the landing, veered left.

It was time for breakfast and she wanted to check that the children were awake.

She reached the end of a corridor when she heard Harriet through the door, having what sounded like a conversation, and paused. Although she could only make out the odd, innocent word, she analyzed the fluctuations in sound: this question, with the telltale rise in pitch at the end, that pause left for a response, the inexplicable laughter that followed. It definitely had the structure of an exchange, but who could be in there? Alistair was in the bathroom, Riika had already gone downstairs and James and Louise still needed waking. If someone was in there, that person shouldn't even be in the house, let alone in an eight-year-old's bedroom.

As she never entirely forgot, there was a serial killer on the loose. The frontiers of evil had advanced to potentially engulf them all. Because, as the murder of that woman in her bathroom in Chiswick showed, people weren't even safe in their own homes anymore. He violated both property and person.

Valerie pounced on the handle in front of her and dashed into the room. The door banged into the wall. As Harriet's

"Morning, Mummy," was succeeded by faint salivary clicks, Valerie swung her vision this way and that.

The curtains were open and her gaze ranged over pink walls, plum carpet and hulking furniture, with nothing to latch on to. There was no one in the room. Her daughter sat up in bed, smiling at her.

She suddenly saw herself from the outside: a multicolored mum twisting and turning like a Rubik's cube. She'd never even heard another person. It had been more like a telephone conversation. Only, it couldn't even have been that, because Harriet didn't have a phone.

"I thought I heard you talking to someone." Valerie wasn't so much accusing her daughter as defending herself.

"Oh, that was my friend."

"Friend? Here?" Her gaze flitted hither and thither all over again.

"He often comes here."

"Who comes here?" Her voice went all shrieky because of that "he."

"My friend."

"What blasted friend?" Her insides were stretched tight, and this time her use of that parental prerogative, the raised voice, was entirely deliberate.

"The one who only shows himself to me."

"Oh, you mean he's imaginary." Her insides relaxed.

Harriet's ponytail shook from side to side. Valerie could have sworn her daughter stared at her with knowing eyes. What lay behind it? Where had a child learnt a look like that? Who from? Valerie's stomach lurched.

"He's real," said Harriet. "He just only appears to me."

Valerie hit the buffers of herself. There was no one here, no one hiding, her daughter was safe and that was all that mattered.

"I see, dear." She didn't, of course, but she could discuss it with Alistair later. "Come on, get up now and hurry down to Riika."

Harriet hooked the spindly arms of her glasses over her ears, eased herself into a pair of yellow slippers, wrapped a daisy-patterned dressing gown around herself and they left the room together.

They both turned left at the end of the corridor.

Upon crossing the oak landing, Harriet trotted down the stairs while Valerie continued straight on.

She still had to wake up the twins.

Breakfast was later on a Saturday, so they usually made the effort.

Arriving at James' door, she knocked once, loudly, and tutted when there was no curt "What?" no Neolithic groaning—no sound of waking whatsoever.

"Come on, James." Opening the door, plunging into the dim interior and striding straight over to the light-crowned curtains, she yanked open the day. "Nearly time for brea…"

She'd turned to face the room, now replete with light, and noticed the empty bed.

———————

Louise opened her eyes. "No-o-o…"

Normally she had nightmares and then woke up. On this occasion it happened the other way around.

One second she was being rowed down a green-banked river with an arm out over the side, dipped up to the wrist, trailing in liquid sky; the next she was in bed with her brother, with her mother knocking at the door about to burst in.

It was morning, full-blown. The curtains were undrawn and light had invaded every corner of the room. So, what was James doing here? She ignored the pressure building high in her nose and leaned over and shook him by the shoulder.

He'd no sooner rubbed his eyes than she clamped her hand over his mouth and whispered in his ear, "'S Mum."

She expected him to spring out of bed and dive under it, or something equally dramatic, but he didn't. He just lay there.

"Wha-?" he breathed hotly into her hand.

"Louise, breakfast," shouted Mum.

James jumped.

Belatedly galvanized, he tore her hand away and mouthed, "Speak to her."

Of course, if she said something—it didn't matter what; anything, just to demonstrate that she was awake—her mother would go away again.

Why hadn't that occurred to her? Maybe she was the one thinking in slow motion; which wouldn't be surprising really, given the shock she'd had and the aftermath of flu.

"It's all gight, gum—"

She couldn't get any further. An obstruction in her nasal passages made talking painful and sustained speech impossible. So, to try and clear the blockage, she pulled her handkerchief out from under her pillow and quickly blew her nose.

What emerged had the fluorescent quality of ectoplasm. And there was more to come. There were skeins upon skeins of it.

The opportunity to avoid a family-destroying morality check had passed in any case.

"What's wrong with everyone this morning?" asked Mum, as the door swung open.

Louise crashed back down next to James. He pulled the sheet up to their necks to hide their nakedness and she clutched his hand beneath it and silently prayed to a God she no longer even believed existed.

CHAPTER 7

"There you are, James," his mother said, in her usual singsong. "Are you keeping your sister company while she's not well? Aww, that is sweet. You two had better hurry if you want breakfast, though."

And then she left.

For a moment James couldn't understand what had just taken place. He and Louise had escaped punishment. Only, how was that possible when they'd been discovered together, like this?

Then it dawned on him: it was beyond Mum's comprehension that there could be anything more to the sight of him in his sister's bed than a touching demonstration of fraternal concern.

Looking at Louise, who stared at the empty doorway with wide eyes showing lots of eggy whiteness, he whistled his relief.

His twin went to say something, choked and immediately started coughing.

When she sat up, clutching the sheet to her chest, he patted her bare back.

Eventually she collapsed, silent apart from a sigh.

Cured of the cough, she lay motionless, with eyes half closed.

He preferred the carbonated Louise to this still one, so he decided to shake her up a bit.

He snapped back the sheet, exposing their nakedness — while the open door faced the wrong way and anyone could have passed in the corridor outside.

The idea was to sabotage her introspection by appealing to her love of fun, and it worked. His sister caught his mood. By the time they were padding down the stairs, in dressing gowns and slippers, both of them were sniggering at their mother's innocence, which in his opinion wasn't so much proof of respectability as lack of imagination.

Following a quick embrace in the hallway, they arrived in the dining room, where they sat down opposite each other, stirred cups of tea, buttered slices of toast and took it in turns to yawn, loudly.

Harriet continued spooning Shreddies into her mouth. Dad looked up from his *Telegraph*.

"I don't understand it," he said, lowering the paper as he turned a page. "How can people who sleep as much as you two still be tired?"

James glanced from his father to Louise and back again. He noticed that while ostensibly addressing both of them, Dad directed his gaze solely at his sister.

James had ignored Dad, as far as practicable, ever since that eventful Sunday lunch with the Moral Policeman. Despite patching things up with the Maces and wangling his way into the Lodge, his father had adopted the same policy with him. Even when he had to address him, he never looked straight at him but always a bit to the side.

Louise jumped and, as if suddenly remembering something, emitted a little "oh".

"I've been meaning to ask, Dad," she said, "what happened at work yesterday? You were telling Mum about it and I only caught the end of it."

"Oh, that, yes, well, I hit something of a raw nerve with one of my clients and he went berserk. Started smashing up the practice."

"Good grief."

Although she put a hand on Dad's arm, James knew that his sister was only really interested in one thing: changing the subject. And he was proud of her, for succeeding.

"Yes, things can get a little out of hand sometimes. And even with a cushion for protection, it's a bit like setting yourself up as a human punch bag."

"Gosh, I didn't realize psychoanalysis could be so dangerous."

"Sounds cool to me," said James, unable to restrain himself. "When can I book a session?"

His father glared at him.

James grinned back.

They remained like that, one smiling, one not, with deadlocked eyes, for the longest of moments.

Time only seemed to pick up pace again when Mum came in with news. "There's been another murder." Everyone turned and stared at her, and she continued, "A woman's body's been found in the Grand Union Canal. It's just been on TV. Isn't it dreadful?" Her voice was taut to the point of breaking.

She'd turned into a news junkie. She didn't even take account of Harriet's presence anymore. They were all getting used to having murder for breakfast.

"So?" replied James. "There's always murders."

"But these are all in West London. All local."

Mum sat down, blinking rapidly.

He tried again. "So far as I've been following, they're all at completely different compass points."

"Exactly. All around here."

Unsure how to tackle her *Alice in Wonderland* logic, he let her carry on.

"They're calling him "The Fiend." Because he's becoming prolific now. No wonder everyone's afraid. I notice it all the time. In the tea room at work, out shopping. People used to discuss the weather, now they discuss this. And nobody knows where he's going to strike next. Deverick and his people should do something. They need to hurry up and catch him, because he can't stop himself now. He's out of control. Don't you think so, Alistair?"

"Of course, by definition," said Dad, barely glancing up from his paper's TV guide. "Ah, good. There's a "classic murder chiller" on tonight."

Thanks to Dad's blatant hypocrisy, James nearly choked on a corner of toast.

He winked at Louise and announced louder than necessary, "Actually, I'm thinking of writing to complain about the level of sex and violence on television."

"Are you?" asked his sister, equally stagily.

"Yeah. There's not enough."

"You're looking better, Louise." Mum took no notice of their double act. "And you look better these days, too, James. How's the sleepwalking?"

"Oh, fine."

He smiled at his sister, but lowered his head when he noticed Dad peer at them.

"I wouldn't say that, looking at the half moons under their eyes," the latter commented.

"Too much reading in bed." James had to avoid meeting Louise's gaze this time for fear that he'd explode with laughter.

"Yes, well, we need to talk about Exeter and Manchester."

James stared at his plate.

Since both he and Louise had applied to go on to higher education, everything had changed. It was a complete mess, because they'd chosen universities at opposite ends of the country, yet they could never live apart now. So, even as they did all the paperwork to keep themselves afloat on the stock exchange of Mum and Dad's expectations and continue drawing on their parents' goodwill, the crash loomed.

But this was prime summertime. Each new day was like a bite from a dripping peach, and James was determined that he and his sister should enjoy as many of them as possible. For, whatever the outcome, soon they would have to go out into society and mix with strangers. And to them, and twins generally, everyone was a stranger.

"We'll talk about it later." James picked up his toast.

Louise picked up hers.

Followed by Harriet, they headed for the door.

———————————

"Guess what," said Valerie, now that she and her husband were alone. "James was keeping Louise company in bed this morning. He must have joined her first thing."

"He what?" Alistair was holding the main section of the paper again and it immediately started to waver and fold.

"What's wrong?" She recalled the sleek heads lifting, the big eyes blinking, the buds of their mouths opening. "I thought it was rather sweet myself. It reminded me of how they used to be."

"Well, it's hardly appropriate behavior now, is it?" Alistair's *Telegraph* had buckled in the middle and he had trouble shutting it. Battering it into submission, then halving it, he dropped it on the table. "No, the sooner those two get off to university the better."

"You're too hard on them." They'd shared the same womb. Why not the same bed?

"You're too soft on them."

Valerie sighed and let it go. It wasn't them that worried her. "I thought I heard Harriet talking to someone in her room."

"You what?"

"Yet when I went in there, there was nobody there. She said she'd been talking to "a friend." Well, at the time I assumed she meant an imaginary friend. It's just, she seemed so convinced he was real that I can't quite shake off the feeling I had before I went in there. And you've heard the night noises." They both had, and often. Could they all just be the sound of the house communing with itself?

"Li—"

"I know, I know—I'm being ridiculous. But when there's a killer about…"

"Love, love, listen. Living in a big old house like this is enough to give anyone the creeps. But if Harriet has an imaginary friend, then it would seem intensely real to her."

"And that's all it is?"

He nodded.

"Oh, thank you, thank you." Valerie leaned back in her chair and sipped tea through a smile.

"So you can stop worrying. It's all psychological."

Bent over, with her hand resting on her knee and her fingers picking at a scab just below it, Harriet cupped her right hand around her ear, just inches away from the other side of the dining room door.

That's what you think, Daddy.

CHAPTER 8

James lay fully clothed on his bed as the wind whipped the window with thin rain.

Where was Louise? They had to make the most of the evenings now that weekdays were work days. Their A-level results had been so poor that they needn't have worried about university.

They wanted to leave The End House, yet didn't have enough put by to move out. So, the plan was to work for a year, save as much as they could, and then elope.

His sister had found employment as a junior legal secretary. He'd got a job in telesales. They were apart for most of the day, five days a week, but their meetings were rapturous, their nights rhapsodic.

Night after night he lay like this, on his bed, drowsily listening for the creak of floorboards in the corridor outside, the rising and falling sound of the door opening and closing, followed by the characteristic rub of her stockinged legs as she walked towards him. Then he'd see her, bending over him, with her long hair falling down as, button by button, and tugging at zips, they relieved each other of the encumbrance of clothes on his squeaky bed-cum-trampoline.

"Hello," she'd say, once her breathing had returned to normal.

And he, still gasping, would make one of his off-the-cuff remarks. Like, "This bed needs oiling."

———

Alistair wandered around the house, sighing and harrumphing.

He was looking for Riika.

He wouldn't normally have been looking for the *au pair* on a Tuesday morning, or at any other time come to that, but Valerie had just texted him with a message for her.

Riika wasn't in the lounge, the kitchen, or the dining room, so he climbed up to her room on the third floor.

He was just about to reach the top of the narrow flight of stairs that led up to the converted part of the attic when he heard a dull clank—a sound that wouldn't have been out of place on-board a ship. It seemed to come from the back of the house, two floors below.

Then he heard it again, and this time managed to get an aural fix on it: the utility room.

He hurried back down to the ground floor, strode all the way up the hallway and turned right.

The cubicle that served as washing and drying room had its own hot, damp microclimate. He was confronted by a light-blue denimed posterior; which for a moment he didn't even connect with a pair of legs.

His brain quickly made sense of the information his eyes crudely garnered. Riika, bending over in a pair of jeans, pulled wet clothes from the washing machine. She had to stick her whole arm in because they clung to the inside of the drum, and tug because they were tangled.

He shuffled around her until he was facing the washing machine. A second door, split in two, stable door-style, with a window in each half, opened onto the garden beyond.

"Er, Riika..."

She continued yanking on the sleeve of a blouse. "Hello, Mr. Glavier."

"I've just had a text from my wife. She left her diary at work yesterday, so she's only just noticed that Harriet has a dentist's appointment today for a quarter to five. She was wondering if you'd mind taking her."

"The dentist is the tooth doctor, no?" Riika stuck her head in the washing machine to retrieve a towel.

"Yes. And the appointment is for quarter to five."

"Certainly, Mr. Glavier."

"Here's some money to treat her to KFC afterwards. I think that's still her favorite." He unfolded his wallet, took out some notes. She swiveled to face him as she stood up; he put his wallet away and held out the notes. Somehow the multi-faceted nature of her movements affected his balance. It felt as if the room's center of gravity was shifting, like being on the bridge of a ship slowly tilting to starboard.

"Thank you, Mr. Glavier." She pocketed the money and smiled.

He tasted metal—as if he had a vitamin deficiency.

"Please, call me Alistair."

"Thank you... Alistair."

"I was just—"

A sudden realignment of reflected light caused him to look up and around. Spots and spokes of light flared on the walls, wheeled about them and then faded into the background once more to the sound of a rubbery rumble and wallop, then a squeak so piercing that it seemed to hang in the air.

Both leaves of the back door swung right open, and an octogenarian with positively fetal posture stood, in black Wellingtons, on the tiled floor. The wind blew through him and he made a noise.

"Sorry, Mr. Glavier, I thought it was you and your wife."

"No, you'll have to make do with me, I'm afraid."

"Oh, I just thought I'd come over to let you know I'm about to put the garden to bed." The reedy voice was redolent of the West Country. "This'll be my last visit 'til next year."

"Oh, right." To compensate for any brusqueness, and especially as Verge wouldn't be around for five or so months, Alistair did what was fast becoming a reflex action: he got his wallet out. "Well, in case I don't see you before you go, here you are. Get a little tot of something to see you through the long winter nights." And he parted with a few more notes.

"Oh, thank you very much, Mr. Glavier." The old man's smile had repercussions for his entire face. He now had wrinkles between his wrinkles. "But I can tell you're busy, so I'll leave you to it. See you again next year."

To show just how busy he was, and demonstrate that it had nothing to do with Riika, Alistair turned around and made it out of the room first.

———

When she looked up at him, James felt as if his brain had been puréed.

Then his sister rested her head on his shoulder and he rested his head against her crown. Supernaturally pale in long black coats, they sat in tilted shadow on the stairs. They'd been on their way out, to see a double bill at Riverside Studios, and this was as far as they'd got.

"I'm so glad you didn't kick me out of bed that time," he said. "I was thinking of doing something desperate."

"Like what?"

"Joining the police force."

She tutted and laughed.

Leaning farther in, she pressed her face against his chest and, somewhat muffled by his coat, quoted (or misquoted), "Only those whose desire is weak enough can restrain it."

"I know what you mean." No more joking now. "You're my sister soul."

She raised her head again. "And you're my lover brother."

"You're my second self."

He was still staring into her chocolate button eyes when the front door opened and their father came in.

They were getting increasingly careless about how and where they demonstrated their closeness, although this probably wouldn't have been a problem if it wasn't for the fact they'd been there when Dad went out.

"What is it with you two?" he asked.

———————

Alistair shut his leather-bound two-year diary with a satisfying click, as the lockable fastener at the end of the short strap engaged. Along with his best pen, he placed it beside his well-thumbed Bible on the cabinet next to him. His gaze slid around the large bedroom with its pink carpet, burgundy bedspread with white flowers and white curtains with burgundy flowers.

It was quarter to eleven by his watch. He and Valerie sat up in bed, him in his stripy pajamas, her in a peachy nightdress, in overlapping circles of light.

He heard the sound of a page being turned and looked round at her. "What's the book?" he asked.

"*The Secret History* by Joanna Trollope."

"Don't you mean Donna Tartt?"

"Oh, yes. Tartt, Trollope—I don't know why, I always confuse those two."

He stared, askance.

As it happened, the question had merely been a way of getting her attention. Now that he had it, he broached the subject he was really interested in. "Have you noticed anything odd about James and Louise?"

His wife shook her head. "No. Why?"

"Their lack of social development is staggering. They behave more like toddlers than teenagers." Judging by what he'd seen this evening, they'd regressed all the way back to a state of shared solipsism and projected narcissism. "Apart from work, they never leave the house. And they're always together. Holding hands, mooning around, whispering in corners. It's not natural."

He would never have got away with behaving like that if he'd had a sister, twin or not. Though, a sibling might have taken the pressure off him a bit. When he was growing up, Grandfather Glavier hadn't been the cardiganed has-been padding around in slippers they'd all known. He'd been strict, authoritarian, always telling him what to do and what not to do—endless lists of "Thou shalt" and "Thou shalt not."

So, it wasn't surprising if the closeness the two of them had managed in later life had been problematic, hardly ever carefree. Alistair couldn't forget how, at the end, he'd been expected to show the very kindness he'd been denied.

No, James and Louise had it easy.

Valerie inserted her magnetic bookmark into her book. "Well, they're twins, aren't they? They're bound to be closer than other brothers and sisters. In fact, I think it's rather sweet myself. A real pigeon pair."

"They're not bloody conjoined." He switched his wall light off with a quick tug of its short cord, then slid down the bed until the back of his head hit the pillow. "It's damn odd if you ask me."

"It's not safe to be socializing at the moment, though, with this "Fiend" out there."

"Valerie, I really think you're overreacting about that. Besides, it's prostitutes who are at risk now, isn't it?"

"The last victim was a prostitute and one of the early ones. But they're all someone's wife, girlfriend, sister, daughter. So, personally I'm relieved James and Louise like staying in."

Alistair restricted his profound disagreement to a sigh.

He'd already told the twins that they should get out more, meet people.

"I can't wait to touch—which, on our new tariff, would save you quite a bit."

James often called his sister from work. It helped keep him going. And she was used to him lapsing into sales talk whenever his supervisor walked past.

"See you later, darling," he whispered, doing a 360-degree sweep from his swivel chair to check that no one had been listening.

Desks were arranged in rows, with five-foot partitions between them. His was near the center, so he had fellow telesales operatives on all sides. The clack of computer keys, the gabble of voices, continued all around.

Their suited supervisor stared out of his office window, so James adjusted the mouthpiece on his headset, looked up the next name on his screen and called the number. Already, telemarketing got on his nerves, because you had to say the same lines over and over again and still sound manically enthusiastic each time.

Hence it didn't take long to decide when, at the end of the day, his neighbor, Colin, leaned over the partition dividing their desks and said, "Fancy a drink?"

"Love one," croaked James, reaching for his throat lozenges.

Colin had joined the firm a few weeks before. He had short, light brown, slightly reddish hair, and blue eyes with blond lashes. Today he wore baggy jeans with rugged hems and a pale blue *White Stuff* T-shirt.

It was easy to get on with Colin. He was a simple fellow: honest, upright. One couldn't imagine him overstepping a blood-bond, for example.

Less than quarter of an hour later they sat nursing their pints at a dimpled brass-topped table in The Dirty Ear.

"Did you see the match on Saturday?" asked Colin.

"No, I missed it." James wasn't even sure which match Colin meant.

"Oh, well, you didn't miss much. Anyway, what do you think of Don?"

Don was their supervisor.

"Oh, he's all right," replied James, noncommittally.

"He would be if he wasn't a Red."

"He's a communist?"

"No, no. A Liverpool supporter."

James quickly tried to steer the conversation onto safer ground. "Read any good books lately?"

"Nah. I mean, who reads these days? Music's disappeared down the digital chute. Books are going. And I suppose we'll be next—soon as we reach the singularity."

James smiled as if he knew what Colin was on about.

"The last physical book I read was ages ago." Colin looked up and to the side. "That book of religious claptrap..." He scratched his temple. "You know, the one that everyone's read..."

"What, the Bible?"

"No, no, *The Da Vinci Code.*"

James wasn't quite sure whether this particular misunderstanding reflected badly on him or Colin. But if he possessed a poor relationship with reality, he blamed Dad.

He tried again: "Do you like The White Lies?"

"Ah, The White Lies; now you're talking. They're from West London, you know."

At last, he'd hit on something they were both knowledgeable about. So they discussed that instead.

Afterwards, Colin gave him a lift home in his classic sports car.

"Wow," came his reaction, as the throaty MG rolled to a halt at the end of Linden Close. "Do you live in that place? It's like a mansion."

The End House looked even bigger in the early dark.

"We haven't lived there long."

The cones of light extending from the front of the car bleached the hedge and everything in the gap in it white. James could tell from the way Colin craned to peer through the gate that his drinking companion wouldn't mind a peek at the interior. This was the downside of work being less judgmental than school. He'd been accepted, shown hospitality, and now he was expected to reciprocate.

"Do you want to see inside?"

"Yeah, why not?"

Colin turned off the headlights, cut the engine, and silence—or what passes for silence in a city—enveloped them as they got out and made their way through the gate and up the strip of concrete to the front door.

James had barely got it open when it caught on the mat. As he beckoned his companion through the narrow gap first, his stomach tightened. Louise would be home. He hadn't seen her all day and here he was letting a stranger gatecrash their twins-only world and walk freely amid the trip-wire of their love.

CHAPTER 9

After escorting Colin into the lounge, James hurried up the hallway to the kitchen.

He'd just put the kettle on and spooned coffee and sugar into two mugs when he heard a rustle of clothing. Turning, he saw his sister, who now favored smart pencil skirts and leather ballerina pumps.

"Ahh, you're making me coffee," she said. "That's nice. But guess what, Mum and Dad aren't home yet. And Riika's taken Harriet to her ballet class. So it's just us."

Louise's hands burrowed inside his clothes; he grabbed them and placed them down by her sides. She stared at him, goldfish-mouthed.

"We can't," he whispered.

Suddenly he saw their love as an outsider would see it: against nature, and equally contemptuous of civilization.

Yet Louise was scowling, so he quickly explained, "I've got a friend round."

"A friend?"

Only when he heard her say the word did he realize how odd it sounded, which wasn't surprising. The last time either of them had used it had probably been at primary school. Little things like this reminded him how divorced they were from mainstream life. Not only was what they got up to aberrant; what would be perfectly ordinary for anyone else—having a friend round—was weird in their world.

———————

"Would you like to meet him?"

"O-kay."

For Louise, this was like swallowing a rock. She had no desire to meet him and only acquiesced for James' sake.

They went through to the lounge and the guest's gaze crossed from her twin to her, then ricocheted back and forth between them.

"Louise, this is Colin. Colin, this is Louise."

Colin grinned dementedly. "Good grief, I'm seeing double."

"Hi."

This was her smileless greeting. While James went to finish making the coffee, she slouched over to the armchair left of the fireplace.

She kicked off her pumps and sat down. Colin perched on the edge of the sofa. His hands cupped his knees. "It's a nice place you've got here."

"Thanks."

She didn't bother trying to make polite conversation in return. She just stared at the empty grate, and beamed a testy thought across the room. *Hurry up and go...*

James came back with three coffees. After handing out two, he placed the third on the table and fell backwards into the arms of the chair by the window as if he were a ball caught by a glove.

"I heard a fox outside my window last night," said Colin.

James nodded. "Yeah, we hear them here too."

"Terrifying cry, isn't it?"

"Excruciating."

"Especially given all that's going on at the moment. I even tweeted about it. Are either of you on Twitter?"

James shook his head. "Nah."

"Facebook?"

"Er, no."

"Regular email then? I've just got to send you a link to this video I saw the other night."

"Oh, Dad won't let us have the internet in the house," Louise said. "He says it's a mirror of human consciousness: nine tenths filth."

James stared at her as if to ask where all this was coming from. But at least it closed down that particular channel of communication.

"Harsh," said Colin.

"Oh, we're lucky he lets us have a television," she said. "Not that we watch it much."

"So what do you do with all your free time?"

"Charades, crosswords, cribbage…"

Colin tipped his head back to drink his coffee and James mouthed, "Cribbage?"

Yet on a roll, she'd just thought of further Cs when the visitor said, "Right, I've got to go, I'm afraid."

He gave her a lingering look and added, "I'll call round again sometime, maybe."

She forced a smile. *Not on my account.*

Her brother saw him out and then rushed back. "What the hell's cribbage?"

Before she could upbraid him for wasting what they called "twin time," a key turned in the front door.

Mum rushed through to ask, "Who was that young man?"

"You didn't tell me she was so sexy." Colin leaned against the partition.

"Hey, that's my sister you're talking about," said James, as he swept the evening shift's detritus off his desk and into the bin—plastic cups with dried coffee dregs at the bottom and a pungent polystyrene foam food container.

"Yeah, it's a pity she looks so much like you."

James lifted his gaze. "Hey, watch it. But you're right, for fraternal twins we're remarkably alike."

"Twins, right..." Colin's head tilted to one side. An incipient smile twitched on his lips. "So, what, was there a special offer on that week or something? Two for the price of one? Buy one, get one free?"

"Something like that. And I've got another sister." James likewise suppressed a smile now. "She's more your type. A real babe."

Colin's eyes gleamed. "Really?"

"Yeah, she's still at primary school."

They could have ribbed each other in this fashion indefinitely, but their dark-suited, yellow-tied supervisor knocked on the window of his office and made a phone-to-ear gesture with his clenched hand; managerial sign language for "Get working."

"Guess what," said James. "It's Colin's birthday next week and he's having a party on Saturday."

"That's nice for you," his sister replied.

"You're invited too."

The same flat tone: "I can't wait."

*What have I—*He didn't like to look at her directly because he was finding it hard to focus.

She sat in the chair in her room. He sprawled at her feet. It saved falling over. Reality had developed a paused-VHS wobble.

He'd gone to the pub again with Colin and a few of his colleague's friends. This time he'd got home much later—by bus. Yet the alcohol hadn't left him completely insensible.

"What's wrong, Lou?"

"Nothing."

"Come on, love. What is it?"

"It's just..."

"Yes?"

"Well..."

"What?"

"Colin."

"Colin? What about Colin?"

"I'm sick of hearing about him, that's what."

James propped himself up with his elbows and stared at her.

"What do you mean?" He tried to smile at her, before his head dropped.

"All of a sudden it's Colin this, Colin that. What about you and me?"

James' erratic vision took her in again. "Oh, come on, Lou. Don't be like that. I was just telling you about an invitation to the guy's party—which applies to you as much as me."

"Well, at least we'll be together. That's one thing, I suppose."

James gave a beery laugh. "He fancies you."

"Who does?"

"Colin."

He watched her breathe in sharply as if taking a fortifying drag on a smoldering cigarette. "I suppose he's quite good-looking."

James levered himself into a right angle and his eyes ceased their roving and locked on to hers. Her remark had sobered him up.

"In a boring sort of way," she added.

"Phew," he said, lying back down. "You had me worried there."

She laughed.

He frowned up at her. "There are some things you shouldn't joke about, you know."

"Why would I want to love a stranger?" She slid off the chair and to the floor at his side. "When I've got you." She put her arms around him. "My own flesh and blood."

"So I don't need to start getting jealous?"

"The only person who's jealous round here…" She nibbled at his left ear lobe. "…is me."

"And what about Saturday? Are we going?"

"Where is it?"

"Hell."

"The nightclub?"

"Yeah."

"Yep, I think I can safely assure you that we're going to Hell."

Alistair turned up the collar of his thick winter coat and held it in place with one hand, to protect against the raw wind, while opening the driver's door of his car with the other. He was about to dip his head and get in when he heard click-click-click in the darkness behind him. He turned to see Riika, in a short black skirt and black jacket, stepping out of the garden gate.

"Can I give you a lift anywhere?" He couldn't just drive off without asking.

"Oh, thank you, Mr. Glavier. If you're going anywhere near Packers Lane…"

"I know the name but you'll have to remind me where it is."

They got in and she gave him directions as they belted up.

"Right, no problem. And it's Alistair, remember?"

"Oh, yes, sorry… Alistair."

He smiled round at her. "I was just on my way to Friends of the Friendless."

"Really? I like this car."

They joined the main road and the automatic Mercedes went up through the gears Pianola-style as the road whooshed underneath them.

Sticking up from the front of the bonnet like a gun sight, the Mercedes-Benz emblem swung across the road as—following instructions to the letter—he took a right turn at a crossroads. Despite traffic lights at green and enough of a gap in oncoming traffic, he still got tooted at.

"I think they must have put up a "no right turn" sign there or something. Never mind. We made it. Your English has improved dramatically by the way."

Synchronizing glances Riika-ward with the slow strobe of successive streetlamps, he saw her blush.

And now he couldn't understand why he'd ever disliked her, because she was refreshingly straightforward. She didn't harbor a shadow self, or conceal a cast of selves, Russian-doll-like, within her. Her sudden silences were as genuine as her bursts of speech. And if he criticized the twins for staying in, it hardly made sense to complain about her going out. One mode of behavior had to be acceptable, and she was just a normal, fun-loving girl.

She sat beside him, all hair and eyes and nails and mouth, with her heady perfume filling the car. In the sweep of a passing streetlamp, he caught a glimpse of her long, slender legs, today sheathed in black ribbed tights.

He could taste his own mouth, and it had a metallic tang.

"I was wondering," he began, before he'd even considered what precisely it was he was going to say, "do you fancy a meal sometime?"

They glided to a halt near the entrance to the cobbled side street she'd asked him to bring her to. She opened the door before he even had the handbrake on and got out. *Oh, hell.* How could he have been so stupid?

And then she spun around and leaned back in, with a smile. *It's okay. She's all right.*

Out-smiling her, he made the invitation more specific: "What about Saturday night?"

Valerie would be attending the promotion of her company's new product during the day and the celebrations in the evening. Harriet had asked to spend the weekend at a school-friend's. And, incredibly, James and Louise were going to a party.

If all this seemed somewhat surreptitious, he was only inviting a long-term guest of the family's out for a meal. And what could possibly be wrong in that?

"Maybe," she answered.

Adding, "Thanks for the ride, Mr. Glavier."

"Have a—" The car door clunked shut. "—good evening."

Late to begin with, he was ridiculously late now; and he'd come out of his way, so he had to turn the car around.

He'd just set off again when his Bluetooth headset vibrated. His hand jerked up to it. "Hello?"

"Ah, Mr. Glavier."

He recognised that leathery voice. It was his voyeur client, Godfrey. They'd made some progress recently. Yet unscheduled calls were at his discretion and he really didn't feel able to give him his full and proper attention at the moment.

"Listen, I know I said to phone before rather than afterwards—the minute you felt the urge coming on—it's just, this really isn't a good time. So stop whatever it is you're doing, remember everything I told you and we'll talk tomorrow."

"But I need to talk *now*."

"I'm sorry, Godfrey."

"Mr. Glavier, I swear, if you hang up on m—"

A black car slows, but doesn't stop.

"Isn't it amazing how one man has brought the city to its knees?" Rachel says. "How one man has made men and women mistrust each other, even more."

"Don't worry, Rach. We've got each other's backs."

"I don't think I could have come out otherwise, I really don't."

She and Kathy stand either side of a lamppost near the entrance to an alleyway: their escape route, should they require one.

A red Alfa Romeo rolls up, with the knock-knock-knock of loud music coming from within.

"Here's my lift," jokes Kathy.

Her cracked voice gives her age away. Yet any false impression of mannishness is amply compensated for by lit-up looks painstakingly applied, stick-on lashes, blond extensions, her cloud-white fitted coat, black leggings and four-inch heels.

"Are you sure? He looks shifty to me."

Rachel studies the driver, who can't be much older than she is, with slicked-back hair and sliding eyes that seek out her friend. It's funny how the younger ones go for Kathy and the older ones go for her.

"They're all shifty, love."

"No, I'm serious. I've a really bad feeling about this one."

"Trust me; he won't give me any trouble."

"Please, just be careful."

"See you in a bit."

Kathy gets in the Alfa Romeo. It roars off, and Rachel's fears crystallize—*I'll never see you alive again.*

It's only then she realizes she's forgotten to make a note of the registration.

Along with taking it in turns to go off, this was one of the two main safety measures they agreed on. Now she won't have anything useful to give the police.

She's mentally shuffling through the various horrors that could be waiting at the end of her friend's journey when a hand seizes her throat. She can't breathe in. She can't breathe out. Her arms are trapped. Her legs thrash.

He lifts her up. Now she's running, off the ground, as she's borne backwards up…

———————

No, it was no good. Valerie's imagination gave out.

She'd switched the radio on in the kitchen, for Radio 4's *Today* program, only to learn about the body found in a

Shepherd's Bush alleyway and how it looked as if The Fiend had got the better of police and prostitutes by going back to arriving and leaving on foot. Straight away, she'd extrapolated out from the few facts given and amplified them to create the semblance of a whole in her mind. Yet maybe one could never successfully re-imagine someone else's last moments.

The attempt had helped her come to a decision, though, about the children's social plans for the weekend.

None of them were setting foot outside. She wouldn't allow it.

———————

Getting up late, as it was Saturday, James smiled when his sister came trotting into his room bobbily, on tiptoes, wearing only her pants.

"I just want to borrow that old pair of jeans," she said. "You know, that tatty pair that fit us both? I don't know how."

"We share the same duff genes."

He heard the scrape of clothes-laden hangers and the triangle-like tinkle of free ones as, obviously unamused, she rummaged through his wardrobe.

Once ready, they made their way downstairs in silence as they listened out to determine whether they were alone or not.

He was just starting to hope that they had the place to themselves when they came across their father, sitting at the kitchen table drinking a coffee as he read the *Daily Mail*—their mother's paper. She, presumably, had already left for the big *Zing!* promotion. Apparently, the more deleterious side-effects had all been addressed.

James put the kettle on while his sister put some bread in the toaster. Then he fetched the juice from the fridge while she got the plates and cutlery out.

He poured them each a glass of orange juice.

Taking the glasses over to the kitchen table, he sat down opposite his father and studied the front page of the *Daily Mail*, which had an angry plea for the incarceration of The Fiend and photos of the six murdered women.

"There's no escaping it, is there," he said.

"I know; it's all over the inside too." Louise peered over Dad's shoulder as she waited for the toast to pop up. "'The 38-year-old man from the Amberly area who has been helping police with their inquiries…' Hey, I didn't know about that. Did you?"

"No, I didn't." He and his sister really were shamefully out of touch. "I wonder who it is."

"'…is believed to have had links with Alison Claye, the fifth murder victim. The pressure on police to make an arrest is enormous. There have been calls for Detective Chief Superintendent Mace's resignation…'"

James sniggered. "I can't see the golf-playing pillocks of society letting it come to that. The Lodge needs someone to bin their parking fines."

The screen of newsprint dropped away, leaving him staring at two black pinpricks at the center of deep-set eyes. The eyes remained fixed on him even as the head to which they belonged turned to face Louise. Only at the last moment did they dart in her direction.

"Do you two mind? I'm trying to read this."

James returned to his corner of the kitchen, his sister to hers—he to make the tea; she to see to the toast.

"Let's take it through to the lounge," Louise said thirty seconds later, as James strangled the drawstring tea bags and she stabbed the butter. "We won't be in anyone's way in there."

They picked up the mugs and plates and James followed Louise through the doorway.

"Yeah, we can watch that program we recorded about sinister religious cults and all the *Jesus hypocrites*." James raised his voice to make sure his father heard.

———————————

Louise's mind fizzed. "I can't believe they've caught the killer."

"Well, they might not have yet," said her brother.

"But "Helping police with their inquiries" is just a euphemism, isn't it? It means they've got their man."

"They need actual evidence to charge him, though, and they haven't yet."

"Mum must think they're going to. That's obviously why she had a change of heart about the club."

Shortly before four, Louise and James were sitting on the floor in her room when they heard Dad leave, somewhat early, for the Saturday evening service. With Mum at the Zing! event, Harriet at a friend's and Riika out for the day, they had the house to themselves until time to leave for the nightclub.

They sprang to their feet and into each other's arms. Her mouth glued itself to his. His hands and her hands blindly unbuttoned, unbuckled, unzipped. Turning and turning, they stumbled forwards, sideways, backwards, across the room.

One day they wouldn't always have to wait for other people to leave before their own lives could begin. It was that thought alone that kept her going in the unremarkable in-between times. Especially during the dragging hours of separation as they both worked hard to save enough to be able to afford to live, as a couple, out of range of God's spies.

Knocking into the bed, they crashed onto it.

By now they were down to their underwear. He'd just climbed on top of her when the phone rang.

She groaned.

"I thought this only happened in films," he said, rolling off her.

He got up and ran out of the room.

A few seconds later the phone stopped, mid-ring, and she could hear him faintly at the foot of the stairs.

"Hello."

"Oh, hi."

"Yeah, course."

"You're joking."

"No, I definitely don't remember that."

"Yeah."

"Mm."

"Well, maybe."

"Okay, I'll tell her."

"To be honest, I'm not sure."

"Don't worry about it."

"Okay."

"Yep. See you."

It took him ages to come back up. When he did finally return, still wearing just his boxer shorts, he crept in.

"That was Colin. About the party."

She didn't like the sound of this. "Well?"

"He wanted to know if we were still going."

"Of course we're going. Why do you think I bought that dress?"

"And..."

"Yes?"

"He asked if he mentioned it was "Fancy Dress Night" at the club."

"Oh, James..."

It felt as if a weight on a pulley had dropped — plummeted — inside her chest.

She hadn't taken much interest in Colin's party until they'd been told they couldn't go. Ever since they'd been told they could, she'd been quite looking forward to it.

Her brother rushed up to the edge of the bed. "I'm sorry, Lou. Either he mentioned it and I forgot, or he forgot to mention it."

"Well, it's pretty bloody important, because where are we going to find costumes now? There's nothing for it; we'll have to cancel."

"I'm really sorry, love." He climbed into bed next to her. "Can you forgive me?" She stared up at the ceiling. "I'll pay for the dress." With no room to bend his body, he had to lie on his side, perfectly straight.

She turned her head. Her eyes completed the motion. Then she smiled. And soon she was laughing.

"What's so funny?"

She composed herself, hooked a strand of hair out of her mouth and sat up. "Come on, we've got to get ready."

"We have? What for?"

"The party, of course."

"How? We haven't got costumes."

She smiled. "Hell, here we come…"

———————

The lantern of the moon hung in the dark sky, illuminating, in black and white, the house, the lawn and the trees.

As Alistair neared the house, the polychromatic palette of the flaring security light rendered the milk-and-water moonlight redundant.

Whistling despite the flesh-withering cold and clutching a gift bag, he got his key out. He let himself in and, knocking the door shut with his heel, took his coat off. He'd just hung his coat up on the stand when, arm-clamping the gift bag to his side, facing front and looking up, he noticed two figures: one male, the other female, in faint silhouette at the top of the stairs.

He stopped whistling, smiled instead, and flicked the switch for the hallway light. As soon as he turned it on from below, one of the twins turned it off from above. They headed down as he headed up. So the moon was their only night-light.

"Oops," he heard, from Louise; though whether with a hiccup or a giggle he couldn't tell. At last, they had a social life.

"Have a nice evening," he said, as they passed him mid-way between floors in the second-hand light.

For a moment he had the sensation of looking at them in the wonky world of a fairground mirror as a very tall Louise, in high heels, waggled her fingers at him as they continued, whisper-giggle-whisper, down the staircase.

He quickly turned away and continued up it, because he had a social engagement of his own to go to—one that made his stomach flutter.

He was just getting his clothes together when his mobile phone rang.

"Hello?"

"Mr. Glavier, it's me."

"Ah, Godfrey. Good to hear from you. How have you been?"

Even Godfrey's verbose response couldn't dent his smile today, as he pulled the perfumed note from his pocket and read it again:

Dear Alistair,
Is your offer still open?
I would like to come.
Yours
Riika X

The flat-screen TV was on mute. Instead, Lady Gaga played on the surround-sound music system as a gallery of windows with lurid signs slid by in the neon night.

"Get your bottom out of my face," said a man in a red Devil costume.

"Sorry," replied a waiflike woman, attempting to hold down the back of her tutu as she bent over in front of him in the mauve and turquoise interior with mirror ceiling and squiggly fiber optics. "I was just getting a drink."

She wobbled slightly upon straightening up. "Ooh, I think I've had more than I thought."

"We're moving," he reminded her.

"Oh, yes. Course we are."

She giggled as she rejoined him, and two other women, on the side-facing, curving-in-and-out leather sofa.

"Why didn't we take the four by four?" asked a dark-haired woman in a leopard-print top.

She directed her question to the man, who now turned to her.

"I wanted us to arrive in luxury."

"Where is it we're going again?" asked a woman with an Eastern European accent and short dyed red hair.

"Hell," he said. "And we're going to do some serious celebrating. Because I've been released without charge."

The women smiled.

"There are no stains on my character."

Now he smiled, and the women laughed.

And they all clinked glasses, as the long black limousine swept on through the murderous night.

CHAPTER 10

Under a sky the color of Coca-Cola, complete with slice-of-lemon moon, a red double-decker pulled up at a bus stop. A few moments later, it heaved off again, leaving a couple of wrapped-up teenagers standing outside a red and white KFC with a stripy awning.

"I'm not getting the night bus home. When it's time to leave, I'm taking a taxi."

She had a low voice.

"All right, take a taxi."

He had a soft, fluty voice, which really ought to have broken by now.

They crossed the road and walked along on the other side. And although he stepped onto the pavement and she remained in the gutter, in her high heels she was still the taller of the two.

They turned up a dark side street with cobbles like hard, tightly packed loaves of bread. She was picking her way past a stretch limo when her left shoe went on one side and she stumbled and fell.

"Are you all right?" he asked, helping her back up.

"Bloody stupid shoes."

They didn't have far to go. Just the other side of a shuttered entrance, stone steps led up to a door above which flashed the legend, in red neon, "Hell."

A silver Mercedes-Benz pulled up outside Delph's, the restaurant.

The dark-suited driver walked around to open the passenger door. A long leg in patterned tights appeared as a young blonde woman stepped out. He shut the car door and rested a hand on the nape of her neck as if to hold in place the baby blue stole draped around her shoulders.

Turning, they walked along side by side. The sound of her stilettos ricocheted off the pavement until he stepped ahead and pushed on the half-glass door.

Louise handed her coat to the cloakroom assistant. Spinning around, she faced her brother. He stared back with burnished eyes—the artificial effect of lashes clotted with something as thick and black as boot polish, and shadow-brushed lids in turn set off by powdered paleness. His lips, covered in a waxy, oily residue a shade or two darker than his natural color, formed into a smile. His black Lycra dress (hers) clung to his non-curves, and rippled when he transferred his weight from one hip to the other.

She looked down at her blue tie, white shirt, dark grey suit and old school shoes (all his). She didn't have any make-up on and her hair had been cut boyishly short, by him, at her request. She didn't even have a bust, because she'd wrapped a bandage round and round her chest to flatten it.

Her brother, by contrast, did have a bust. She'd padded out his bra with balled tissues.

"'Scuse," said a giant Duracell bunny-rabbit, heading up a pristine angular corridor, like the gangway in a spaceship.

Louise and her twin set off up it as well. He lurched as he stilt-walked beside her in a pair of heels from Riika's shoe collection. Her shoes had all been too small, so they'd let themselves into the attic room and taken—borrowed—some of the *au pair*'s.

They'd make sure to return them tomorrow.

Louise looked round at her brother. He had on the long dark brown wig she'd worn as an extra in a school play. He kept sliding bits of the fringe out of his eyes. In addition to the clatter of his heels, she could hear a nylony chafing sound as the end of the corridor loomed.

He turned suddenly and bent over with his hand flat against the wall, propping him up. "I don't know if I can do this."

"Oh, come on, don't be such a baby, you'll be fine." She grabbed his hand with its painted fingernails and hauled him the rest of the way.

They passed through—it felt as if they were sucked through—a pair of sound-proofed doors, and it was like walking into a dream. Black decor, pricked with light; a goose-bumpy operatic intro. The song turned out to be Dario G's *Dream to Me* with its thrumming beat, which vibrated in her chest, and vocals that swooped and soared. The asymmetrical partitions only stretched so far. Beyond, an expanse of dark air, relieved by patches of colored, light-reflecting smoke that smelled of just-opened cans of pop and drifted under the metalwork of a studio-like ceiling.

Drawn towards the silver railing, they stared down at a spinning mirror ball the size of a small planet. Beneath that was a pit—obviously the hub of the club, because beautiful and grotesque beings, fantastical creatures, pumped the driving beat for all it was worth.

Swaying vertiginously, in his high heels, James turned away from the balcony.

Louise followed.

The red, yellow, blue, green and orange exhalations from the disco lights were as beautiful and useless as distant supernovae. The minute white lights in the partitions and ceiling were as pretty and ineffectual as stars; so, most of the time they were in semi-darkness.

Turning a corner, they came across a little oasis of light featuring a recess with comfy chairs and a staircase.

"This way, Louise," she said.

"Okay, James," he replied.

Louise assumed they must be getting close to the bar because the platform became crowded. A whole perfumery's worth of scents assailed her nostrils. The effect reminded her of walking into the White Chapel on a Sunday morning. Though these aromas hit her harder than that. She isolated vanilla, now almond, now musk, now woodiness, while all the time a hundred others clamored for her attention.

Batman and a female Robin held hands by an aquarium; Lara Croft threw up over a potted plant; Bob the Builder relaxed with a joint. And Louise wasn't sure but she thought she counted more than two sexes. She even thought she spotted an extra-terrestrial.

She and her brother squeezed past two women, one with dyed red hair, the other a brunette, both posing as gum-chewing prostitutes. The red-haired one wore a white midriff top tied at the front, red hot pants and black boots, and clutched a micro-handbag.

"Which one do you fancy, Hels?" she asked, with a Polish — or possibly Russian — accent.

The brunette, who'd gone for a leopard-print top, a PVC miniskirt and pointy Cruella de Vil shoes — considerably longer than they needed to be, yet doubtless ideal for tripping up small children, on the other side of the street — leaned towards them with garish eyes and lurid lips. "Both."

"Cocaine really gets up my nose," said a giggly angel with a tinsel halo bobbing above her short, babyish blonde hair as she bopped on the spot in a tutu and a dinky pair of ballet slippers.

Behind her, an exceedingly tall man in a shiny red Devil costume held forth: "So they showed me this beautiful corpse. Then they asked me, 'Did you ever have sex with the deceased?' So I said, 'No, I've never seen her before.' And they shut the refrigerated drawer."

Louise made it to the brightest part of the platform, the bar. Her brother hung back. Sighing, she leaned in and gave their orders.

She took them over to James and put them down on a small high table so that she could put her wallet away. He picked up the lager and she picked up the white wine. Laughing, they swapped.

After his first sip, he shout-whispered in her ear, "What are we doing here, with a bunch of bisexual, coke-snorting necrophiliacs?"

She thought for a moment. "We can talk."

A smile flickered across his lips.

They headed inwards and stopped five feet short of the edge. He stood half behind her.

To their right, a blonde goth accosted Dracula's daughter. "Oh, the corpse look is so in this year. You must tell me the name of your mortician."

Louise shook her head. "I'm going to have weird dreams tonight."

"See Colin anywhere?" asked James.

She glanced round and pointed over her shoulder. "Probably that bloke in the NBC suit."

He turned.

Standing against the outer wall, by a red fire extinguisher, was someone wearing a nuclear, biological and chemical warfare suit, who obviously knew something that the rest of them didn't.

Louise heard something, like a scratch on the record, which sounded uncannily like her brother's name being called.

Colin, dressed as a pantomime policeman, waved from the next gantry along from theirs and mouthed, "Wait there."

When Colin rounded the corner, his eyes alighted on her. With a "Sorry" here and an "Excuse me" there—in between shouting out "All right, mate?" and "Couldn't get a costume, then?"—he made his way over.

She had to suppress the laugh that bubbled up when Colin turned to her brother, with what could only be described as *hot eyes*, and said, "Louise, lovely to see you again. Don't worry about not having a—"

Scrutinizing James as if he had a monocle lodged in one eye, Colin stopped, recoiled. "Bloody hell. You look even more like each other than you normally do."

"It wasn't my idea," said James.

This is going to be fun.

Colin blushed. He appeared to have shrunk inside his tunic. When he'd recovered, he addressed them again, the right way around: "Hi, mate. Hi, Louise. Thanks for coming."

Louise failed to understand what her brother saw in his colleague. She had to resist the temptation to do something outrageous. Yet as well as endowing her with a thrilling sense of freeness, James' togs provided the perfect protection against unwanted advances. The only downside was having to wear three pairs of socks to make his shoes fit. "Thanks. Happy birthday. And, um, witty outfit."

"Oh, do you think so?"

No, she didn't think so at all.

Fortunately James took over ego-massage duties—with hearty congratulations on the choice of venue.

"Yeah, great, isn't it," said Colin. "You can get to the dance floor via the lift or stairs. The stairs leading up are to chill-out rooms or private rooms."

"Where's the alien from?" asked her brother.

One silver-numbered epaulette was replaced by another as his friend looked around, first one way, then the other, straining to get a glimpse of the green chap with one eye in the middle of his forehead. Colin's neck unwound. "Oh, somewhere just outside Ursa Minor."

"Who are all the others?" Louise said.

"Well, you see that guy in the Devil suit?" He raised an arm with a miniature zebra crossing around the sleeve and pointed.

Satan's pair of sleek red horns gleamed in the light from the bar as he conversed with a bin-bag Catwoman.

"Yeah, we saw him when we came in," she said.

"Well, I just had the most extraordinary conversation with him," continued Colin. "Because you know this killer that everyone's talking about?"

"You mean The Fiend, or whatever his name is?" Louise asked.

"Yeah, that's right—The Fiend. Well, guess what? He's the latest suspect. He told me so himself. The police recently took him in for questioning but had to release him."

"Then that can't be him," said James. "The police are still interviewing someone. We read it this morning."

"Yeah, him. They released him this afternoon."

"They did?" Louise glanced at the man again. "Well, if he's a suspect, why did they let him go?"

"Because, apart from the fact he knew one of the victims, they didn't have anything linking him to the murders. So it was a battle of intellect and he came out on top, he said."

Louise peered over at the Devil. When he looked up, she looked away.

A drop of sweat dripped from her right armpit and, landing just below her bandaged ribcage, trickled down her side. Tundra-melt-water cold, it tortured her with its slow progress until eventually it was absorbed into the waistband of her brother's boxer shorts.

She shuffled around, away from the bar. "So what's he doing here?"

"Celebrating."

"But how do you know him?"

"I've never met him before in my life."

"But it's your party."

"I know. He must have come up from one of the lower levels—either the lounge area, in the mezzanine below this, or the dance floor—and decided to gatecrash it."

"Well, aren't you going to chuck him out?"

"Oh, I can't chuck him out. If he left, that would be the evening over. Half these people are his friends. Besides, it's not every day you get a possible serial killer at your party, is it?"

When he was relaxed he sounded almost as flippant as her brother, which at least solved the mystery as to how, why, they got on.

He even added, "I'll introduce you if you like."

Why on earth would I want to meet a murder suspect?

Yet before she could decline the offer, James accepted it.

Was he mad? Taking advantage of the fact that his friend had peered off to the right, she shot him an admonitory scowl.

Colin waved to a couple of corpulent Teletubbies, who started jiggling as soon as they saw him. "Just got a few new arrivals to welcome, then I'll introduce you."

Perfume mingled with wood smoke as the volume rose at some tables, fell at others. Multiple conversations overlapped, filling Alistair's ears with background babble.

Seated opposite Riika, in a lounge chair by the stone hearth at the bar end of the restaurant, he watched as she got as close to the fire as she possibly could. She held her foot out and let the spiked shoe dangle. Only inches away, amid crackling and sputtering, yellowy-gold flames fed on orangey-red logs.

Black lace hosiery stretched this direction here, that direction there as it charted the contours of her leg.

"They're very expensive," she said.

He looked up to find her pale eyes focused on his face. He subjected his voice-box to a change of gears, double-declutched, to buy himself a tad more time as he tried to recall what it was they'd been talking about.

Of course—the pashmina wrap he'd got her as a little present.

He'd bought one for Valerie, several years ago, and it was the only gift he'd been able to think of that didn't involve jewelry.

"I'm just…glad you like it." Left leg jiggling, he gripped his knee. As soon as he realized that if he appeared schoolboy-flushed he could always blame the dry heat of the fire, or the wet heat of the whisky, his hand relaxed along with his leg. "It's thin enough to fit through a wedding ring, you know."

"What about the eye of a camel?"

"Ah, I'm not sure about that."

She won that rally, and he didn't begrudge her the accomplishment one bit. He laughed—then felt hollowed-out inside.

Taking his cue from Riika's lifting eyes, he glanced over his shoulder and jumped when he discovered that there was someone standing there: a man in black and white whose features somehow failed to cohere, as if he had one man's chin, another man's nose, a third man's forehead. "Excuse me, sir, madam, if you'd care to follow me this way…"

Alistair gulped down his drink and they got to their feet, so the waiter could show them to their table.

"This is Louise and that's James," Colin shouted, over a pounding beat. "Or should I say, *this* is Louise and *that's* James."

Talk about a cack-handed introduction. The real Louise hung her head to stop herself shaking it. The irony wasn't lost on her that, just when she wanted to demonstrate confidence, she found herself dressed in men's clothes and staring at the floor.

Thankfully, she didn't attract so much attention in male attire.

"I think it's obvious who I am," said the Devil. "But you can call me Nick."

Looking up, and then higher up—Nick was a head taller than anyone else—she started when she saw his eyes. They were red; and not from fatigue, or drink. They weren't bloodshot. The irises were red, and only the fact that they weren't quite as bright as what he had on made them seem in any way normal.

His all-in-one costume—seamless from built-in boots to skin-tight hood—was a garish red. He looked as if he'd been molded out of some kind of plastic.

"I've been to Hell and now I'm back," he added, with a flourish of his cape and a one-step-forward thunk of his right boot. "Do you like my tan?"

Chatty, charming, amusing—he wasn't as she'd expected at all.

Something brushed her shoulder. Seeing that they'd been joined by the angel with blonde, wispy hair, she realized that it was her white, feathery wing.

The young woman had on a bodice, a tutu, tights and ballet slippers, all in white. Except for a bar-code tattoo across her upper arm, she was flawless.

"Daddy," she baby-voiced, "can I have some more sherbet?"

Nick squeezed his fingers into a small pouch-like pocket half way up his side.

The angel turned her gaze on James and Louise. Her face retained its rigid, doll-like cast as she looked from one to the other. She either failed to notice they were wearing each other's clothes or she didn't find it odd at all.

"Cynthia," said Nick, taking out two twisted foil wrappers, "for you, angel, anything."

He was about to give them to her when he paused. "By the way, I know someone who'd like to make your acquaintance."

Cynthia raised an eyebrow in the direction of the big brown bear that prowled around, on hind legs, in the background.

She nodded, and the Devil handed over the foil wrappers.

"Just got to powder my nose," she said, giggling as she spun away.

"I run what you might call a…" Already standing close, Nick leaned closer still. He looked at them each in turn as if filming them with his eyes and moved his hands apart as he slid his tongue around his lips. "Sweet shop."

"I can get people to do whatever I want," he continued.

Colin nodded and giggled and put his hand up to the side of his head and, briefly, frowned.

"I get them to sell me their souls."

James glanced at her. He gave his twisted little smile. Though today it had a different slant. She still couldn't get used to having a twin sister.

"By giving them what they crave."

Colin laughed, a little too loudly. He corrected for this with a wink at her and her brother as if to say, "See, I told you he was good."

With predictable naiveté, her brother's friend had assumed, or he hoped, that Nick was a harmless joker. James, she knew, would react this way whether the guy was joking or not. But they were skirting around the central issue here. Was he the murderer or not?

Nick put his hand out and brushed her breast pocket.

The thought of what had just happened stoppered her breath. She stepped back—needing space, space.

Teetering on his heels, James advanced.

"You had a speck of dust there," said Nick.

She exhaled.

James wobbled to a halt.

"I think I need the bathroom," she said, breathing hard.

"Going to spend a pound, eh?" Nick turned and pointed. "It's there."

"Thanks."

She was on course for the Ladies when she heard the clunk of steps behind her and, "Uh-uh. You're in there."

One nudge was all it took to send her flying through the next door along.

With her eyes on the tiled black floor, not daring to look at the man standing with his legs apart at one of the urinals, she headed straight for the nearest cubicle. She slid the lock behind her.

Wiping the seat with a wad of toilet paper, she dropped her trousers and boxer shorts and sat down. But she couldn't go.

Eventually she heard the man's steady stream reduce to a trickle, the tug of a zip and the singing of a tap. A paper towel got extracted and rustled with, footsteps passed and the door to the Gents opened and closed.

Louise flushed the toilet, pulled up her boxers and trousers and opened the cubicle door.

She stepped out and walked up to the silver-bolted mirror—and saw James. She kept forgetting from one moment to the next she was dressed as him.

Leaning over one of the sinks, she splashed water into her face while the sound of the flushed toilet receded to a high hiss.

When she looked up, the Devil was standing behind her.

She gasped.

James came in. His heels clattered on the tiles. "Are you all right, Lou?"

"Yes…"

Nick clapped James on the shoulder, laughing. "Shouldn't you be next door?" He looked from her brother back to her. "So what's going on with you two?"

She stiffened. "What do you mean?"

"The clothes." Nick smiled. "Why, what did you think I meant?"

She blushed, and knowing she wasn't wearing any makeup, blushed even more. "Let's talk about you."

"Me?"

"Why, what's wrong?" She tugged a paper towel from the dispenser, dabbed her face and dried her hands. "Got something to hide?"

He pointed at the door. "Maybe my reputation precedes me."

"Oh?" She threw the paper towel in the bin. "What reputation's that?"

He grinned. "What is it you want to know?"

Her curiosity tore at her. "Is it… Are you…"

"Yes…?"

"Is it you?" she said, breathlessly.

He fixed her with his red, alien eyes. "What you mean is, am I the serial killer?"

She blinked.

Although this was exactly what she meant, she hadn't expected quite such a brazen response.

Her chest heaved. "Yes."

"Oh, you'll have to do better than that." He smiled, turned and left the room.

Louise and her brother hugged. Nick's lack of a denial was as close as she was going to get to a confession; and much closer than she'd expected.

But, to find out for sure, she needed to spend more time in his company. So she hoped the sense of invulnerability James' clothes gave her wasn't entirely illusory, because for that she had to put all thoughts of her own safety aside.

Red candle, white cloth. Man, woman. The images replicated, as in mirrors, at the tables around them. Ambient conversation. Rich food. Lulling wine. Faceless waiters came and went in the low, flickering light. Every now and then they trailed hot food smells.

Alistair had been so busy talking he'd barely touched his steak.

Riika leaned in to ask a question in her velvet voice, her face and arms glowing in votive candlelight. Her eyes were points of light.

Of course, he knew how all this would look if a colleague or acquaintance happened to pass the restaurant and peered through the window. Yet that person would be judging them without sound.

"Yes, it is quite unusual," he said. "But the primary goal of Christian psychoanalysis, or "inverted Freudianism" as some of my critics in the profession insist on calling it, is actually very simple. It's to get the individual to police his or her own thoughts, censor them, to guard against temptation or the memory thereof—to have, if you like, a self-cleaning mind."

The man he was now was the same man he'd been at the Doomsday Church an hour and a half earlier. There was no break in continuity.

He'd invited an honorary member of the family out for a meal, given that, until very recently, he hadn't had any time for her. Worse, he had said horrible things about her, behind her back.

What for a lesser man would be a seduction supper was, for him, expiation.

"Do you control your desires?" Nick the Devil leered at Louise and James in turn. "Or do your desires control you?"

His eyes flashed like silent lightning out at sea at night.

Louise felt little quivers inside her. "Well, our dad's a preacher."

"Oh, a preacher, eh?" Nick smiled. "That must be rather difficult for you."

She turned away and took a sip of the vodka and coke Nick had bought her.

If she'd suspected he knew about their rebellion beneath the bedcovers, now she was sure of it. They lounged either side of him on a squeaky sofa under three converging beams—one vertical, another slanting in from the left, a third from the right. Although only separated from James by one person, Nick's bulk blocked her view of him completely. She couldn't even hold her brother's hand.

The clean guitar riff and swoony swelling synths of The Killers' *Human* drifted up from the dance floor.

A policeman paced in the shadows, jerked spasmodically around (*squeak*), paced, jerked spasmodically around (*squeak*).

Louise giggled as Colin frowned at his rubber-soled shoes.

A man in a purple one-piece terrycloth costume with an upside-down coat hanger sticking out of the top of his head waddled over.

"Eh-oh!"

A green one joined the purple one and they bounced up and down.

"Eh-oh!"

"Eh-oh!"

Nick came back with two syllables of his own.

In fact, it looked as if Tinky Winky and Dipsy were under arrest.

Colin dragged them away by the backs of their onesies.

Thank God he's gone.

Suddenly she realized this meant she and her brother were left alone with Nick. Her heart beat faster, pushing the blood through her veins, priming her limbs ready for flight.

"I wasn't always like this," he said, as his arms snaked around her on one side, her twin on the other. She squirmed. Nick squeezed tighter. "I was pure of heart once."

She stopped struggling. *Is this it?* Was he going to unburden himself, confide in them?

"You don't believe me?" He ran his tongue around dry lips, to little or no effect. "Really, I could not have been more different. But did it do me any good? No. And do you know why?"

His head wagged from side to side.

"Why?" enquired Louise, feeling as if she was getting closer to the truth, yet acutely conscious of the pressure of his arm. For if she and James had spent the last half year in moral free fall, then surely now, in fraternizing with someone who could well be The Fiend, they'd hit the bottom.

But she was intrigued, despite herself. She wanted to know his story.

"I was too fucking nice, that's why. Because, you see, kids, Christianity doesn't work. The nicer you are, the worse you get treated." Nick stretched. She could have run if she'd wanted to, but she didn't. "I mean, look at Christ. He was so nice they crucified him. That's all it comes down to if you think about it. Fortunately I realized there isn't any point being good—that sometimes life won't let you be good."

James shot to his feet. "Yes."

She found herself nodding. *You can say that again.* It was like when she read a book or heard a song and a line jumped out at her, expressing a thought she'd had but never articulated.

Her brother clattered around in a circle on his high heels.

Lifting one up behind him to adjust the strap, he almost toppled over.

Nick chuckled. "Yes, I thought you'd understand."

She dropped her gaze, kept it fastened on a floor light.

"Anyway, where was I?" Nick rested the heel of one bright red boot on the toecap of the other. "Oh, yes, standing a foot away from a sheer drop, one step away from Game Over." James sat back down. "But then I thought, Hey, hang on, if I'm going to die, I might as well enjoy myself first." *Can't argue with that.* "So instead of suicide, I chose a new identity. I decided if I can't be good, I want to be bad." *But how bad?* "Fuck morality, I thought." She heard James laugh. "I'm going to go to sleep tonight and tomorrow I'm going to wake up a different person. And that's exactly what I did." Nick's raised boot clomped back down. "I reinvented myself. I acquired a taste for evil. I found I have a talent for it. And I murdered the old me."

He was easily the most disturbed human being she had ever met. Yet for all his bounce and swank, there was a—and she couldn't believe she was thinking this—strange vestige of innocence.

"Evil is individuality," he said, as if reading her mind and demurring, "and I'm vain, I'm egotistical. I admit it. I'm proud of it." *I can believe it.* "Only passionless people find it easy to be virtuous. And I decided quite consciously that I was going to be rapacious." *Uh-oh.* "Because to be completely free you need to abandon all notions of goodness. After all, what's the law other than a list of things you want to do and can't?"

"Good one," cried James.

"What no one tells you, though, is that if you reject one plank of morality, you often have to jettison more. Yet take away too many and the whole edifice collapses." He made a chopping motion with his arm, and she jumped. "Then there's no way back."

A woman in blue Avatar body paint came up the spiral staircase from the dance floor, took one look at James dressed as her, her dressed as James, the Devil between them, and said, "Christ."

She skedaddled.

"That's a bit much, from a Smurf." Nick guffawed.

Louise could see James' stretched-out stockinged legs shaking and heels clacking as if he was being electrocuted and hear his hoots.

She sighed.

Society was pushing her and her brother further to the edge. *I guess we've found our level.*

Nick had come pretty close to admitting to some serious-sounding stuff. Such early trust on his part elicited feelers of trust from her; which put her in the rather ticklish position of both starting to believe that he was The Fiend — and hoping that he wasn't.

They were joined by the prostitutes, and the whisper of a sigh leaked out of her because she wouldn't be able to get anything more out of him. Not that she'd ever want to be left alone with him again.

"Come and dance with us, Daddy," said the red-head, in her flat singsong.

"And bring your beautiful friends," added Hels, the brunette, turning to them with the leer of a smile.

"Ah, my girls." He bounded to his feet, kissed first one, then the other, on the lips, and turned around and linked arms with them.

Addressing her and her brother again: "You see, I'd thought, 'I want to be loved. And if I can't be loved, I want to be hated.' Because if you're going to be unpopular, you might as well be really unpopular. But now people are drawn to me. So perverse is human nature, I'm adored."

"Come on," called the prostitutes, disengaging and walking backwards away from them.

"No shame, that's my trick," he said. "No shame."

Louise jumped when he reached out and grasped her left hand, and yanked.

CHAPTER 11

Candlelight-delineated, shadow-adumbrated, Riika's face turned this way, that way. Waiters swooped in and bore off dessert plates cleared of tiramisu and chocolate ginger torte, together with used and unused cutlery.

Alistair tried to remember the last time he'd spent such an enjoyable evening.

It had probably been when he and Valerie were courting.

Ironic, really: in the days when they hadn't been able to afford it, he and his wife had gone out two or three times a week. Now that they could afford to go out every night if they wanted to, they hardly ever bothered. Instead, here he was dining out with the *au pair*.

He pulled a wry smile.

Yet it can't have been too contorted, because Riika returned it. He sat as if for a photograph as her eyes played over his face.

"Oh, I forgot," she said, frowning, "my window leaks. Above the TV."

"Hm, water and electricity—not a good combination. I'll take a look at it as soon as we get back."

Her mouth curved into a smile.

He smiled back.

Was it a contrivance? Was she trying to give him an excuse to accompany her to her room? Because if so, she'd misjudged him, misread the situation.

Far from withdrawing the offer, however, he relished this test of his moral stamina.

Just the bill to settle, then in a couple of moments they would be leaving.

The waiter with the photofit face, in his black suit, white shirt, black tie, appeared.

"Would sir and madam care for coffee?" He hovered obsequiously.

"Riika?"

"Urm…"

Will she, won't she…?

"Yes, please."

"And sir?"

Alistair stuck two fingers up.

———————

Shooting from wall brackets and suspended racks, strobe lights strafed the smothering, choking gloom. Each flash illuminated colorful clubbers as smoke wafted, before darkness swallowed them, or reduced them to shifting silhouettes. The mirror ball petaled the heart of the dance floor with colors, and the chill note of pure sound coming from the speakers got steadily louder.

For some reason the film clip in James' brain was of an articulated lorry with a lethal load and no brakes emerging from an Alpine tunnel, orange sparks streaking and white ice chippings fountaining, air horn blaring.

The beat kicked in and he felt his internal organs vibrate when he strayed too near a speaker.

He slid his heels back and forth, and left and right, and gently swung his arms.

The wig felt as hot as a Grenadier Guard's bearskin hat. And stretched at the shoulders instead of the hips, his dress kept riding up. He'd paused to tug the hem down when the woman called Hels gripped his shoulders, pressed her body against his and planted her lipsticked lips on his. The notes of lemon in her perfume went straight up his nose, right up into his cranium, as her tongue squirmed its way into his mouth and flipped around like a small fish.

So, this is what it was like to get off with someone at a party—someone you've never met before, who you may never see again, after tonight, or may end up having a proper relationship with; all that exciting uncertainty. Everybody accepted it. It was the norm. Yet the forced intimacy made him gag.

He freed himself from her clutches, and the sucker of her mouth, but felt something stuck to his left eye-tooth.

Plucking it out, he held it up, away from him, and squinted at a ball of chewing gum.

"Yours, I believe," he said, handing it to her.

"Oh, thanks, love." She popped it back in her mouth.

The only woman to have been so familiar with him before was his sister; and she was drifting over to the other side of the dance floor, dressed as a bloke, in the company of a possible serial killer.

"Louise," he wanted to call out.

He didn't. She wouldn't be able to hear him.

Yet what was she doing? They needed to stay close. If they lost sight of each other, how would they find each other, in this crowd?

Straightening his dress for the umpteenth time, he saw spots—leopard-print ones—as Hels launched herself at him all over again, and pawed, and tickled.

He shook with laughter-sobs, swayed, tottered, first one way, then the other. In order to try and protect the sensitive flesh of his flanks, he bent over with his elbows clamped to his sides. It felt as if he'd been speared laterally, right through.

Rearing up to fill his lungs, he just made out the left-hand side of a red cape rise up Louise's back like the wing of some hell-born bird of prey spreading for flight. Nick hustled her towards a dark doorway at the back of the dance floor.

Where was the red one taking her? For what purpose?

Similar questions had obviously occurred to her, because she peered over her shoulder. What stood out, in the dark light of the club, were her fear-enlarged eyes.

Just before the mantle enveloped her, she twirled down the length of Nick's outstretched arm. She tried to ward off his hand with a panicky bat of her own, but he caught her wrist.

He held it up as if in victory, almost lifting her off the floor in the process.

A circle of people stood around watching. For one second they weren't silhouettes, they were vividly individuated, as a stripe of light ploughed through that corner of the crowd.

Maybe they thought it was some kind of floor show, because a couple even clapped.

James wasn't laughing anymore, because his heart was being squeezed, stretched, torn.

"No," he cried, breaking away from the Hell-hag.

At the same moment, Louise wrenched herself free from Nick's grip. They rushed towards each other through the human forest writhing in the sonic storm, and came to rest in each other's arms. She clung to him and he clung to her. Her head went back and her eyelids shut, as if loaded with hidden counterweights, as they kissed with famished mouths.

Opening her eyes, she looked around, and he followed her gaze.

When they weren't being blinded by disco ack-ack, they saw another pair of eyes flaring like live cigarette ends.

"It's him, James. It's him."

James nodded. "I know—the killer. I had the same feeling too."

"Did you see? He tried to abduct me."

"Yeah, I did."

Nick slid towards them, towered over them. "Don't mind me." Something snagged at his top lip as his mouth curled into a smile. "Though I can't help wondering what Mummy and Daddy think…"

Where was the lift? James couldn't see it. Fortunately, each circle of Hell had its own bar. He used the one down here to orientate himself.

"Come on." He grabbed his sister's hand. "Let's get out of here."

"He nearly got me," she panted. "But we've got *him* now, haven't we."

"Yes," he replied, getting his phone out of his small across-the-body bag.

He didn't have any reception down here. They needed to get out.

The battle between light and darkness raged on as he put his phone away and they pushed their way through the human zoo.

They reached the brushed metal door. James jabbed the black button. "Come on, come on, come on."

Ping.

One half of the door trundled behind the other and both halves retracted into the wall. They darted into the stainless steel cavity with lit-up white plastic ceiling. Louise pressed the button for the next level. The door shut. The lift rose.

She leaned against the back-wall mirror. "Phew, I thought he was going to come after us."

James stretched his hand out, took hers. "Me too."

The lift stopped.

Ping.

The door slid open.

They stepped out.

A brilliant red cloak unswirled to disclose something that had not, could not, have been there before: an equally conspicuous costume and a pair of radioactive eyes.

James' heart thumped. *How the...?*

Nick stepped towards them. They retreated.

James could see the exit. Only, how could they get there? He looked wildly this way and that. Nick had them cornered. They tried to edge around him.

Nick put a hand out, curtaining their view with his cloak. "No need to rush off. There's something I want to tell you both."

James' heart had been placed in a vice, and each moment that passed resulted in another crank of the handle. He started to reach for his phone.

Spotting movement off to the side, he clutched Louise's hand as a throng of new arrivals meant the crowd surged their way, taking them with it.

At first he tried to alter course for the exit but sheer numbers, and the fact that far more were arriving than leaving, made it impossible.

One of his heels tripped over the other and he almost went down.

"Careful," said Louise, taking his arm, holding him up.

Where is he? James checked over first one shoulder, then the other. He couldn't see Nick anywhere.

Oh. He stopped shoving and elbowing and allowed the press of bodies to determine their course.

The sea of people swept them against the wall—bump, bump, bump.

James lunged at an opening. It was the foot of a staircase that led up at right angles. A sign on the wall to the side read "Private". He caught hold of the edge and pulled himself in. Spinning around, he hauled Louise up.

"Have we lost him?" she said, looking back.

James peered into the crowd. "I think so."

"Phew."

A cough made them jump. They turned their heads—turned their bodies—to see Nick standing on the first step.

James flinched. *How did he…?*

Louise squeezed his hand.

They couldn't even make a run for it. The mass of bodies bulged at the entrance to the staircase. Nor could they get up the stairs. Nick blocked their way. Though no doubt the door at the top would be locked.

Laser eyes raked their faces. Nick addressed them from the step as if from a pulpit: "Don't you ever feel like throwing off society's shackles, its straitjacket, and running amok?"

Louise enunciated slowly. "Some-times."

James dripped with sweat.

He held onto his wig, with his free hand, as he nodded.

Lizard-like, Nick's tongue flicked. "Of course you do. Aren't you tired of that voice in your head…?"

James leaned back as Nick's forefinger came towards him. It tap-tap-tapped his forehead.

"The one that's been drilled into you by endless repetition, always telling you to do the right thing. Wouldn't you like to start thinking for yourself?"

Nick's tongue slid from one side to the other, making James' own mouth dry.

"Of course you would. You're special." He clapped them each on the shoulder.

James looked at his sister. One glimpse of her stoked the furnace of his heart.

"Normal rules don't apply to the likes of you." *True.*

"I mean, why should people as beautiful and intelligent as you bother with *pet*-ty laws or res-*pect*-ability?" Nick spat these words out as if they were the foulest imaginable.

James and his sister continued to steal synchronized glances, with, in her case, noticeably bigger eyes each time.

Nick rested his hands against the staircase's sloping ceiling. "You've got to celebrate your capacity for evil, liberate your vices. After all, it's fun being naughty, isn't it?"

Louise gave half a giggle. James turned from her emblazoned cheeks back to Nick.

Heat consumed his being, which bubbled over as laughter.

"Children of darkness get everything they desire." Nick stooped towards them. "What I'm about to tell you is not for ordinary mortals to hear."

They leaned in. "I'm about to invite you to join a secret society. It's called..." He paused, smiling. "Satan's Fan Club."

James knew that alcohol alone couldn't account for his tingle of terror, his shudder of joy, and that his reaction wasn't so much confused as compromised. Because he only knew of one person who talked like this, went around tempting people like this. Dad had always told them that God's arch-enemy existed. So could it be that, now, they'd met him? Devil or not, Nick was the antithesis of the God-Dad. He'd even offered them a way out of their moral impasse: turn morality on its head and they'd be at the top, not the bottom.

With the area in front of the doorway clearing, they could have fled if they'd still wanted to.

But they didn't.

"The only way—"

James glanced at his sister. With her mouth twisted to one side and brow double-clefted, she stared at the angel with wispy hair. *Damn damn damn.* Cynthia's return had cut short the Devil's sermon.

She pirouetted in her tutu with her arms forming a graceful arch over her head.

"Wheeeeee!"

Someone had damaged one of her wings. No wonder she went around in circles.

She stopped spinning, suddenly. Her upper body swayed. Her haloed head rolled.

Feeling a body brace against his, James turned to find that he and Louise had been joined by the two harpies. Hels squeezed past him and her companion squeezed past his sister.

Cynthia grabbed the Archfiend's hand, and tugged.

"I eat serial killers for breakfast." She purred—licked her lips.

Nick chuckled. "Oh, Cyn, Cyn, Cyn."

The two prostitutes joined in the struggle.

"I like to surround myself with evil angels," said the Devil.

Knocking James and his sister out first, they all spilled out of the stairwell.

It was as if Nick knew his potential recruits would want to follow in order to catch every last sentence. He raised a red arm as his little band crossed the platform. "It's a highly exclusive club. In order to gain admittance you have to prove your worth." James teetered like a man walking a tightrope, over Hell.

What does that mean? What kind of worth?

Nick and his dark angels entered the lift. He turned around, held the door open. "So being bad isn't good enough." His leer lingered upon James and his sister as they stood outside. "You need to revel in the glory of being unequivocally evil. Because only those who are truly free—beyond society—can join for life."

James received a pointy-elbowed jab in the ribs from Louise. He didn't need reminding that they still didn't know what the entrance requirement for Nick's club was.

"You haven't told us what we have to do," he called out. His voice had a desperate edge to it.

"You expect me to shout it out?" Nick pointed a long forefinger at them, upside down. It crooked and uncrooked.

James glanced at his sister. Her head wobbled.

Nick put his arms round all three women, who peered out from his capacious embrace.

Louise nodded.

She and James scuttled across the threshold and crushed into the lit-up capsule. The door sealed itself shut behind them.

Nick nudged the "down" button. "You've got to kill them."

What the—Who?

"You've got to kill your parents."

James tottered as the floor sank beneath him.

CHAPTER 12

Each time he thought about it, the answer crashed over James like a wave, winding him.

His lungs re-inflated. Suddenly a whole lot lighter, murderous dreams shot back up to the surface of his mind.

Kasabian's *Club Foot* pounded in his ears. The mirror ball twinkled overhead.

Surrounded by subterranean wildlife, he danced with his sister. If you could call it dancing. He felt as if he'd grown hooves.

Old Nick's head stuck out above the rest as he danced with his fallen angels.

James smiled at his sister.

She closed the gap between them, in one step. "Did he really say that?"

Between gouts of smoke, James spotted Nick grinning at them. "Yeah, he really did."

"Mum and Dad?"

"Yep, Mum and Dad."

"The frightening thing is, it almost makes sense."

"That's because it's personally tailored to us." He could feel her unnaturally fast heartbeat. "Are you all right?"

"Yeah, I think so."

Though normally too circumspect to indulge in public displays of affection, for the second time that night, under the influence of alcohol and doubtless something more satanic, their mouths fused.

"I've been looking for you every—" That was as far as the voice—male, youngish, nigglingly familiar—got.

Breaking off the kiss, James turned his head to see Colin stood just three feet away, with open mouth and crazed eyes.

He got a jolt, as of electricity, like a cattle prod in the back. He'd relied on the fact that he and Louise were among strangers, most of whom were even more way-out than they were. It had slipped his mind he'd been invited by a friend and had to meet that person every day at work.

His sister didn't help, smiling brightly as if to say, "See? We're lovers."

Colin turned and knocked a woman's glass of red wine over Eminem's white vest in his haste to get away.

A Teletubby's aerial made a beeline for the birthday boy and he veered off.

James sighed. "Let's go."

"Okay." Louise waved bye to Nick.

His eyes glowed red-hot.

Grin gone, he leaned over and poked a card inside Louise's breast pocket. "Don't forget our little arrangement." He stared at them each in turn as he patted her pocket. "Your Uncle Nick'll be waiting."

In the splash of artificial daytime the security light provided, Alistair followed Riika up the path to The End House.

The cold hit him in the chest, specifically his breastbone, where the cut of his coat and jacket left a deep V and his only protection was a thin shirt and tie. She unlocked the front door and, after a slight delay as it rubbed the mat up the wrong way, shut it behind them.

Once he'd disabled the alarm and hung up his coat, the external light had gone off. They climbed up through the empty house.

With her leading the way, it felt as if he was in her house rather than the other way around. The impression was heightened by defamiliarizing darkness. By the time they turned up the second staircase, darkness obliterated the last visual trace of them and their surroundings. Only their choppy breathing, the creaky stairs, her floaty perfume and his equally ethereal consciousness testified to their continued existence.

At the top of the stairs, Riika crossed the landing to open the door to her room. Monochrome moonlight infiltrated the passage. He stepped inside, through the beams that poked through her window like the fan of rays from a cinema projector.

Everything went from black and white to color when she switched the light on. The whole mood of the room was completely transformed. Even if the pink of the carpet, the yellow of the walls and the blue of the duvet clashed somewhat, he considered the randomness homely.

Not that the decor had anything to do with Riika. She'd inherited it like that. She'd stashed all her belongings away in the squat chest of drawers and the narrow wardrobe; apart from a copy of *Fifty Shades of Grey*, an MP3 player and a chunky scarf.

She took off the pashmina and he maneuvered around her in the smallness of the room. The front half was even more confined, with the segment sheared off it. First stooping, then crouching, and finally on all fours, he made his way over to the dormer window. He reared up to drag the table with the TV on it as far out of the way as the cable for the aerial allowed.

"Coffee?"

Another? One more and he'd be up all night.

Yet peering around, he saw her paused in the act of taking a white plastic kettle with the lid off to the bathroom, with sunshiny hair and eyes turning their light on him.

"Go on then."

Now able to stand up in the extra space the dormer window provided, he had a clear view of both the window and the wall under it. He examined the area in minute detail.

The only anomaly he could see was a hairline crack that started at the bottom right-hand corner of the window, passed above the aerial socket but stopped just short of the power point. Was this the leak she meant? The painted plaster was dry.

Then again, it wasn't raining.

The kettle bubbled away on the tray on the floor just behind his right foot, gradually getting noisier. Then it quieted, briefly, before a more violent knocking started up within. Eventually, that died as well, following a click, and he heard her rattle around behind him.

"Coffee's ready."

At last, an excuse to come away. "There's not a lot I can do at the moment. I'll get some sealant and fix it another time. Just don't watch any TV when it's raining."

She handed him his mug of black coffee and smiled. "What else am I supposed to do in the evenings?"

Uncurling a long finger with a pale nail, like enameled eggshell, she pointed at the ancient armchair—khaki now; he couldn't remember what color originally—indicating, with only the minutest of movements, that he should sit on it.

So he did.

She perched on the end of the mattress, facing him, and his heart went pit-a-pat.

He'd taken a sip of her incredibly strong coffee.

Luckily, she got up again, so she didn't see him wince.

She went over to put on some music.

Louise shivered as the taxi driver turned his truncated hearse around. She and James ran—skated, on the ice-plated bits—over to their garden gate.

The little winking red light on the plastic barnacle of the burglar alarm, in the top right-hand corner of The End House, was the only point of interest.

The hoary, wiry trees were photograph-still, petrified, in the icy moonlight. Some washing left out in the yard to the left wasn't just motionless, it was positively rigid. The taut, two-dimensional shirts would have made decent dinner trays. The stiff elongated socks could have doubled as cricket bats.

They hadn't got very far up the garden path when the breath clouds that mushroomed from their mouths like ascending souls lit up as if from within. It was as if the bulb had gone on inside a giant fridge. The white lawn glinted like the inside of the freezer compartment. Louise and her brother crushed whole clusters of the proportionately-oversized ice needles underfoot as they struck out, on a detour, across it.

If the face of the house was an Advent calendar, then it was the second day—with Riika's dormer attic window and the lounge window the only ones illuminated.

Dad must have put the lower light on. His car was outside.

On reaching the lounge window, Louise leaned against the ledge, peered in, and saw Harriet. What was she doing home? She was supposed to be staying over at a friend's. Instead here she sprawled on the carpet near the standard lamp.

Where's Dad?

Harriet chattered, gesticulated, even though there was no one else in view.

"Who's she talking to?" asked Louise, pressing her forehead against the smooth, hard ice that was the glass, rolling her head from side to side in an attempt to see into the near corners of the room. It didn't help that the standard lamp was the only light on.

James pressed his nose against the adjacent window pane. "I don't know. I can't see anyone."

"What's that shadow on the wall?"

"Where?"

"There."

"A plant pot."

Yes, it could be a plant pot. But in addition to her sister's voice, she thought she heard the crackly voice of a man.

"Who's that?" she whispered.

Straining hard to listen, she even held her breath.

"The TV."

Louise released her breath in a sigh. Leaving a patch of mouth mist on the window, she followed her brother to the door. He let them in. As soon as they'd shut out the cold and taken off their coats, they filed through to the lounge.

Harriet rolled onto her side and gawped at them through her spectacles as they entered.

Louise wished she knew what was going on behind those keen brown eyes. The glasses magnified them to an alarming extent. So much so that when she blinked, it made her jump.

"What are you doing here?" Louise strode into the corner and switched the TV off, before advancing.

"Hi." Harriet's mouth broke into a smile that there didn't really seem to be any reason for.

Until she asked, "Why are you wearing the wrong clothes?"

Louise looked down at her dark grey suit and the dull black mirrors of her toecaps. She'd forgotten there was anything odd about her attire.

Her brother obviously had too, because he scuttled back behind the door.

Just his eyes, and fringe, peeped around it.

"We've been to a fancy dress party," she said. "Anyway, don't try and change the subject. I thought you were staying at your friend's. What are you doing here?"

"Lucy's granny had a fall. She's in hospital."

"Did Dad bring you back?"

"No, I haven't seen Daddy. They dropped me off on the way over there."

"So, who were you talking to? Lucy?" Louise couldn't see anyone, just Harriet's two dolls propped against the foot of the sofa.

"No. She went with them."

"Who then?"

Louise peered into the wedge of darkness that gave the other half of the room a deep-end feel, before turning back to her sister who blink-, blink-, blinked.

"No one."

"We saw you, through the window. Now, who were you talking to?"

Harriet wrinkled her nose and screwed up her brow.

Louise glanced around at her brother to see if he'd witnessed this grotesque display of petulance. He had. The whole of his coloring-book face stuck out from behind the door.

"Forget it," he said. "It'll just be her imaginary friend."

"He's not imaginary," a pouting Harriet mumbled.

"Well, we've never seen him."

"That's because he hides."

"Yeah, right."

"Where?" asked Louise.

"I can't say."

"I mean, the cellar, the attic…"

"He doesn't want me to tell you."

"Well, what does he do then, this friend of yours?"

"Do? He doesn't do anything. It's not him who's doing it, it's you."

Louise's limbs seized up and her mouth dried. Her little sister grabbed the pair of dolls and started knocking them together as if they were anatomically correct.

The timing was too much of a coincidence to be artless, surely.

Louise got a twinge of the soul ache she recognized from one of her dream-loops. She felt, again, as if she'd been struck across the face with something cold, wet and dead.

Her face even darkened in the mirror above the mantelpiece.

"What does the little brat mean by that?" she cried.

"Just ignore her," said James. "She's only a kid. She doesn't know what she's talking about."

Still lying on her side, Harriet stared up with eyes like keyholes.

And Louise stared down.

For a moment she thought she was going to lunge at her, but she didn't. She backed towards the door and muttered, "Horrid child," as she and her brother exited.

"What *did* she mean by that?" she asked James, out in the hallway. "Do you think she knows?"

"No. She's bluffing. She's just trying to scare you."

He seemed so certain that self-doubt breached the bulkheads of her brain. She wondered whether perhaps she'd over-interpreted Harriet's actions because of her own lost innocence.

"Yeah, well, she succeeded all right. Her and her invisible friend."

"I think she genuinely believes in him."

As they climbed the stairs, Louise stopped and stood in the slanting darkness.

"You mean you think he really exists?"

Her brother stopped too, and descended a step so that they were on the same one. Then another, so that they were roughly the same height.

"No, I mean she does."

"God, sometimes this place gives me the heebie-jeebies." Louise shivered. Her jaw juddered. And she got the back-of-the-neck prickles she normally got when stared at from behind. "There it is again. Can you feel it?"

"What?"

"I don't know how to describe it. It's like something cold rushing past right behind you."

"I think they're called drafts. You get them in big old houses."

"No, I'm being serious. You don't notice it when you're here all the time but as soon as you come in, there it is again, waiting to assail you."

"Some kind of subliminal smell maybe—like a gas leak?"

"No..."

Now he was trying too hard.

Then again, her account had been rather cryptic.

"What's the name of the bloke who used to own this place?" she asked.

"I don't know. Why?"

"I think it's him."

"A ghost?" His voice rose higher than it had when he'd been imitating hers. "Don't be silly. I reckon it's old Verge."

"There you are, you see, you have felt it. Me, I've never liked this place. I wish we'd never come here. I'll be glad when we leave."

"Will you stop it?" He pressed her against the wall and leaned in to kiss her.

"What's that?" She turned away at the last moment and gazed into the half-darkness at the top of the stairs. Muffled music came from somewhere up above.

"Probably Riika's stereo."

"Right."

They continued up the staircase.

"Stop worrying, love."

Easy to say, but what if they ran into Dad again and he reached the light switch before they did? He'd see them, like this: a female James; a male Louise. Thankfully, she couldn't hear any footsteps, only the music.

Her brother caught hold of her hand as they wheeled right upon reaching the landing. "Your bed or mine?"

"I'm sorry…" She rested her back against the wall. She even let him take the whole weight of her arm. "I think I'll sleep on my own tonight."

They were alone in the breathy dark, smooth, unbounded, space-like; with neither up nor down, left nor right. And apart from their sawing breathing, the only isolatable sound was a rhythmic creaking gathering pace.

A final, desperate urgency, then James subsided with a sigh.

Eventually, he reached out to click on his lamp, maneuvered his bottom around to the edge of the bed and let his feet fall. This jerked him sideways into a sitting position. He sprang upright, strode over to the hook on the back of the door and wrapped himself in his dressing gown.

Just about to open the door, he paused and turned: "So, were you joking when you said you wanted to be on your own?"

"What do you think?" his sister replied.

He laughed.

She was right; it was a vacuous question. They could never get enough of each other. Was that why they'd made the relationship physical—not just to try and recreate the closeness they'd enjoyed in the womb but so that this craving could be satiated?

For a little while at least.

Louise had rolled over onto her knees, and now leaned over the side of the bed to retrieve something from the floor wearing his flappy white shirt, and nothing else.

"Don't go away," he whispered, slipping out into the corridor.

———————

Clubbers made their way down Hell's front steps into a world that had gone glam rock. Glitter dust coated cobblestones, pavement, sleeping cars, all the street furniture.

Yet that was the moonlight, working its magic. Really, everything was glazed with frost.

Nick's travelling companions were already outside.

Two of the women had just lit up. The cold air gave them all smoky breath.

Hels twisted and turned in her miniskirt. "Where's he got to?"

Cyn's whole wing flapped, and her torn one fluttered, as she shivered. "I d-d-don't know."

"Ah, speak of the Devil."

Footsteps rang out in the crystalline night as Nick descended the steps and crossed the street in a long black leather coat and black boots, carrying a black hold-all.

The limo's engine and lights came on simultaneously at his approach.

He opened the rear door and held it open. One by one, the women stepped inside.

When they were all in, he threw his bag in after them, said "Bye, my loves," shut the door and started walking.

He turned left at the junction and hadn't got far when the elongated car caught up with him.

A window whirred down and Hels' head appeared.

"Where are you going?" she called out.

He smiled an elastic smile. "To paint the town red."

CHAPTER 13

James unscrewed his eyes open with those primitive implements, his knuckles, then jumped because there was something on the back of his right hand.

Holding it further from his face to get it into focus, he made out the blocky representation of a tiered black palace.

A tattoo? How the hell had that got there? He would be marked for life. Then he remembered having his hand stamped on the way into the club, and chuckled.

His winter pajamas fitted snugly. Louise had got all the gunk off his face and nails before they'd gone to sleep. They'd got high together on nail varnish remover.

His sister had left hours ago.

If the window was a lock gate, then it was now equally full on both sides. Light inundated the room. He was still getting used to it when his door flew open and Louise bounded in.

"Mum just told me that a body's been found in a wheelie bin outside a block of flats the other side of the high street."

Before he could respond, Mum followed her in.

"Nobody can tell me they're not local now. This one happened just down the road from that nightclub you went to. I told you both you shouldn't have gone. It could have been you, Louise."

James turned back to his sister as, eyes sparking, she turned to him.

Neither he nor Louise had shared Mum's obsession with the serial killer until now they knew who it was. The latest murder was, if anything, proof. They knew Nick had been a suspect, and they knew he'd been in the vicinity. Yet they said nothing.

They had gone from trying to catch a killer to covering for one.

———————

That night, Valerie turned off the kitchen radio and picked up the two mugs of decaf coffee with the fingers of one hand looped through both handles.

Noticing as she passed that the stone steps down to the cellar appeared tilted where light fell across them at the angle of the partially open door, she shut the door and then switched the kitchen light off.

She'd intended to just check the TV for news—there hadn't been much on the radio—but couldn't quite face the prospect now. So she turned up the stairs and, once at the top, crossed the landing.

She didn't get very far up the corridor. Hearing childish giggles, she walked backwards until she came level with the short corridor that led to Harriet's room.

The instant she heard her youngest whispering, she went hot. Once again, no one should be in there. The twins were in their rooms, and in any case never called on their sister. Riika had gone out and Alistair was writing his diary in bed. So who was Harriet talking to? Surely she should have outgrown imaginary friends by now.

And the killer still hadn't been caught.

Valerie set the mugs down on the floor and jogged towards the murmurs.

Shadows flooded the corridor at an acute angle. Their tidemark rose up the walls to the ceiling as she ran. They submerged the door ahead of her as if the passage itself were tilted. The handle jounced closer with each alternate lurch. She wanted an accurate snapshot of inside, so she barged straight in.

"Who were you talking to? Who, Harriet?" She shouted. Exactly like before, her daughter sat alone, cross-legged on the floor at the foot of the bed under the glossy black, room-reflecting window.

The big light burned brightly. As Valerie stepped under it, she swore she could feel the heat of the bulb singe her crown.

"No one, Mummy."

"Yes, you were. Now, who was it?"

"A friend."

Valerie huffed. "I'm not stupid. What friend?"

The lenses of Harriet's glasses flashed reflected light with every jerk of her head, then whited out completely when she looked up. "My best friend."

"Tell me his name, Harriet."

"Oh, Mum…" The lights in the lenses winked again as her head bobbed and swayed.

"Now, Harriet."

The small face dipped. "I can't."

"What do you mean, you can't?"

"I promised."

"Promised? Who?"

The nine-year-old looked up at her with large, open eyes. "My friend."

"Harriet, this has got to stop. It's more than my shredded nerves can take. It's got to ruddy well stop."

Valerie turned towards the door.

Her daughter scrambled onto one foot and one knee as if about to jump up, then collapsed sniveling against the end of the bed.

———————

"It's not our fault if the police let him go, is it?" said Louise.

Her voice sounded small, distant, even though they lay facing each other, breathing in each other's carbon dioxide. In bed.

"Of course not, love." He addressed her eyes. In the dark, they were all he could see.

"And they can always have him in again if they want to, can't they?"

"Of course." Under the covers, he took her hand, held it and squeezed.

She squeezed back. "It's true what he says, you know…"

"What?" he asked.

"We're like him. We can't be good. All we can be is bad."

Exactly. Why try and be good when their very relationship meant they'd be bracketed with evil? Far better to do what their immoral tutor had done, surely, and turn negative into positive. "Yeah. So we have to excel at that."

"And be as bad as him?"

"You're still looking at it the wrong way round, Lou. Evil is good now, good evil."

"Evil is good?" She laughed. "Actually, that's not bad."

"Yeah. Should get a couple of T-shirts printed up with that on."

She laughed again, then stopped. "But it shows how far beyond the mainstream, or whatever you want to call it, we are already, doesn't it. The only place that'd welcome us is a bloody crime academy."

"Thank God for Satan's Fan Club's what I say." Maybe it was just the outcast's desire to belong, yet he needed something to cling to.

"Well, yeah. I'm hardly likely to kill anyone, though, am I? No matter how much I wanna join."

"Killing's just the logical conclusion of being bad without limits."

"Even if that's true, I mean, Mum and Dad—the two people responsible for us being here." Her glow-in-the-dark eyes blinked. "I can't even imagine that. Can you?"

"Well…" His anger had abated since he and Louise had broken through the fetters of convention. He hadn't had any more murderous dreams. Yet, once again, simply by existing, his parents stood in his way. "You never know."

After a while, his sister's left leg jerked, once, as if trying to take a free kick.

He waited until he heard sounds of sleep, which didn't take long. Then he prayed, to the Devil.

Draper toolbox in one hand and small bag of filler in the other, Alistair made his way up the stairs. He'd been meaning to fix the leak in Riika's room since before Christmas. He hadn't wanted to do it with her there because he hadn't wanted to cause her any inconvenience. Valerie had told him a few days ago that the *au pair* would be out Saturday afternoon, though, so he'd decided to get it done.

He turned the corner at the end of the corridor.

Light had already started draining from the day and dusk had arrived early. As he trudged up the steep stairs to the attic, he remembered the last time he'd climbed them. The stylus of consciousness jumped, skipped a bit, and he thought instead about how he'd barely seen Riika since that evening. He'd been busy organizing Church events in the run-up to Christmas. When he'd made time for family life over Christmas itself, she hadn't been around. She'd gone to stay with a friend. Since Christmas he really hadn't had time for anyone. He had stacks of work to do, so much that sometimes he even ate in his office.

He scaled the stairs and tramped over to her door.

Surprisingly, it was ajar. Yet whether it was left open or shut probably didn't matter much when Riika had the whole floor to herself.

Widening the gap with a gentle knock from his knee, he crossed the threshold.

From the window came a faint, TV-like glow—which merely made the room seem darker. Elsewhere the air had a grey, grainy quality, like old-fashioned newsprint held too close.

So it wasn't until he flicked the light switch with his elbow that he saw her.

Yes, he'd been aware of a greyed-out patch of room to his left, yet the idea that it could be Riika scarcely had time to jump the gaps of his synapses before she was reified by light.

What was she doing home? She was supposed to be out.

Dressed in skinny jeans and a lead-colored tunic, she sat upright in the chair, pulled out her earphones and stared at him.

"Sorry," he said.

Her gaze felt like sunburn.

From the leftward list of her head, he could tell she wasn't sure whether the apology was for bursting into her room this time or for leaving it, leaving her, last time.

Alistair buckled and dropped to his knees as images of that night cascaded and collided in his mind. After they'd got back from dinner, it had all been above board until he'd got up to go, when a good-night kiss had failed to end.

"I've totally ignored you, haven't I?" he said. "I'm sorry."

He'd looked down to one side. He looked up to see the flash of a smile. Didn't she understand? Had she mistaken an apology for a fresh advance? How?

Then again, her knees acted as his armrests. His hands calibrated her waist, and toolbox and filler sat, forgotten, on the carpet behind him.

Maybe he'd been right before. They should've avoided each other.

As he stared at her skin, her eyes, her mouth, he experienced a slight lift, a giving way. It felt as if the floor fell, fell, fell, even as he knelt on it.

Now that he'd sinned once, would he always be susceptible where she was concerned?

"No," said his conscience.

"Yes," said her eyes.

Did he lean forward, or did she?

Either way, their lips met.

———

"Why did Nick say that we could join his club, then set a test impossible to pass?" asked Louise, thinking aloud.

"It's difficult," said her brother. "I don't know about impossible."

They lay face up on his bed, with their heads at the foot of it and their feet on the pillows.

She placed her hands under her neck, with fingers interlocking, to elevate her gaze and avoid having a ghostly X-ray-like image of the big light's bulb burnt into her retinas.

"We talking about the same thing?" She shuddered. "Well, technically, it's possible, I suppose. But there's an emotional barrier to anything of that kind that can never be got over or round. Or, only in the most extreme circumstances."

"There'd have to be rules of engagement, naturally."

Supporting her head with one hand now, she brushed a strand of hair out of her eyes. "I mean, if Mum and Dad interfered in our relationship, then possibly there might be a case for action of some—"

"They don't know about it."

"Exactly." She placed her hand back behind her neck, with the other. "There's no need."

His head swiveled to face her. "So we just do nothing?"

"But you're still missing the point." She massaged her neck with her fingers. "I think Nick set the bar deliberately out of reach."

"Why would he do that?"

"I don't know."

A nearby floorboard creaked.

"Who's that?" she said.

"What?"

He remained on his back, but she propped herself up on one elbow with her head half turned towards the door and closest ear cocked. She could see the upside-down crucifix he'd put up. It glinted, dagger-like, just inside his open wardrobe door.

Slippers flapped and flopped faintly past the bedroom.

"Alistair, I need to talk."

James jumped on the mattress—causing them both to bounce.

Mum had called from the foot of the attic stairs.

"I can't turn a blind eye to it any longer," she shouted again. "Not when it's going on under our own roof."

"Oh, God, Mum knows." Louise's whole body shook as she dragged herself up off the bed. "She knows."

"Are you ready?" asked James.

"Ready?" Her heart punched her.

"Yeah. For what we might have to do. Because it sounds like we're about to be put to the test."

Leaving Riika, Alistair felt as if the floorboards' creaks came from his ankles, knees and hips as he walked, woodenly, across the top-floor landing to the head of the stairs.

He stopped and stood, rocking slightly, to look down at his wife.

She'd turned the light on from below. Her gaze was pinned on him. Her body was at a slight angle to the walls, yet as upright as a flame. Maybe it was the house that was leaning.

"Do you think I could have a word with you?" Her voice was hard, her gaze sharp.

"Of course."

She turned and he followed.

Damn. She knows.

He rounded the corner on reaching the first-floor landing. Still one staircase ahead of him, she hit the ground floor and turned left into the lounge. She'd been flicking wall switches all the way, and by the time he joined her every light in the room blazed.

She sat down in one of the armchairs. Unable to speak, hardly daring to breathe, he remained standing.

"I need to talk to you about something." Her voice had softened, turned plaintive. He realized that far from being the cause of her troubles, he was to be her confidant. Breathing freely again, he made himself comfortable in the other armchair.

He'd just adjusted the cushion behind him when James and Louise entered.

They walked past him, moving as one. Then they wheeled around to the sofa and, only spinning independently at the last moment, sat down next to each other.

What did they want?

"It's your daughter," said Valerie.

A ripple ran through the twins.

They looked paler, because they'd dyed their hair darker. Where Louise now kept her hair short, James seemed to be letting his grow.

"I always knew there was something wrong with those two," said Alistair.

"Not that daughter. The other one."

"Harriet?" He couldn't keep up with this.

It was as if the twins had been tied together and now the ligatures had been loosened. They sat up and shuffled from buttock to buttock as if shaking themselves free. Their sister was the one in trouble this time.

"What's wrong with Harriet?"

"It's happened again, exactly like before. It's been happening a lot lately. I keep hearing her talking to someone in her room. Well, with this killer still on the loose and everything, one can't afford to take any chances. I always dash in there, and she always fobs me off. But today was different."

Alistair's back left the cushion. "You mean there was someone in there?"

"No. Just her."

"Well, what then?" He merged once more with the chair.

"I pressed her and I pressed her and finally she admitted it."

He turned his hands up. "Admitted what?"

"That she does have a friend. That he's not imaginary. He's real. And do you know what she said his name was?"

"What?"

Valerie stared at him for a moment. "God."

"God?"

"But that's precisely what God is," said James. "An imaginary friend."

"Stay out of this, you." Alistair found the twins' manners appalling. He dreaded to think what their morals were like.

Valerie turned to James. "That's just what she calls him. I'm not saying that's who she's talking to."

"Listen, listen." Alistair considered his youngest daughter's friend the least of his worries, yet he couldn't tell Valerie that. "I'll take Harriet into work one day next week and get one of my colleagues to do a psychological evaluation of her that'll establish once and for all what we're dealing with here."

James sat up. "Hey, hang on a minute. Louise and I are a disappointment because we don't believe in God and our sister's one because she does? Where's the logic in that?"

Alistair wasn't in the mood for his son's impiety. Already on his feet and heading for the door, he quickened his pace.

"Fore!"

"Oh, bad luck." Alistair's cloudy breath hung in the clear gelid air as he waited for his friend, Deverick Mace.

The two of them set off up the outsize lawn of the fairway, long enough to land a plane on, trundling their golf bags behind them.

"How's your lovely lady?" asked Deverick.

A flinch of cold. "Valerie? Oh, fine, fine."

The dew at their feet sparkled in the ineffectual sunshine.

"And Harriet and the twins?"

"Oh, don't ask."

"I see. Like that is it?"

"Afraid so."

"Do you know, it used to bother me but these days I'm almost pleased Charmaine and I never had kids. I mean, it's such a pitiless world. We don't have to watch it gradually corrupt them as they simply do what they're programmed to do: soak up experience."

Alistair had been staring at the course, with its artificially rough and smooth patches, yet now he glanced at his friend. Alistair was the one who normally delivered the jeremiads.

"I haven't seen you much at the White Chapel lately, or the Lodge," he said. "Everything all right?"

"Well, this is my first proper weekend off in ages."

"You mean because of the murders?"

The Detective Chief Superintendent nodded. "Everyone wants to know how we can let a serial killer run loose, for months on end, in London, as if we're not working day and night to catch him."

"I suppose tensions are running high."

"They certainly are, with women disappearing, turning up in wheelie bins. The public is outraged, naturally. Politicians are asking questions in the House. And the papers are baying for my blood. In fact, reporters won't leave me alone. You'd think

I was the killer. I've even considered early retirement, you know."

Alistair knew what it was like when the whole of life just felt like work. While it was a little like work for him, talking seemed to do Deverick good. "Do you think you're getting closer?"

"Well, we've implemented strategies to hit the ground running—speed up identification et cetera—should, God forbid, a new one occur. And we're currently reviewing all the information we've already gathered to see if we might have missed something. But then he's clever, and careful. And he varies aspects of his MO. That's about all I can say at the moment. No doubt the details will come out later, at the trial. Because we're going to catch him. That's the only reason I'm hanging on now. To make sure of it."

CHAPTER 14

"**M**y God, they've found another one," cried Mum. "Lou, quick." James abandoned the cup of tea he'd been making and he and his sister ran around to the lounge.

Their mother pointed at the TV. "They're coming thick and fast now. Look."

"Where this time?" he asked.

"Local again."

Louise perched next to Mum on the sofa and James sat in the armchair facing the TV. They stared at the vast stony plot with the white tent pitched, medieval-like, in the middle of it.

James shifted to the edge of the seat to get that bit closer. "Are you sure that's round here? I don't recognize it."

"It's the patch of waste ground where that condemned block of flats used to be, between here and the high street," replied Mum. "You never see inside it because it's all boarded up. Look there, you can just make out the multi-story car-park in the background. See?"

"Oh, yeah," from Louise.

"Oh, when's he ever going to stop?" Mum's right hand shot to her mouth.

James' heart thrilled to the news that Nick was still outwitting the law. *Yes—he's out there, waiting for us.* James clenched and unclenched his hands.

His eyes had eagled right, to meet his sister's, when Riika put her head around the door.

"Good-night," she said.

Instantly her head receded.

Mum called out, "Riika, Riika."

Riika re-emerged, inch by inch. "Are you sure you wouldn't rather stay in? There's been another murder. This side of the high street."

"Really?"

"Yes. Aren't you afraid?"

"I will have company. Good-night."

"Morning, Miss Querty," said Alistair.

"Oh, hello, Mr. Glavier."

"Good grief. What's been going on here?"

Alistair had been showing Harriet and Riika around the practice when he'd come across his trim, sixty-year-old secretary in the waiting room nimbly turning and stepping and bending in a white blouse and black slacks. At first glance he'd thought that she was doing calisthenics, but on closer inspection he'd noticed her right a potted plant and pick a book and a magazine up off the carpet and place them on the central table.

"Mike had another rough session with Mr. Richardson," said Miss Querty.

"How is he?"

"Oh, all right physically, just a bit shaken. So he's taken the rest of the day off."

"Fine, no problem. I'll phone him after lunch." He gestured for Harriet to take a seat, then kissed her on the top of the head. "Mia will call you in when she's ready, darling. She should be finished soon."

Turning, he ushered Riika into the pale blue sanctum of his office.

Shutting the door behind them, he led her past the bookshelves, the large potted plant and the couch over to a seat in front of the wide walnut desk.

He took his usual place on the far side and switched on the brass desk lamp with the green shade that wouldn't have looked out of place in some plush library. It didn't look out of place here either because of the presence of his books.

He'd seen their different-colored, different-sized spines so many times he didn't even notice them anymore, and certainly not today. His attention had been claimed by a pair of ice-blue eyes in a face that could have been compacted of sun and snow.

It had just struck him that there was something different about Riika's appearance this morning when his mobile vibrated in his pocket, and continued vibrating.

"Excuse me a sec," he said, taking the call. "Hello?"

"Oh, you simply wouldn't believe some of the things I witnessed this weekend. I mean, it's not my fault if people leave the curtains open, is it?"

Alistair tried not to sigh. "Listen, Godfrey, I'm a bit busy at the moment. Do you mind if we talk later?"

"Well, I…"

"Thanks. It's much appreciated. Bye."

Only now, as he met Riika's Arctic eyes for a second time, did he realize what was different about her. Her head looked smaller, because her hair was up. She'd scraped it back and tied it in a bundle at the nape of her neck.

"What would you like to do while we wait?" he asked.

"What do you suggest?"

"How about a free consultation?"

She grinned. "Really? Free?"

"Of course. Because you should never trust professionals. They only do it for money. Amateurs, on the other hand, do it purely for pleasure."

He barely recognized himself in Riika's company.

He'd just giddily got to his feet when Miss Querty's voice, over the intercom, held him back. "Konrad Palinski on line two. Says it's urgent."

Not another one. Pressing the hands-free button, he leaned over the microphone. "Tell him to call back, please. I'm in the middle of a consultation."

"Certainly, Mr. Glavier."

Riika waited with her head to one side as he made his way around the desk. "Are you an amateur?"

Joining her, he led her over to the couch. "A perfect quack."

I looked through a keyhole and saw an eye.

Harriet tried to remember the details of her dreams from the night before.

Daddy always said dreams could reveal a lot about a person, so she wondered what that one, and the one about a skull being covered in *ratatouille*, revealed about her. She probably wouldn't have long to wait to find out.

A door opened and a woman with long blonde hair and a deep tan stepped out. Harriet couldn't help thinking that she looked rather like a negative.

"Hi, Harriet. Sorry to keep you. My name's Mia. Would you like to come in? And then we can have a nice chat."

Harriet felt her insides wibble-wobble, jelly-like, as—trailing a pocket of mintiness—Mia led her inside.

The room had lime green walls and a leaf green carpet, with a desk under the window and a black couch against one wall. The bookshelf had plants on it, and a box of toys sat in the corner.

Mia patted the back of a chair. Harriet sat down, and the long string of pearls around Mia's neck clacked faintly as she joined her. The low square table in the middle of the room had an odd collection of objects on it: two miniature footballs that would fit snugly in the palms of the hands, a large bowl of potpourri, and a much smaller bowl of mints.

Mia held out the mints, but Harriet shook her head. She already had one of her own sweets in her mouth.

"Now, what are your three most favorite things in the world?" asked Mia. "What makes you happiest?"

Harriet sucked on her buttery sweet. "Urm, ballet... T-TV..." The question could hardly be any easier, only Mia's scratchy note-taking distracted her. "My dolls..."

"And what makes you unhappiest?"

"Being on my own."

"On your own? But you've got a new friend, haven't you? What about your friend? Tell me about him."

Although not aware of any movement on her part, Harriet heard the chair squeak excitedly beneath her.

"My friend?" She wasn't sure why she'd worried now. Someone actually took her seriously for once. "Oh, well, he's the bestest friend that anyone's ever had."

———————————

Valerie put down the phone in her third-floor office. Taking a sip of coffee, she savored one of those contemplative moments essential for replenishing creative reserves—stared out of the window—when a man plummeted past.

She clapped her hand over her mouth, shot to her feet.

Stumbling over to the window, she opened it as far as it would go and leaned out.

He lay motionless on the flagstones, with one leg bent back on itself. Figures poured out of the main door towards him.

"Oh, God..." she muttered.

Hearing cries from other floors, she staggered out into the corridor. Roger from HR ran past.

"Who... Who is it?" she called after him.

"Konrad. Konrad Palinski," he shouted back, before plunging down the stairs.

Konrad had been one of the volunteers in trials for BraxPelling Pharmaceuticals' latest antidepressant.

"What's going on?" asked Mary, looking up from the water cooler.

"It's... He..."

A sob lodged itself in her throat.

Unable to swallow it, unable to breathe, she dashed towards the Ladies and clattered inside, where it burst from her.

She stood heaving over the sinks as tears spritzed her shaking hands.

The room smelt, in part, of summer meadows.

Plip ...plip ...plip, from one of the cisterns.

Rearing up, she spotted the window in the mirror.

Memory-projected onto it; she saw again the cruciform figure fall past her office window and heard his truncated cry.

157

"Oh, God." She rushed into a cubicle, pulled out a yard of toilet paper, dabbed her eyes and blew her nose.

Hearing voices out in the corridor, she locked the door behind her, put the seat down on the loo and sat on it.

What would the consequences be for the company? All that was certain was that, like cracks in ice, the incident looked set to ramify.

Her husband, too, would be affected. The jumper was one of his clients.

She hugged her stomach, as if to stop herself flying apart, and rocked backwards and forwards, backwards and forwards.

―――――――――

Unquestionably occupied, but typing rather than talking, James had clicked "Send" and minimized Outlook when a pair of elbows jutted over his cubical wall and into his left-hand peripheral vision. Late in on account of—of course, that was it—a dentist's appointment, Colin leant over the partition dividing their desks.

James pressed the wrong button on his keyboard and heard a crash in his headphones that sounded like a piano falling down a staircase.

He'd just composed an email to Louise, the frank contents of which would be explosive if read by someone who knew they were related. It would be cruel if Colin turned out to be their nemesis; especially when, thus far, and despite drunken provocation on their part, he hadn't been any trouble. The first Monday at work after the party he'd just laughed, and he'd been teasing James since.

"Not wearing the dress today?"

"No, I left it at home today."

"You had me worried for a minute towards the end there, mate." This was as close as Colin ever came to mentioning his and his sister's amorous antics prior to leaving the party. Thankfully he'd assumed it was all part of the gender role-play. "I bet you and Louise had a right old laugh at my expense."

"Yeah, you're right, we did," replied James, with a two-ply smile.

———

Back in the waiting room, Harriet sat flicking through an old Rupert annual.

She preferred the books at the dentist's, yet it gave her something to look at other than the carpet. *That* had off-white loops in a pattern that lassoed your attention. The comma-like tails curved back on themselves. Spiraling inwards, they drew you in, further and further, dragged you down, deeper and deeper, unless you made a superhuman effort to resist. Thankfully her feet didn't quite reach the floor.

Someone rustled through from reception and she had no intention of looking up until, despite a roomful of empty chairs, the new arrival sat down next to her.

Raising and turning her head, she saw a man so thin as to be almost two-dimensional—like a human coat-hanger. Straight away, she put her hand in the pouch-like pocket of her top, pulled out a packet of Werther's Originals and offered him one.

He shook his head of long straggly white hair and tutted. "Didn't your mother tell you? Never offer sweets to strange men."

He took one anyway and, as soon as he'd unwrapped it, popped it in his mouth. As he did, she saw that he had transparent teeth.

"Are you strange?" she said.

"Oh, very."

"Is that why you're here?"

"No. Being strange is quite normal. I'm here because I suffer from writer's block."

Under the chair, Harriet's feet swung backwards and forwards as if running—just without touching the ground.

"How romantic. A writer…" She sighed, wistfully.

"No. I just suffer from writer's block."

Her leg-swinging stopped abruptly.

Realizing that he was being totally serious, she gazed and gazed at the door to her father's office. *What are Daddy and Riika doing in there?*

"You don't have to be a writer to suffer from writer's block," her neighbor continued, "just as you don't need to be an athlete to suffer from athlete's foot."

"Right…"

"Mind you, if I didn't suffer from writer's block, I might actually be a writer. There's just no way of knowing."

"No, there isn't. Bye." She jumped up and ran to greet Daddy as he stepped out of his office, followed by Riika, pinning up her hair. They both beamed back at her as widely as the people in commercials.

———————————

"Can I see?" said Morris Louche, picking up a sheaf of papers from Louise's desk.

She groaned inwardly as he tilted them towards the droplet-dappled window.

Leaning over her, he plunged her into olfactory overload with his aftershave fumes.

Where's a match when you need one?

She looked away, stared instead at the white tulips poking up from behind the printer at the far corner of her desk. They had a petrified appearance in the bluish light. Changing focus, the tongue-and-groove flooring and shelves of box files visible beyond likewise had a stony hue.

He merely flick-flick-flicked through the papers, which rendered his compliment as he put them down again, "Good work. Flawless," as worthless as it was unwanted.

"Just doing my job." She looked around and up at the thinning hair, colorless eyes, bony nose and pale, unctuous smile of Collard Gradden's junior solicitor.

"And what are you doing tonight?" He perched on the edge of her desk in his God-awful brown suit.

"Um, let's see. Oh, I know. I've got to paint my nails tonight."

"Well, it makes a change from washing your hair, I suppose. Not that there's a lot of it left. I don't know what made you cut it all off."

"And that makes a change from compliments. I was going to let it grow back. I don't think I'll bother now."

His golden tie-pin glinted at her as he leaned in closer. "Oh, come on, Lulu. Don't be like that. You can take this coquettish game too far, you know. I might just give up eventually."

"Don't get my hopes up."

"Oh, well, not to worry. I can wait."

He stood up, turned and headed back to his office. She didn't even care if her jinky bracelet gave her away as, under the desk, her right hand executed a vulgar valediction.

———————————

"Oh, it was awful," said Valerie, mouth fretful, eyes intense.

"I can imagine." Alistair slumped down next to her on the sofa. "I got a message telling me about it when I got in. It never even occurred to me you might have witnessed it. How ghastly."

He tried to put his arm around her shoulders but it didn't quite reach. He'd left too much of a gap between them.

She shuffled closer. "It must have been a shock for you, too."

He took a fortifying breath. "Yeah, it was."

The light they sat in came from the standard lamp to her left and the table lamp to his right. Gaze sinking floor-wards, he noticed that he had two shadows, one darker than the other.

Clearing his throat, he tried to sound upbeat. "Anyway, my news is I had a chat with Mia and apparently Harriet's just indulging in a spot of attention-seeking. Because she feels left out of things."

"Left out?"

"Well, I mean, she's certainly excluded by her brother and sister. So she invented her own private friend. Calling him God was for our benefit. To make us take notice. But you can set your mind at rest—we're not dealing with intruders or anything like that here. And it isn't just me telling you this now. What we've got is simply a nine-year-old's overactive imagination."

"Okay, thanks, love. That's exactly what I needed to hear." Her gaze softened and he saw the crease of a smile.

Then, slowly, the smile stiffened. "Now all I need to find out is why James keeps giving me such funny looks."

James licked his sister's make-up off as, gently grappling, they rolled around on her bed.

He was half clothed, half skin. She likewise, only the opposite way around. He had a shirt on and no trousers; she had a skirt on and no top. Heading first one way, then the other, they kissed with mouths open, until their teeth clashed with a click.

"Ow," from Louise.

Yet it couldn't have hurt that much.

As if the first rupture wasn't bad enough, she ended the embrace as well, staying put next time her back was on the mattress, then turned away from him. Having rolled off her and come to rest facing the ceiling, he went into reverse to end up on his side right behind her. He drew his knees up into the space vacated by hers and they lay like that, doubled.

"What's the matter?" he asked. "Don't you want to play anymore?"

Mumble-mumble into pillow.

"What's wrong, Lou?" He sat up, leaned over her. "Tell me. You know we never have secrets."

A long sigh, then, low and moany, "It's this creepy guy at work. He's getting on my nerves."

"Why? What's he doing?"

"Trying to get me to go out with him."

A mini-conflagration flared up brightly inside him, like a struck match—prompted by her colleague, not her. He knew he could trust his sister. "What's his name?"

"Morris. Morris Louche."

"And you see him every day?"

"Yeah." She nuzzled the pillow. All he could see was the back of her head.

He smiled. "Right, tell him you'll meet him tomorrow night."

"Hey?" She twisted around and looked at him now. "Haven't you been listening? I don't want to meet him. That's the whole point."

"I know that. Just tell him you will. Say, seven thirty. Outside The Dirty Ear."

"And then what?"

"Stand him up."

She rolled over, onto her back. "Oh, okay. Hey, good thinking."

When she slid her buttocks up the bed to sit up, he did the same, and put his arm around her. She, in turn, undid the top three buttons of his shirt, to expose "I Hate God" emblazoned in green ink on his chest.

He'd got it done in the same spirit that he'd put up more Marilyn Manson posters: as parent-bait.

"I wonder what Nick's doing at this precise moment," he said.

"I don't know."

"D'you know he's up to eight?"

Her hand fluttered inside his shirt. "Eight?"

"Yeah. And I'm sure it won't be long before he's hitting the newsstands again." Because not for one second did he believe that that paragon of vice, their Hell-sent friend, would stop there. He drew her closer to him. "We need to decide what we're doing."

She withdrew her hand. "What do you mean?"

"Well, we still haven't done anything."

She turned away. "We haven't any reason to do anything."

CHAPTER 15

Maybe it was just because they'd been talking about him the night before but James thought he saw him. He thought he saw the Devil, on the Underground.

On their way home from a Horrors gig, ears still ringing with thrashing guitars, he and his sister filed through the automated barriers and stepped onto a moving metal walkway that broke up into blocky steps and descended sharply. Getting bored with the same three or four digital posters in different permutations, he spotted a seven-foot figure in black stepping off the other end.

"Quick, come on," he cried, pointing him out to Louise.

They dashed past those letting the escalator do their walking for them and, pitched off at the bottom, hurried through tiled tunnels to a subterranean world of sooty mice, lost people, and ghost trains. When James dreamt of Hell, it generally had the decor of the London Underground. Like a dream, there was no sign of the one they sought, on either platform.

"Where'd he go?"

Two thirty-nine in the afternoon in his office at home, Alistair stood back from his mahogany desk with his mobile clamped to his ear.

"Privacy is, or should be, sacrosanct." He had to give his phone clients his full attention: stop and speak no matter what; even if, as now, he had company. He couldn't afford to lose another. "It's one of the most basic human rights of every man, woman and child."

"What about wrongdoers?" asked the caller. "Do they forfeit that right?"

Alistair nodded, though to the person on the phone rather than the person in the room. "Okay, yes, maybe they do."

"Good."

"Why?" He wiped his brow with the back of his only available hand, the one holding the phone, and returned it to his ear.

"Because through this window—"

Now he shook his head. "Godfrey…"

"I can see a front room—"

"You're—"

"That's been turned into an office. It looks as if it's built out of books. And there's a man with his arm round a young woman who's definitely not his wife holding a mobile up to his ear with his other hand."

Alistair felt a fluttering, as of wings, inside him. "Godfr—"

"And guess who he's talking to…"

Alistair's body shook, exactly as if a bird flap-flap-flapped in his ribcage.

Bookshelves blurred as he spun to face the window — too late.

"Godfrey," he shouted into the mobile.

Yet Godfrey had already terminated the call.

"What's wrong?" asked Riika.

He turned to his companion.

She gave a sideways jerk of the head that sent her hair flying over her shoulder, then looked at the window, and back. "What is it?"

"I've got a client who's a voyeur," he said, "who's started spying on me now. On *us*."

On his way up the garden path, Alistair heard a voice call "Mr. Glavier" from the shrubbery.

He whirled around.

Spending the day at the practice had made a welcome change from working from his office at home, especially after yesterday. Yet, he didn't expect to be able to avoid exposure so easily. He'd been waiting for Godfrey to make contact. Maybe this was it.

A head popped up from the midst of the laurel. An old man in wellies and ancient tweeds shuffled out into the open carrying a gardening fork.

"Oh, Verge, it's you. I forgot you were back with us today. Nice to see you again."

"Thank you, Mr. Glavier. Good to be here." The gardener's wrinkles lengthened and deepened without warning.

"You should find everything pretty much as you left it." Alistair noticed as he spoke that Verge had deteriorated, in only five months. He'd always had the posture of a man locked in the stocks. Now when he blinked, his eyes stayed shut nearly as long as they stayed open. They leaked cloudy tears, and the area beneath each one was dark and baggy. Elsewhere his skin was as pale and thin as paper, with shadowy watermarks, and his temples were embossed with violet veins. "I must say, you're looking a bit strained, Verge. Are you all right?"

The transplanted countryman nodded. "I'm all right now. Had a hard winter of it, though. Right low, I was. Nothing to keep me occupied, see. But then I met Mrs. Glavier out shopping and she suggested some tablets. Pep me up right proper, they do. Put a spring back in the old step."

With potential blackmail campaigns to worry about, Alistair turned to go. "Glad to hear it."

"Thank you, Mr. Glavier."

The phone rang indoors, and Alistair ran up the rest of the path.

He made it inside, grabbed the receiver and lifted it to his ear. "Yes?"

"Hello again."

As expected: Godfrey. He must have got the landline number from the phone book.

"I was wondering when I'd hear from you. So, you've decided to start spying on me now, have you?"

"It's The End House I've been watching all along."

"Right."

"No, really."

Alistair fleetingly wished he'd paid more attention to Godfrey's ramblings, but it was precisely this tendency to observe uninvited he'd been trying to treat.

"Why don't you get to the point?" He lowered his voice— though, apart from Riika, no one else should be home yet—and stood with his feet apart and head on one side, braced for the worst. "What is it you want?"

"It's actually your daughter I was calling."

"My daughter?" Hot needles pricked his brain. What did Godfrey want with Louise?

"I often speak to her."

"You speak to Louise?"

"No, Harriet."

Alistair was all ready to call in friends in the force when he realized that what Godfrey claimed didn't make any sense. "When? Harriet hardly ever has any calls."

"I talk to her in her room."

Alistair allowed himself a smile, because he knew that those with the most deep-seated delusions had their own logic, their own schema, and the more elaborate such a system was, the more likely it was to contain inconsistencies. "Er, I don't think so somehow. She hasn't got a phone of her own."

"I don't always use the phone."

"How do you communicate then?"

"Directly. It's cheaper."

Alistair felt as if his brain had been well and truly skewered now. "You mean to say" — massaging his temples with the fingers of his free hand — "her friend isn't imaginary, it's you?"

"That's right. She always told you her friend was real."

"Well, true, but she also said that it was God."

"Yes."

Alistair rocked, as Godfrey invited him to, "Picture a World Brain that knows everything from the universals to the particulars — because chaos is just order too complex to understand. Any item of information can be retrieved; any strand can be followed, if you have access to the whole of objective reality. The question is simply one of relevance. Okay, now factor in a moral dimension — the ability to separate right from wrong. And there you have it. I am that entity. The recording consciousness is me."

Alistair breathed in deeply. Even though Godfrey's sense of omniscience had tipped over into delusions of the grandest proportions, he had his family to consider. "This ends here. All right? You've got serious issues requiring urgent attention but I can't work with you anymore. And if you ever try to communicate with my daughter again or I catch you snooping round here or I hear your voice on my landline or mobile one more time, damn confidentiality, I'm calling the police."

He banged the receiver down, then bounded up the stairs.

Louise and her brother got off the bus—for once they'd managed to catch the same one—and turned up the close.

Ahead of them, Mum parked her Peugeot at right angles to Dad's Mercedes and got out. Doubtless having been picked up from ballet class, their sister clambered out of the other side. By the time Mum had got The End House's front door open, they'd caught up. Amidst "hi's" and "hellos," they filed through it after Mum and Harriet.

The latter trotted up the corridor. Mum leaned around the doorway of the study, recrossed the hallway and trudged up the stairs. Once they'd hung up their coats, Louise led James into the lounge.

"I forgot to tell you," she said, as both of them sank back into the sofa. "Morris, at work, has been no trouble. For two days now he's virtually ignored me. Your idea to stand him up must have worked."

"Good." The corners of James' eyes were notched with laughter wrinkles and his mouth was tightly pursed.

She sat up, reached for one of Mum's lifestyle weeklies and leafed through its prismatic, surprisingly modish pages, not so much searching for the most entertaining items as letting them grab her attention.

Flick, flick.

Conscious of the waiting-room atmosphere she'd inadvertently introduced, she resolved to undermine it. "Hey, look at this. They do pashmina boxer shorts now."

"What's pashmina?" James peered over her shoulder for a moment, before leaning back again.

"That's what they're made of. I think it's goat fur. You must have seen Riika's pashmina stole."

"No, I don't think so."

"They're a bit passé now, so I don't know why she'd want one."

"Okay…"

Flick, flick…flick.

"It's amazing, some of the stuff in here. Scented paint for children's rooms. Ha, and listen to this. Vanilla-scented knickers."

"Those sound good."

"Yeah, you'd wear those, wouldn't you?"

"Mm. On my head."

She listened to check that all was quiet out in the hallway, then brought up the subject they always came back to, eventually.

"I was sure something was going to happen the other night, you know."

"Which night?"

She leaned closer. "The night we saw Nick."

"You said yourself, we can't be certain it was him."

"Well, I think it was and he's stopped."

He stared at her. "What, killing?"

"Yeah."

He frowned. "Can you see someone like that happy with a tally less than double figures?"

"But you've got to admit, the frequency's dropped. Almost since the night we met him."

"Well, in that case, maybe…" He glanced at the door.

She touched his arm. "What?"

"Maybe you're right and he's gradually handing over to us."

She heard a short sigh, or a long breath, outside the lounge door, and quickly put a forefinger to her lips.

The door creaked open. Louise held her breath. James glanced at her. Harriet entered, carrying a glass of orange juice and a packet of Monster Munch, with her dolls under her arm. Louise exhaled.

Their sister picked up the remote off the coffee table, then sat on the floor. She placed her drink and her snack and the two dolls, which nowadays wore a mixture of each other's clothes, at her side, before pointing the remote at the TV.

A cartoon came on.

James got up.

"Didn't you want to watch the headlines?" Louise asked him.

"Nah. I saw them yesterday."

She laughed.

The news only really held any interest for them when it involved their infernal friend and his antisocial hobby.

They moved to the other end of the room.

"Do you think Nick really is the Devil?" she whispered, once they'd got settled.

"Yeah, fancy dress parties are the only parties he can go to without being found out."

"No, I'm serious. Is he?"

"Well, I think you know what I think. But I wouldn't beat your brains up with questions like that too much. Because in a sense, does it even matter if he's everyone else's Devil? What matters is, he's definitely our Devil."

CHAPTER 16

The white net curtain rendered the back garden a scene from early Japanese art—all hint and suggestion.

Valerie filled the kettle. *Funny how kitchen sinks are always under a window. It can't just be for the sake of people doing the washing-up; can it?*

Not long now and she'd be sitting down with a cup of Echinacea and raspberry tea and maybe a bit of mindless TV. She'd changed out of her work things. She stepped to the left to plug the end of the power lead into the back of the kettle and flick the switch.

Sliding back along the counter, she stopped level with the draining-board to extract her cup from the overladen rack. The net curtain moved in the breeze and she looked out at a figure crossing the bottom of the garden as if in a snowstorm.

Hunched over, it stopped, staggered, slumped to its knees and pitched forward.

Oh, my God—Alistair.

She swept the flimsy veil aside and, all too clearly, saw Verge, motionless on the grass.

Oh, heavens.

Rushing over to the back door, she yanked it open.

She'd no sooner made it outside than the lounge's patio door popped open like a hatch. It slid back, and James and Louise charged out through it. They ran down the lawn to Verge much faster than she could have done, in her slippers.

"Mummy, what is it? What's happening?" she heard.

Harriet stepped out of the patio door.

Valerie hurried over to her and blocked her view. "Nothing for you to worry about, darling. Just find your father."

"But—"

"Now."

Harriet withdrew.

Valerie spun around to see the twins carrying Verge up the garden stretcher-style. Only, without an actual stretcher, his body sagged in the middle like a sack of potatoes, and his head hung back. It jounced in time to their short, quick steps, rolled with every lurch. As they passed the cherry tree and covered the remaining ground towards her, her stomach, or was it her bowels, bubbled as if boiling. The day could be going along quite normally and then a man could fall past your window.

The twins shuffled around on the moss-matted concrete slabs that made up the patio, laid Verge out at her feet and stepped back.

"Is he…is he all right?" Valerie asked. Starting with the dear old wellies, her gaze slid up past the equally familiar tweeds to take in the face and instantly veered off again. What she saw reminded her of sightless gargoyles, the blank stares she got from creatures plucked from the depths of the ocean lying on crushed ice at the fish counter. The sorts of things she normally preferred to keep at the back of the cupboard of her mind.

"Dead," said James.

Valerie shook to the muffled crump of her heart, like distant heavy artillery; felt rather than heard. It was bad enough knowing that murders took place locally without people queuing up to die right in front of her.

Where was Alistair? Hadn't Harriet found him yet?

As soon as she heard the deep, hollow knock of the lounge door bumping against the side of the sofa, her stomach relaxed and her heart rate slowed. It was almost Pavlovian

Instead of Alistair, her youngest daughter burst out onto the patio, announcing "Daddy's in bed with Riika in the attic and they've got no clothes on."

Harriet's wail upon noticing Verge no sooner reached Valerie than it receded—almost as if it caromed off her.

A buzzing in the ears.

A blackness behind the eyes.

"She's going," shouted James.

Hedge and trees and lawn tilted, slid completely away.

———————

Louise held Harriet back to one side of the patio, so that the man and woman in green uniforms could do their work. She wondered when—if ever, now—life would return to normal.

"Is Mum dead too?" said her sister, between sobs.

"No, she's just fainted."

"Ow."

"Sorry." She must have tightened her grip on Harriet's shoulders. Her own emotions had been given a shake by the bombshell about Dad. *An affair? With Riika?* When had that started? How? And what would James make of it?

Where had her brother got to, anyway?

The patio lights flaring into life around her at least answered the latter question. The switch was in the kitchen. James must have turned them on.

In all the light, she saw that Mum had come to. The ambulance woman knelt next to her. Behind them, the ambulance man covered Verge with a blanket.

Dad stepped out of the patio door wearing his dark suit. As he turned, his white shirt-tails flapped obscenely in the breeze.

Mum sat up, but as soon as she saw him, her eyes rolled to white and she flopped back into the ambulance woman's arms.

Valerie had been slumped at the kitchen table for so long that the faces of miniature goblins grinned at her from whorls in the grain.

How could he do this to her? *Twenty-four years.* He'd always made such a show of being faithful, upright, devout. *Bloody hypocrite.* What was he thinking? *In their own home.*

Although she'd stopped crying, moans still issued from deep within her.

She sat up and rubbed her jaw, which ached from where the patio had slammed into it.

Getting her compact mirror out to have a look, she barely recognized the red eyes, blotchy cheeks and pouchy mouth. She almost forgot to check out the tiny abrasion to the side of her chin.

Could one get dehydrated from crying? She didn't know. But it felt like it.

She checked her cup… Empty.

The world outside the net curtains had ceased to exist. Night had long since engulfed it. While she'd rather have been back in her room, lying in the dark with the door locked, the thought of the stairs defeated her.

A crack from the doorway, as of a tiny stone under a tile disturbed by the pressure of a foot, made her jump. As Alistair entered, her heart clenched.

She listened to him, behind her, get a glass down from the cupboard and fill it at the fridge.

He brought his drink over.

What are you doing?

He pulled back a chair.

No... You can't.

He joined her at the table.

If he'd plonked himself down opposite, she would have got up and left the room. As it was, they sat at right angles under the humming strip light. Her clamped heart gave her the strength she'd prayed for up in her room. When he cleared his voice for speech, she forestalled him: "Whatever you've got to say, I don't want to hear it."

"But I need to—"

"I think we're past apologies, don't you?" She refused to allow herself to be smothered with words. "To be honest, I don't even want to talk to you." Hence she still hadn't turned her head in his direction. "Though I suppose we do need to discuss arrangements."

"Arrangements?"

This time she did look, and noticed his sheeny forehead.

"Yes." Now that she had the upper hand, she was determined to keep it. "Don't expect me to do anything for you, because I won't. And don't think you're sharing my bed, because you're not. There are plenty of other rooms in this house. You can move into one of those."

"All right, I'll sleep in one of the spare rooms; let you have some time on your own. And I'll get onto the agency about a replacement for Riika first thing in the morning."

"Oh no you won't." She couldn't believe it. He blamed the *au pair* when, both in terms of age and social situation, she was the one who'd been exploited. Besides, what if the members of the Doomsday Church found out and it became a public scandal? She didn't want that any more than he did. "Riika can see out the rest of her time. But stay away from her. Understand?" She omitted to mention that she would be ensuring that he did.

"I don't want to talk about Riika. I want to talk about us."

"Us?" He seemed to be under the impression that, however long it took, he would be forgiven. Yet how could he appeal to a bond he himself had betrayed? "There is no "us," remember? You saw to that."

Now possessing all the impetus she needed to get her up the stairs, she slung her handbag over her shoulder and rose to her feet.

As James and his sister descended the staircase, Mum opened the front door and entered.

Unfortunately, Dad was getting ready to go out.

With every step, James felt as if he descended into a thick gluey medium. Everything slowed down and stopped, including him and his twin on the staircase, as their parents ignored each other at close quarters at the bottom.

He still couldn't believe he'd missed something as seismic as Dad's relationship with Riika. Then again, he and Louise had met Uncle Nick. They'd been invited to join his murder club. Morality's poles had flipped. And of course, they'd been distracted by their own illicit relationship. But at least they really loved each other. At least they didn't say one thing and do another. No one could accuse them of double standards.

Signaling the return of normal viscosity, their sister ran through from the lounge in a stripy top, pink trousers and her yellow slippers.

Dressed in black leggings and a long white top, Mum had been to her slimming club.

"How did you get on?" asked Harriet.

"They praise you if you've lost and fine you if you've gained," said Mum.

"But how did you do?"

"I've lost pounds."

"In weight?"

"No, money."

Wearing jeans and a sweater, Dad had just put on his Gibsons. He now donned a Berghaus jacket.

James stifled a snigger.

Dad swung him and his twin a look. Digging his chin into his chest as he zipped up his jacket, he said, "Please give your mother a message." She took her shoes off right next to him, so the request was superfluous, but the two had separate conversations nowadays. "Tell her Charmaine called."

He turned and opened the front door.

"Be good," Harriet called after him as he stepped outside.

Evidently disconcerted not so much by the advice as the source, he flung a panicky glance in her direction as he pulled the door shut after him.

As his footsteps receded, Mum released a sob and instantly lost a couple of inches in height.

Harriet led her through to the lounge.

James and his sister continued down the stairs and around the post at the bottom with the giant carving of an acorn on top.

Harriet came straight from leaning rooms in dream palaces to find Mummy still on the sofa in the lounge—only this morning slumped sideways on it, with an empty bottle clutched in one hand.

The grown-up's face had a blue tinge. Then again, the whole room had. The light making it through the navy curtains dyed everything that color.

"Wake up, Mummy."

Just the whiffle of a snore in response.

Harriet prized the fingers from the bottle, placed it on the floor and got down by the head resting on the arm of the sofa, right up close. "Wake up."

It worked. Mummy reeled backwards and ended up still on the sofa, but upright.

She delivered a burst of speech in the nonsense language of sleep. Now she groaned.

"Mummy, you've got to get up or you'll be late." Harriet stood in front of her, took her hands and tugged and tugged to encourage her to make the effort, and it worked. If groaning even more, the grown-up got to her feet.

Harriet turned around to act as human crutch, and they hobbled to the doorway. Passing through it, they emerged out into the hallway, where splayed sunlight, streaming in through the window down the side of the door, half-blinded them.

"Oops, careful. Come on, that's it."

They turned up the stairs, and Harriet planned what had to be done and what could be skipped. As soon as she got Mummy to her room, she'd borrow her mobile and call for a cab. Then she'd get her ready. They'd probably have to forget breakfast.

Twenty minutes later and dressed for the day, if not fully washed for it, she and Mummy re-crossed that indoor bridge, the landing.

Turning right, down the stairs, she wondered whether there might be time to make a hot drink, but a car horn tooted out front. As soon as they reached the ground floor, she made sure Mummy had her handbag, opened the front door and shepherded her outside.

The morning was less glary than it had been. Doughy clouds had risen already.

She led the way up the pathway and out through the gate to where a white car waited with its engine idling. She opened the rear door, helped Mummy inside and leaned in to strap her in.

Finally, she closed the door.

And as the cab pulled away, she flapped her hand.

With all the blood in his body going *oomph, oomph, oomph,* James ran up the stairs and down the corridor.

He burst, panting, into Louise's room: "There's been another murder. It's just been on the news."

The blazing light shade hung UFO-like between them. Sitting at the head of the bed, propped up by pillows, his sister let the magazine she'd been reading fall and looked up. "Where?"

He dashed over to the bed. He dropped to his knees on the rug at the side of it with his forearms out in front of him, parallel on the coverlet.

"Larksmead Avenue."

"Larksmead Avenue? That's just up the road."

"I know. And that's not all..." He pulled out the map of London he had stuffed in his back pocket, opened up the left-hand half. As soon as she'd moved back, he laid it out on the bed between them. "I've marked and numbered each of the murder sites." He spun it around so that she could see properly. "Look at the recent ones, in order."

"What am I looking for? Some kind of pattern?"

"You could say that."

"My God, each one's a little nearer than the last."

"That's right. The Devil's closing in, Lou."

She lifted her gaze, locked eyes with his.

"Wanna check out the crime scene?" he said.

She blinked, swallowed.

He touched her shoulder. "Don't if you don't want to." *One of us has to.*

"O-kay."

"You'll come?"

She nodded.

They hurried downstairs, slipped into their shoes and threw on their jackets. James yanked the front door open and they stepped out into the night.

Harsh, unearthly high-pitched cries issued from it.

James' heart thudded.

It's just an animal. Isn't it?

As soon as they stepped outside, the garden turned into Wembley Stadium—which at least silenced the cries.

They'd tripped the security light. As they made their way up the path, he thought he spotted a pair of red eyes stare at them from underneath the hedge. He raised his arm to point them out to Louise but they disappeared, and the light clicked off.

He kept a lookout as he and Louise turned left out of the gate, and again when they turned up the alleyway that ran down the side of the property. Yet the light from the last streetlamp on the cul-de-sac merely sheared off a bit of the entrance. The levitating white and colored squares—the clear or curtained illuminated windows in the upper stories of black-backed houses—didn't add much. What had been pockets of night murk back on the cul-de-sac engulfed them in the alleyway.

They picked their way along it.

The clattering drum and bass of a helicopter gathered around them. Then a cone of light slashed through the night like a spotlight from heaven.

Solid black against nebulous city sky, the sleek rig slowed, stopped and parked in the air above dark, jagged rooftops, with a jewel-like white light, a tiny winking red light and the massive twitching searchlight.

"Honestly, it's like Gotham City, isn't it?" Louise raised her voice to be heard over the yammering of the rotors.

"Except the searchlight should be directed upwards, not downwards."

The chopper tilted, flung itself off.

They came to the end of the alleyway, crossed a road and continued, right, up the opposite pavement.

A pair of kids raced past, and two girls strolled hand in hand the other way under the streetlamps on the opposite side of the street speaking French.

"Hard to believe there could have been a murder anywhere around here," he said.

"It is a bit."

"Funny, though…"

"What?"

"We're the murder-obsessed ones now, not Mum."

"Got too many problems of her own to care anymore, I suppose."

"Yeah, s'pose."

Footsteps ringing in the hollow night, they turned left up Larksmead Avenue and, sure enough, there ahead, silent blue rotor-blades of light whirled atop silver vehicles with yellow and blue checks down the side.

Parked at a slanty angle across the road, the nearest police car's front doors hung open. The lettering on the side read LICE.

Onlookers clustered around the front of the house. More arrived, beating James and Louise to it. They jogged the rest of the way, to join them.

Fluttering blue and white tape kept everyone back. White plastic sheeting hung from the porch. A constable stood sentinel. James looked up at the play of police lights across the front of the house, like blue flash photography.

Glancing around at the other bystanders, he noticed a yellow-haired woman with her back to the building. She stood at the far corner of the tape, where it had been wrapped around and around a lamppost. She held a microphone, and a cameraman got into position opposite her.

Kids rode around on bikes. And conversation crackled and spread.

James' neighbor, a short woman in a camel coat, saw him peering around.

She cleared her throat. "Waited till she was crossing the threshold. Charged in after her... Katie, her name was. Lovely girl... Her husband died in a car crash last year."

James' mouth dropped open.

"What kept her going was the fact she'd fallen pregnant beforehand. Of course, that only made the miscarriage even harder to bear."

The woman's voice quavered on the last word and something twisted inside him. Where the previous murders had all seemed peripheral, tabloid-sized, more like entertainment than news, this one left him with a stitch in his side that wouldn't go away.

He glanced at Louise but she had her head down.

She walked off, pulling him with her.

"That was a bit awkward," he said, "for friends of The Fiend."

She stopped, looked up, with wild, flashing eyes. "It isn't just that we could have told the police and reporters who committed the crime, though, is it? We could have prevented it." She clapped a hand over her mouth, turned away.

He caught a glimpse of the filmy eyes she struggled to keep averted and he coughed to clear the choking tightness in his throat.

"Hey, it's not our fault if the police can't get it right." *We can't help knowing. Can we?* "They've got Nick's address. They've already questioned him. And they can again if they want to." He shuffled round to face her. "We're on the Devil's side, remember, not the Moral Policeman's. And it's too late to change allegiances now." He patted her arm. "Listen to me. If we just keep our mouths shut, we'll be safe."

"From which side?"

He sighed, and his arm dropped.

When they got home, he led the way through to the lounge, switched the rolling news on and they sat on the sofa and watched it all again.

"Look," he cried, as he glimpsed two figures with the same profile standing next to a woman in a camel coat.

"Why do you think he's getting closer?" asked Louise.

"I don't know." He could feel her gaze on the side of his face. His was still fastened on the TV. "Perhaps he's trying to tell us something."

"What do you mean?"

"It's as if he's using murder as a form of communication. The latest is like a message, a reminder, to us."

"Saying what?"

"Well, maybe he's egging us on—egging us on to do it."

"Do what?"

He turned. And importunate eyes stared back.

"You know. *It.*"

CHAPTER 17

No, no, please, it was just a thought experiment.
    With her mouth a zero, her eyes minus signs, Mum lay, unmoving, on the bathroom floor.
Just theoretical talk.

Yet while his intellect might be satisfied with this gloss, his feelings were much harder to fool; hence the sensation of something clawing at his viscera.

Squatting down beside her, he nudged her shoulder. "Mum, wake up."

Not even the faintest flicker of a response.

In her best nightdress—long, white, cotton, with an embroidered neckline—she lay profiled with her back to the bath and her legs at right angles to it as if she'd been sitting up and had slid sideways.

What had happened? Had she fainted again? Why would she have, for no reason?

The bottle of Bell's whiskey aslant in the crook of her arm might have provided an explanation, except it was mostly amber, with only a bit of clearness sliced off the top.

Then he noticed discarded packets all around her, and foil strips with little windows torn out of them.

The design of the empty boxes looked familiar. He picked one up and red lettering on a green background jumped out at him: *ZING!*

"Christ," he said, in a voice made deeper by bathroom acoustics.

A creak at the top of the stairs signaled the return of his sister.

"Lou, quick, call an ambulance," he shouted.

Humming a song by James, the band, Louise set four minutes on the microwave and hit "Start". The light came on and the plastic tray slowly rotated.

As she turned, a bar of blackness passed the window.

Lifting a corner of the net curtain, she glimpsed an epic shadow all down the lawn, before whoever it belonged to skedaddled around the side of the building.

She ran through to the lounge.

Riika was teaching Harriet a card game on the carpet.

Harriet looked up. "What's for tea?"

"A Wei..." Louise coughed and strained to keep the shakiness out of her voice. "A Weight Watchers meal and oven chips." She turned to Riika. "Did you see that?"

Riika shook her head. "No. What?"

"See what?" said Harriet.

"Never you mind."

Louise beetled out of the lounge and up the stairs to James' room.

She barged in. "I just saw someone in the back garden."

Her brother sat at his desk. His head shot round. "You're sure?"

"The shadow was half way down the lawn."

He almost knocked his chair over in his haste to get up. "Nick?"

"Who else?

James crossed the room to the door. "What was he doing?"

She followed him out into the corridor. "He must have been watching."

"Who?"

They cantered down the stairs.

She realized she was panting. "Me or Riika."

James flung the front door open, charged outside and dived down the side of the house.

Shielding her eyes from the security light, she stood on the doorstep, peering that way.

When footsteps came running from the other side, she swung her gaze in that direction. Her heart knocked.

It was as if someone had pushed a plunger in her soul. Something inside her went down and then came up again.

"Nothing," said James.

She followed him as he pushed on into underwater moonlight.

The light clicked out behind them and she halted.

To either side, smothering darkness. Ahead, streetlamps squinted through the trees.

A gap yawned where Dad's car should be. He still hadn't got back from the hospital. Mum had very nearly saved them half the trouble.

She glimpsed James poking around the close and up the alleyway.

He came trotting back.

"Gone," he said.

Harriet had her face pressed to the lounge window, inside the lit-up curtains.

Louise shivered.

James came up to her, placed his hands on her shoulders, gripped them. "Love, we've got to stop Hamlet-ing around and act. We've no choice. We have to do it, to stop him." He looked around at the window, where Riika now stood behind Harriet. "Time's running out."

Louise glanced at Riika, then back at James.

She couldn't speak. Her heart hammered at her ribcage.

What have we done?

At the window, a succession of smoky clouds drifted across the face of a lustrous moon, like a screensaver: vivid, idealized, endless.

Everything else: shadowy, marginal.

Where am I? Valerie turned one way and found her exit blocked, turned the other and, in her haste, almost rolled off the edge of the lounge sofa.

The clock on the digital set-top box said 20:03.

She hated waking up. Each time took her back to that first time in hospital.

Even now, she struggled to understand how it had come to getting her stomach pumped. Emotions had lurched back and forth inside her like the drum of a washing machine, leaving her unable to resume the relationship, unable to end it; in control one minute, crying the next, still with feelings for

Alistair but stifling them in his presence because she couldn't forgive him, until eventually she must have sought the nearest available means of release. For that was the funny thing. Swallowing the tablets had wiped the memory of taking them from her mind. Since her return a blur of days ago, Alistair had cooked her meals, covered her with blankets and brought her hot drinks. Yet she found it even harder to trust him now. A whole Grand Canyon had opened up between them. How did she know that he hadn't paid nightly visits to the attic, and Riika's bed, while she was in hospital?

She could have asked him earlier. She'd listened to him rattling around in the kitchen for ages. Now all she could hear was the ticking of the clock on the mantelpiece and the distant laboring of the fridge.

Then again, would she really have asked him? How could she believe any answer he gave?

She didn't feel any better for all the rest. Most of the time her brain felt like alphabet soup, yet every once in a while a feeling bubbled up into a thought.

He could be up there with her now.

Her neck jerked as it happened again. She almost gave herself whiplash.

He couldn't, could he?

He has before.

She stood up, hooked her slippers onto the ends of her feet, shuffled out into the hallway—darker than the lounge; if not quite as dark as the office—and turned up the main staircase.

There was no more auditory evidence of her husband on the first floor than there had been on the ground floor. She just heard the twittering of the twins as she passed James' door. This hint of normality caused her will to waver. She wanted to turn around, go back downstairs, because she told herself that she was being ridiculous; paranoid.

Or was that merely an excuse so that she didn't have to go through with it?

She'd come this far. Surely it was better to settle the question now rather than get down to the lounge and have the same suspicions all over again. And anyway, whose fault was it if her trust was in tatters?

She turned the corner at the end of the corridor, kicked off her slippers and climbed up into nothingness. The darkness here was total. She felt her way up, coarse-carpeted block by block.

Near the top, the gloom started to thin out.

Scaling the stairs, she saw a foggy glow down and around one side of Riika's door. She crept towards it until, holding her breath, she peered through the gap.

The curtains weren't shut properly. Discernible in the back-of-the-cinema light, the gargantuan heaving of a duvet under the sloping ceiling uncovered a heft of arm here, a V of knee there. The worst thing of all, she could hear her husband's breathing, as familiar as her own.

She felt as if she'd been punched in the chest and the kinetic energy had nowhere to go. She almost fell over. She just managed to pull a foot back to stop herself and turned away.

Her heart choked her, as somehow she made it back down to the lounge.

———————

Double whiskies muffled the world, such that the sudden *drrrring* of the doorbell could have been a fire alarm and Valerie wouldn't have budged.

"I'll get it," shouted her youngest daughter, who'd come down to check on her a little earlier and then wandered off to the kitchen.

Before she'd gone, Harriet had closed the curtains and switched the lights on. Holding her cut crystal glass up to the standard lamp beside her, Valerie stared at the honey-colored contents and needly glints of light, spellbound.

She'd always considered herself an amateur drinker, but thanks to the man whose rigorous and challenging brand of morality she had admired for twenty-four years being on more than speaking terms with temptation, she was ready to turn professional. Hence her toast: to the end of thought. Or the end of turbid feelings, emotional gloop. The whiskey sluiced away all that.

"It's someone called Colin, Mum," her youngest called from the hallway as the visitor entered.

"Oh, hello." While his name hadn't meant anything to her, his face did. He owned that charming MG.

"Sorry to trouble you…" He stood by the doorway in blue trainers, old or pre-worn jeans and a light grey T-shirt with a white stripe down one side, as if he'd been lying in the middle of the road, slightly off-center, when the council had been painting the lines. "…only I was just passing and thought I'd call on James and Louise, if they're home."

"Come in, have a seat."

He made for the armchair nearest the door. She wouldn't be able to focus on him all the way over there. "No, here. Next to me."

He sat down, with his hands on his knees and his arms as straight as struts.

"Drink?"

His right hand blurred, or at least her eyes made no attempt to keep up with it as he waved it in front of her. "No thanks, Mrs. Glavier."

"Please, call me Valerie."

"No thanks, Valerie."

She reached for the whiskey bottle. "Sure?"

He nodded.

So, with a somewhat unsteady hand, she replenished her own glass.

Finally she put the bottle down and picked the glass up. Slowly lifting it to her lips, she took sips. In between, she studied the young man at her side, taking in his sandy hair, fulsome mouth and frank, steady blue gaze.

A gulf of time and chunks of experience clearly separated them; he looked as if he'd been freshly cast that morning.

"Funny, really..." She put her glass down. "I spent most of my life convinced I wasn't attractive. It was only maturity that brought me round to the view that youth itself is attractive. Unfortunately the arrival of the one rather implied the departure of the other." Her laugh echoed, hollowly. "And yet people your age and people my age have relationships."

Up to this point, her neighbor had mostly stared ahead or, every now and then, glanced at the door. Now he turned in her direction and leaned back as if long-sighted.

She hadn't meant to open up to a stranger—only, his silence, stillness and impartiality meshed perfectly with her needs at present. Patting his hand, she gave it a grateful squeeze. "Even if one of them's married, you know."

She jumped as Colin sprang to his feet. "I think I'd better be going."

She watched him scurry out of the room.

"Oops," he said. "Didn't see you there."

"Upstairs, to the right, on the right," came Harriet's voice.

"I... Oh. Thanks."

Valerie cupped her chin in her hand. *What did I say?*

Shocking woman.

At the top of the stairs, Colin fumbled about for a light switch, yet couldn't find one. So, turning right as directed, he entered the mouth of a tunnel. The darkness deepened several shades at once. After that, it intensified incrementally until eventually it engulfed everything. He had to feel his way. Trailing his fingers along the cold, matte wall to the right, a recess alerted him to the possible presence of a door.

Sure enough, he found one. Interpreting the utterance he heard on the other side as an invitation to enter, he groped for a handle and gave the door a push.

Darkness rolled back around him to be replaced by lunar light. Transfixed by the spectral paleness of the moonlight, a full second passed—a long time in the circumstances—before it struck him, *that's a bare back.*

Immediately afterwards, he noticed a pair of hands in the small of it, just above the covers. *Two people. In bed.*

Realizing that they'd seen him before he'd seen them, he dropped his gaze and, mumbling his apologies, had already started retreating when something made him raise it again, to the female's face.

When he saw who lay stretched out in the pale night, he experienced the familiar sag of disappointment. But when he tugged his gaze up a notch, to the person she preferred, he got a kick of shock.

"What the—?"

He even got the acrid back-taste of his stomach juices.

Flick-flick went his eyes, from one to the other.

Flick-flick, from Louise to James.

In a desperate attempt to insert a wall between them to replace the one that they had torn down, he could only look at them one at a time.

Boyfriend-brother.

Girlfriend-sister.

How they must have laughed at his expense.

Both slid from view as he turned.

How long had it been going on? He loped back up the corridor. How had it started? He couldn't even begin to imagine. He skidded round the corner. And how come he hadn't twigged? He scrambled down the stairs. Was his naivety so capacious that their depravity could fit inside it? His fingers slid down the banister. The only time he'd suspected anything had been at his party, yet he'd been correct to think the unthinkable.

The light dangling from a bit of flex to his right came on and a figure staggered through from the lounge.

"Oh, hell—Mrs. Glavier." Colin halted.

"Oh, it's you," she said. "What are you doing up there?"

He responded with a carefully nuanced shrug of the shoulders, as if to suggest it was a perfectly unremarkable evening and there was nothing unusual about him loitering on someone else's staircase.

I'm loyal, even if they're not.

"You've seen them, haven't you?"

"Who?"

"The love-birds, of course."

His mouth seized up. It only formed the shape of a letter, not the sound, and it got stuck on an O.

He wrenched it shut, and open. "You mean you know?"

"Of course. I saw them together shortly before you called."

Colin groaned as decompression sickness set in. His limbs had gone all rubbery, and now his shoulders tautened in addition to his neck. "How can you allow such a thing?"

"It's been going on for ages."

"But it's disgusting. It's…it's…grotesque."

"I don't care anymore."

"You don't care?"

"No."

A wave of nausea swept over him. He'd never met a more debauched family than the Glaviers. First the mother propositioned him, then he came across the older offspring conjoined at the loins and now he learned that the mother knew about that relationship and didn't mind. He really couldn't work out whether he was more appalled with James and Louise for committing crimes against nature or with Mrs. Glavier for countenancing them. "Oh, God…"

"Don't worry about it. I'm not. Want me to show you? Look, I'll phone them."

"No," Colin said with a cracked voice.

Valerie picked up the receiver, punched in a number. "I know exactly what you're up to and I don't care anymore. I don't care." She slammed the phone down.

At the top of the stairs two pairs of legs, one bejeaned, the other beskirted, appeared.

What now? A young blonde woman wrapping a pashmina round her flew past with a flash of holographic eyes. Without a word, she bolted out of the front door.

A man with dark eyes and a black beard bustled down after her.

He and Mrs. Glavier turned their heads in opposite directions as his feet hit the ground floor carpet, but she followed his progress in the mirror on the wall as he likewise headed for the front door.

Colin rushed out after them.

Half blinded by a silent explosion of light, he hung back as the man tried to talk to the girl. She turned away, up an alleyway.

The man got in a Merc.

Colin set off up the garden path.

Nutters.

The moon is drowning. Like a face held underwater, it dims and dims, as layers of cloud rush in.

He pulls his attention back to Earth, where the blonde woman glides ahead of him—silently apart from the footfall of her boots, yet with a stride that has a definite snap and twang to it.

Doesn't she know it's dangerous to be out at this time of night, in this part of town? Shouldn't someone warn her?

Yet there isn't anybody. It's just the two of them, heading the same way.

She isn't even on a proper street, with people, cars, streetlamps. She's on an uneven alleyway with small rocky outcrops, gravelly bits and tufts of grass.

A hundred yards back, a road had bisected the alley. She could have turned left or right, but no, here she is still on it.

There's a high wooden fence on one side and a smaller wire one on the other, with back yards beyond. Here and there, lit windows silhouette gardens lumpy with vegetable plots and compost heaps.

Ahead, a concrete wall blocks off that side, while the other side opens out in the form of garages.

Her spiky boots crunch gravel.

Yes, someone really should make her aware.

He breaks into a run, raising his arm as he does so.

He's almost upon her before she turns.

Glimpsing what's descending towards her, she lifts her hands to protect her face—too late.

A stone struck a window. Alistair opened his eyes. Lit up from within rather than without, the black-leaded stained glass looked intact. Outside, laughter erupted. A can clattered. The shuffle of footsteps receded.

Alistair got up off his knees and his heels clicked on the polished floor as he strode up the aisle of the White Chapel. He headed for the vestry. The door creaked as he opened it.

He had inky fingers from putting out the Bibles. So he rubbed them together under the cold water at the sink and used the brush and the thin bar of soap to get them clean. *A launderette for souls.* Ideas often popped into his head that he could use in his sermons or for posters on the noticeboard outside. He'd certainly been hanging out his smalls a little too publically lately. *How can I make things right?* He scrubbed harder, with the claw-handled brush, until his fingers glowed. Even just being here, alone, helped.

He dried his hands, lifted his coat off the big wrought iron hook and put it on.

Stepping out into the lobby, he turned off all the lights, only pausing to glance into the body of the chapel. Even in darkness, the high-ceilinged space exerted its influence. He imagined it warping the lattice of space and time, calling out to the semi-lawless streets beyond, *Come and be healed.*

He passed on out into the night, locking the door behind him with the weighty key.

His mind stretched like a net over the city, taking in the nighttime stereophonics. If things had fallen quiet here, there was more than enough going on elsewhere, at different points of the compass, different distances away. A lonesome dog howled hoarsely on the next street. An overground tube train judder-judder-juddered to the east. Traffic whooshed out on the dual carriageway to the west. And far off but getting closer, he heard that lasso of sound, a city siren.

The widely-spaced streetlamps and hazy moon barely dented the night. A faded facsimile of the latter shuddered in a puddle as a movement of air made him shiver.

He crossed the small car park and was about to unlock his car when something pleeped out on the street.

It was the cash-machine-cum-pay-phone just up the road, the installation of which had inspired a sermon on the subject of modern telecommunications: "Too much talking, not enough being said."

It didn't let up. *Should he? Shouldn't he?*

He ran out into the street, past a man walking a Rottweiler and between rising and dipping hedges with gaps for garden gates on the one side and cars parked on the other like three-dimensional shadows.

The pay phone stood on the corner of another street, with more shadow-cars. A teenage girl passed right by it. It had been the same all his life. The public-spirited minority had to work extra hard to make up for the self-serving majority. He hurried even more, now that he'd made up his mind to do the responsible thing.

Lifting the receiver off its hook mid-pleep, he put it up to his ear. "Hello?"

"Ah, Mr. Glavier," boomed the male voice at the other end.

Alistair's mind free-wheeled.

Unable to see or think beyond the unaccountable fact that the caller knew his name, he put a hand to his forehead. "Who's this?"

The voice didn't sound quite so unfamiliar, now that he'd had a moment, but who among his acquaintance would know where to find him by calling the nearest pay phone?

A long-distance pause. "God."

James sat a foot away from his sister on the lounge sofa. He wanted to close the gap between them but knew that he shouldn't, downstairs.

Louise sob-gulped, which gave him all the justification he needed. He put his arm out to comfort her.

Leaning in, she rested her head against him. His shoulder became the repository of significant sighs, meaningful moans.

Surely it was his problem they'd been caught out by Colin, not hers. Yet he tightened the band of his hug. "Don't worry, darling. You won't have to see him again."

She lifted her head. "But what if he tells Mum and Dad?"

He stared at her profile, so similar to his, and reached out to take her hand. "He won't. And if it looks like he's going to, I'll talk to him."

She nodded, yawned and stretched.

Glancing left, she jumped up and dashed forwards—a rush of movement that ended as abruptly as it had begun.

In stockinged feet, she dithered on the edge of the Persian rug in her lilac dress.

"Lou?"

She stared off up the room, then bounded up it.

James launched himself off the sofa and sprinted up to where she stood. He opened his mouth to speak.

Louise held a finger to her lips. With her other hand, she pointed to where the floral chintz curtains fell almost to the carpet. An unfamiliar pair of leather tan slip-ons poked out from under the hanging folds.

With his heartbeat picking up speed to somewhere between a trot and a canter, James snatched up a faux Ming vase.

Louise grabbed the cord that would send the curtains truckling open.

———

A cosmic crackle and hiss, like a bad connection between two worlds, then the line clicked and cleared.

"You haven't forgotten our conversations already?" said the voice.

Maybe it was because he was on a pay phone rather than his mobile but he hadn't recognized the gravelly voice as Godfrey's at first. Then again, he would never have predicted that upon picking up a ringing pay phone he'd not used before, nor had ever wanted to, he'd be addressed by someone known to him.

"How did you know where to find me?" His impossible ex-client had obviously gone to extraordinary lengths to get around his ban on his mobile and landline.

"I know everything."

Although he had long since ceased to dismiss whatever came out of Godfrey's mouth as bluff and blather, the status he accorded him fell a long way short of the omniscience of the man's delusions. He had to admit that the most irritating person he had ever tried to treat knew a great deal, not least about the goings-on at The End House. Yet he believed that strictly human powers of surveillance lay behind each scoop and coup—with, presumably, a little help from technology.

But the inveterate voyeur must have access to some pretty sophisticated equipment to be able to locate him and call him on a pay phone.

Either that or he followed me. He heard again, in memory's echo chamber, the tap of a stone against a window.

"Don't look like that."

Alistair felt as if a piece of string starting in his neck and dangling the length of his body had tautened, jerking him upright. "Like what? Are you watching me now?"

"My eye never sleeps."

Alistair peered around the kiosk up the side street and his vision swung up and down the main road.

He couldn't see any suspicious lurkers. He couldn't see anyone else outside at all. Cars passed but never the same one twice. No faces peered from any of the properties round about—the windows of which were all either inscrutably dark or covered by illuminated curtains.

Alistair drummed his fingers against the metal skin of the kiosk. "Why the interest in me?"

"I've seen what you get up to."

"Am I interrupting?" Riika's voice resounded in his head. As if the events of the memory took place outside him, he could see his mahogany desk and the blade of her cheek as she leaned in from the side and, so close he could have done it for her, hooked a long shining lock around her ear.

He even heard his own voice: *"No, I just—"*

The sound of another siren threading through the night pitched him back out onto the street beside a pay phone.

"I know you have," he said.

"On more than one occasion."

The wind arrived in one big gust. Where before it had been negligible, now it buffeted him, actually lifted him onto his toes before setting him down again, with a bump.

The sinuous metal cable coming from the receiver writhed as Alistair turned back to the kiosk. "What the hell do you want from me?"

"I just wanted to let you know that we haven't finished."

Alistair shook his head. "Finished what?"

"Treatment. We were making progress, I thought, and you can't stop mid-way like that. It isn't fair."

Alistair bent the cable back on itself. "Godfrey, we're done."

"No, you and I have a way to go yet."

"Call me again and I'll have you committed." He fumbled to replace the receiver.

Sighing long and deeply, he stooped and cooled his brow on the pay phone's metal housing, before scurrying home through the dry current of the wind.

———————————

"Now," mouthed James.

His heart galloped.

Louise yanked the cord.

The curtains flew apart. Gathered folds swung first one way, then the other.

Only a dull reflection of the room appeared with their reflections in the foreground and darkness beyond.

James looked down.

An empty pair of shoes.

He placed the vase on the carpet. "No one bloody there."

He glanced accusatorily at the stone statue of a woman with praying hands and a silver-framed photo of his parents holding up identical babies.

"Dad must have bought himself some new shoes," said Louise.

"What are they doing there?"

She shrugged and went and sat back down on the sofa.

He joined her.

"I really thought it was Nick," she said.

"I know. Me too."

She cleared her throat to speak again when they heard the crunch of a key in the lock and the front door ran aground on the mat.

Dad put his head round the door of the lounge. "Where's your mother?"

James sat back, turned away.

His sister leaned across him. "Harriet's putting her to bed."

"And Riika?"

"Not home yet."

James listened as Dad shuffled back out into the hallway and through to his office. He heard him opening and closing the drawers of his desk, placing books on top of books, and rifling through papers.

Just as Dad's laptop greeted him with its usual fanfare, the doorbell rang.

Oh, God, please, not Colin again.

James tracked Dad aurally as he got up out of his creaky chair, moved around the desk and out of the office and walked the short distance to the head of the hallway.

What if he does tell Dad about us?

The front door opened.

"Evening, sir." The voice was uniformly flat. "It's Mr. Glavier, isn't it?" No inflection for the question even.

James had already started to switch his attention back to his sister when the man introduced himself and someone else with him. While their surnames couldn't have been more different, they had the same initials. The letters didn't stand for first and second names at all, they stood for ranks. He even recognized this particular combination—DS—from TV.

Nudging Louise's elbow, he strained his hearing to its utmost limit.

"I believe this is the correct address for a Miss Riika Polvi?"

"It is, yes. Though I'm afraid she's not in."

"We realize that, Mr. Glavier, because I'm sorry to have to tell you this but we believe it's her body that's been discovered in a nearby alleyway."

James shot upright in his seat and felt Louise start beside him. "She's dead."

"Dead...? Riika...? How?" Dad's voice had faded to a whisper.

"I'm afraid, in these circumstances, it's a murder investigation."

James stared at his sister and she stared back, with gobstopper eyes.

The Devil had struck again, this time on their doorstep.

CHAPTER 18

"Sir, are you all right? Sir?"

"Yes, yes," James heard Dad reply, eventually. "It's just a shock, that's all."

"I know. We realize that. And that's why we're sorry to have to ask you this but we'll need you to identify her."

"Now?"

"No, no, most probably tomorrow."

"Of course."

"Oh, and, sir, just to prepare you in advance, it may not be that easy."

Dad swallowed, with a clicky sound. "I... see."

"Good night, sir."

"Yes, night."

The front door shut, quickly followed by Dad's door.

Louise let out a massive sigh. "Oh, God. Riika..."

James could hardly breathe, let alone speak. For a moment he felt as if he had a weight, gravestone-heavy, pressing down upon him.

His sister got up. "Come on."

"What, where?" he said, likewise standing.

She pointed upwards, and darted out of the room. He ran after her.

Out in the hallway, he swore he could hear sobbing. But he jogged up the stairs after Louise and by the time they stopped in the corridor outside her room, he wasn't sure if he'd heard it or not.

"What?" he asked.

She shook her head and whispered, "Not here."

He set off after her again, up the stairs to the attic. She pushed the door open into Riika's room, turned the lamp on and sat on the edge of the rumpled bed.

He shivered. "What are we doing in here?" He looked wildly around at Riika's pink hairbrush, her flowery Oyster card holder, her tortoiseshell travel mirror.

Louise stood up. "You were wrong, you know." She spoke at normal volume, stared at him with Steadycam eyes as she flicked a strand of hair out of her eyes. "Nick isn't communicating with us." Her voice rose. "He's playing with us." She flung her hands apart. "I mean, this time it's someone we know, someone we actually live with. We're implicated, inextricably." She glanced out of the window, turned back. "And talking to the police isn't even an option anymore because having known everything and done nothing, we're as answerable for her death as we are those of the previous three." She shook, violently. "Oh, God. Oh, God."

"Stop freaking out."

"Freaking out? How can I not freak out? Riika's dead, because of us."

"In a way, yes. By not committing two murders, we've blood on our hands from even more."

Her eyes flinched shut before opening again. He hadn't meant to express it quite so baldly. But what was the Devil trying to do, apart from mess with their heads? Was he punishing them because they hadn't kept their side of the bargain? Had they made a pact with him without knowing it, merely by accepting his card? Would people keep dying closer and closer to them until they carried out his grim request?

With another big puff of a sigh, Louise leaned against the chest of drawers from three or four feet away, with back arched and head dipped.

He gripped her shoulder and squeezed it.

He was glad she couldn't see his face, which felt twisted out of shape. A murder so close to home couldn't possibly be construed as encouragement. It must be a warning to get on with it.

If they didn't, who would be next?

Dad had always said it was dangerous to trust the Devil.

Alistair followed the officers down a long corridor. Squeak-squeal-squeak went a wheel of the metal gurney they passed coming the other way, mercifully unoccupied. He never wanted to reach the end.

The morning had been no less ghastly. First he'd had to call Riika's parents to express his condolences. Then he'd had to tell the children. Louise and James had heard already. Harriet had howled. Straight after that he'd had to get rid of a reporter who'd turned up. Two more had phoned.

They arrived at the door. The pathologist shook his hand, with cold, stiff fingers.

Alistair shivered as the chilled air penetrated his shirt. He did his jacket back up.

A body lay on the slab, covered from head to toe.

In green scrubs, the pathologist lifted the top of the sheet and carefully folded it back.

It's not her. Red gashes criss-crossed the face, the deepest separating nose from left cheek, right cheek from right temple and right cheek from mouth, giving the whole a cubist aspect. He made out purple swollen eyelids. Otherwise only the teeth were intact, in the drawn-back mouth.

It wasn't until he noticed the matted blonde hair and recognized the soft white neck that he hunched over as if he'd been kicked in the stomach and a sob-gulp escaped his crumpled frame.

Then he had to rear up to stop his lunch propelling itself up his throat at high velocity.

He turned to the two suited officers, who stood with heads lowered, eyes raised.

Swallowing sick, he nodded.

"Thanks, Ahil," the older detective, with a shaved head and unshaven chin, said.

The pathologist raised the sheet and settled it back in place.

Even as Alistair and the two officers made their way back towards natural light, the image of Riika's face—what was left of it—bobbed in front of his eyes like a macabre balloon.

It didn't go away.

He doubted if it ever would.

———

Balancing a teabag on a spoon, Louise placed her foot on the pedal of the bin by the back door and tipped the soggy bit of filter paper full of tea leaves in.

The door opened. A hand grabbed her wrist, yanked her outside. She shrieked.

Her vision travelled up the arm to her brother. "Christ, James." She put a hand to her jumping heart. "What is it?" He pulled her round to the side of the house. "James, what's going on?"

"I was bringing the dustbin round and look what I found." He pointed to a piece of baby blue fabric. Stained rufous, it dangled by a tassel from a brier poking up from the thick bushes.

She put her hand to her mouth. "That looks like…"

He nodded. "Riika's scarf."

She looked around to see if anyone was about. Lowering her voice, "What's it doing here?"

"He left it here." They didn't even use his name any more. They didn't need to.

"Why?"

"Never mind that. We have to get rid of it, quick, before Mum and Dad get home."

She grasped his wrist. "Don't touch it."

"I'm not going to touch it." He pulled his arm away, reached out and plucked up a bamboo cane that wasn't supporting anything and used the end of it to hook the piece of fabric free. "Come on."

She followed him up the side of the house and over the low wall onto the patio.

"Get me a bag," he said.

"You mean you're not going to destroy it?"

"I can't. It's evidence."

She pointed around the corner. "Planted evidence."

"Insurance."

"Who for?" She sighed, ran into the kitchen and grabbed a bluey freezer bag from the bottom drawer just inside the back door. Realizing she was still clutching the teaspoon, she dropped it and hurried back out into the garden.

As she held out the open bag and he tilted the stick over it, her gaze travelled up and across the back of the building. Glimpsing a short static form at one of the windows, her eyes shot back. Yet the window stood empty, as if the figure in a portrait had stepped out of its frame.

"This is serious now," said James.

"I know." She checked the window again. Nothing. "I can't forgive him for Riika's death."

James shook his head. "No, I don't think you understand."

Her eyes latched onto him as his forehead creased.

"He's not taunting us anymore." Her brother's forehead crumpled. "He's threatening us."

Her neck made involuntary jerky movements. Suddenly acutely conscious of her own body, she could hear little ratchety sounds within it. "How do you mean?"

"Remember the map?"

She nodded, and heard corresponding internal creaks.

"How he's gradually been getting closer?"

She nodded. Click-click.

"Well, how can he possibly get any closer now… without coming indoors?"

She followed him inside.

"You mean…" Her head wobbled frantically on the stem of her neck and she couldn't stop it. "Next he's going to be targeting one of the family?"

James took the notebook attached to the fridge that Mum used as a shopping list and sat down at the table. "Yes, I don't know if he planned it that way or if he's trying to force us to act because we know about his club and his crimes and we might decide to shop him, but he's really putting pressure on us now." With the little red pencil that came with the notebook, he drew a gallows with a double crossbeam and a stick-figure hanging from each side. "We have to do it, Lou." Underneath one figure he wrote "Mum", underneath the other "Dad". "We have to. Otherwise he's going to come back again."

"But I don't know if I can."

He stood up. "Well, then we have to clear out of here, as soon as possible."

She nodded, freely, without any clicks. "All right."

"Okay." He tore off the page of the notepad he'd scribbled on. Balling it, he stepped over to the bin and was about to place his foot on the pedal when he turned. "I fancy Venice myself. It's out-of-the-way and we need somewhere decadent, because there can be no middle-class cul-de-sac for us. We could lose ourselves at the heart of its watery maze." She watched him soar on the thermals of confidence. "I'm sure we'd fit right in. What do you think?"

Venice... So potent was his optimism, she got a bit of the updraft. At last she spied a portal, admittedly closing, through which they could escape their parents, Nick, the police, everyone. "Sounds good to me."

"Great." Coming back over, he stuffed the freezer bag in his front pocket along with the piece of paper. "We'll book the first available flight online tonight and one of us can empty our account out in the morning."

"I'll do it."

"Thanks. I'll go into work to keep up appearances so Colin doesn't do anything and then we'll leave whenever the flight's for, either tomorrow night or the day after that at the latest."

"I'll throw a sickie tomorrow and just never go back." She chuckled. "Morris will do his nut."

James rested his hand on her shoulder. "We'll pack tonight but leave our bags here and come back and collect them when it's time." He shook her, gently. "This is it, Lou, or nearly. *Au revoir*, England."

"Don't you mean *arrivederci*?"

She caught the glinting diamond of his smile.

Their time had come. They'd had enough of this grey and unpleasant land and were going into exile, moving closer to the sun.

Just a few more nights to get through.

"Can I..." She touched his arm, wanting to ask, not wanting to. "When you say he's coming back... who do you mean for?"

Her brother's smile shrank to nothing. He looked at her through a cloud of thought. "There's two women in the house, three females. One of them's you."

Through some strange Cartesian inversion, her heart pounded in her head and boxed her ears. *The Devil's coming back for me.* "I thought that was what you meant."

CHAPTER 19

A listair parked up outside work. If only to avoid the heavy weather of Valerie's moods, he tried to avoid his office at home these days. Plus he had to prepare for a new client.

He'd unplugged his seatbelt when his mobile buzzed in his jacket pocket.

He tapped the glossy black surface to take the call and lifted the phone to his ear. "Yes?"

"Alistair."

"Godfrey." *When did he start using my first name?*

"How are you?"

"We're not having this conversation, Godfrey."

"Oh. I'm imagining it?"

Alistair shook his head, sighing.

He was about to terminate the call when he caught, "Harriet's peakiness is really just a pale form of prettiness, isn't it?" Quickly putting the phone back up to his ear, Alistair heard faint salivary clicks. Godfrey smiling? *At Harriet?* "Either that or she's just growing up."

"Godfrey…"

"They do, you know, so fast."

"Godfrey."

"Anyway, I know you're busy, so I'll let you go."

"Godfrey," he shouted.

Time has holes, chasms. One opened up now as a pause stretched out and out.

"Yes?"

"What do you mean? You can see her?"

"Yes."

"Where?" Alistair switched the engine back on.

"On the way to school. You don't expect me to be more precise than that?"

"Godfrey, if you touch her, I swear…"

Godfrey coughed, choked. "What are you suggesting?"

The normally quiet engine roared.

"You on your way somewhere?" said Godfrey.

"Yes."

"I really should let you go then."

"Don't you dare hang up on me."

"Alistair, Alistair, Alistair… Normally you don't want to talk, today you do. I'm getting conflicting messages here." Godfrey chuckled.

Alistair spotted a girl with a flowery rucksack, brown hair and glasses. *Harriet.* He slowed right down, opened his window. It wasn't her.

"So talk to me." He drummed his fingers on the steering wheel.

"What about?"

"Anything you like. Today is all about you."

He passed right by the school, at crawling pace. The traffic wouldn't let him go any faster. But he still couldn't see his little girl. In a couple of years she'd be at the big school. Yes, she might be growing up, yet she was still a child.

Godfrey cleared his throat. "Well, let me see… I know, your wife. Do you think she's going to tell the Church what you've been up to?"

Alistair braked hard as red lights flared in front of him and the gaps closed up between vehicles as between the wagons of a braking train. "No. What makes you say that?"

"I'm just not sure how a man in your position can sustain a secret like that." The traffic started moving again. "I mean, it must be burning a hole in her to confide in someone, and then it'll all get out." Alistair caught a glimpse of his crinkled forehead in the rear-view mirror. "What do you think the Church will say? Alistair? Alistair?"

"Harriet, Harriet, are you okay, love?" He'd wrenched the car up onto the kerb, leapt out.

"Of course, Daddy." She allowed herself to be hugged and then stepped back, swaying slightly.

"Did you see him?" He looked around, wildly.

"Who, Daddy?"

"The man, the man."

"I haven't seen any man."

He stared down at her. "Not even your "imaginary friend"?"

"Oh, Daddy, imaginary friends are for babies. Or loonies."

"You know, if someone's approached you, for any reason whatsoever, you need to tell me." He placed a hand on her shoulder. "It's very important."

"What do you mean, Daddy?"

"No one's been talking to you?"

"No. Just you."

He steered her around towards the car. "Okay, come on."

"Daddy, school."

"Uh-uh. Day off."

"It is?" She clapped her hands. "Oh, Daddy, I love you."

He strapped her into the back of the car and leaned against the door.

Tapping his phone again, he put it up to his ear. "Detective Chief Superintendent Mace, please."

Dodging shoppers under the glare of windows catching sunlight, Louise glanced over her shoulder at the man in the white hoodie twenty or so steps behind. Hunched over with his hands in his pockets, he had a long, loping stride and kept close to the inside of the pavement. She discreetly increased her pace.

The wind had got up. It whipped around her ankles. Where a Costcutter projected out a few feet, a mini-tornado of dust and little bits of litter corkscrewed in the corner as if temporarily strung together, before coming apart. Items lay where they fell or scraped across the Tarmac in jerky zigzags, before every last one of them whizzingly took off and frantically helter-skeltered up and down all over again.

She'd just withdrawn her and James' entire savings from the bank, a total of £3,146.27. James had transferred his money to her account via internet banking yesterday evening, then booked a late flight for today.

She peeped over her shoulder. The man in the hoodie was now about fifteen steps behind. Deciding to let him pass, she turned down a side street, with no one about.

Stupid, stupid. It was him she needed to get away from, not everyone else. She was about to turn back when he rounded the corner. Goosed, rifled, pickpocketed and generally manhandled by a particularly persistent gust, she pressed on.

The man's hoodie was pulled down low, like a monk's cowl. She couldn't see his face at all. *It could be anyone. Even...* Her blood lurched in her veins. She tasted salt.

She darted left at the end of the short street, onto Packers Lane. She held her breath, counted one, two, three, and looked back. *Shit.* A hotness shot through her as he turned her way. *It's him.*

Every few steps she broke into a little trot as if late for an appointment. Breathing raggedly, she willed the next turning to come quickly. *Oh, God.* She should have let James collect the money and she should have gone to work.

James. She fumbled with her phone inside the handbag over her shoulder. She got it in her hand. She wanted to speed-dial him, or dial 999, but Nick would see.

No, it can't end like this... It just can't. A film of tears made her vision go all blurry.

He couldn't be more than ten steps behind now. She could hear him breathing.

Nine.

Her heart pounded, quaked.

Where the hell is everyone?

Eight.

She peered at the back yards of the shops. Most had high fences. You couldn't even get onto the land, let alone inside the building. Others allowed access but to doors that would doubtless be bolted and barred. Without a door she could be sure would open, she'd be walking straight into a trap.

Six.

At last, she spotted a side street coming up, the last before Hell nightclub. She ran and didn't stop running.

He broke into a sprint, bounding over the cobblestones, gaining on her.

"Nick, no," she cried, as he knocked into her, sending her sprawling.

She put her hands out as ground rushed towards her.

Valerie lay on a slab in the morgue with a knife to her bare shoulder. *I'm not dead.* The knife pressed, made a bloodless incision diagonally down her chest. Maybe the cut was just so clean but she couldn't feel a thing. *I'm not dead!* However much she tried, she couldn't get her mouth to work. It hung open. Her tongue lolled, uselessly. The knife made another bloodless track diagonally the other way, till it met with the first.

A pair of latex-gloved hands opened her up like a pair of curtains white on one side, pinky scarlet on the other.

Then a saw buzzed. *No!*

She heard rather than felt the snaps of bone.

Next, the knife made a succession of lateral motions. More cuts, but painless, entirely sensationless.

A hand reached into her from either side. She did feel something then, distantly, as they tugged, rocked, tore, before lifting out…

She yelled, coughed, spluttered. Hearing a whistling in her ears, she put a hand up to the side of her head to try and check it. She opened her eyes and a blinding flash meant she had to shut them again. *Ugh. Morning.*

Her head throbbed and spun in the unremitting sunlight.

She must have forgotten to shut the curtains.

Her twisted back ached.

She straightened and stretched her spine and the back of her head thudded against wood. What was she lying on, a table?

Her skin itched with cold and crawled with gooseflesh. Just air making contact with her body, yet so much of it, all the way around. Where was she, outside?

She studied the ceiling and made out a white roof and beams, two stories up, yet with no floor in between.

Bolting upright, she saw rows and rows of pews, white pillars, white walls, a stained glass window high up.

She let her feet fall to the floor. Bottles clattered and rolled under the pew and the rolling went on for miles, years.

She remembered now. She'd come here for direction, guidance, and must have brought her sickness with her.

Turning her wrist over, she checked the time, before reaching in her bag for her mobile.

"Susan? Hi… No, I'm sorry, I can't, won't be in today… Yes, it was terrible… Yes, a tragedy… Oh, he's fine, thank you… Yes, I hope to be in tomorrow. Bye."

Why was she keeping up this charade? For Alistair? Herself? The family?

How her husband had treated her was like a bruise that had started, just started, to heal. It didn't hurt all the time, only when she pressed it. Maybe in a little while she'd be completely free of pain, if only she could stop probing, poking, prodding.

How strange. Her younger, more attractive replacement lay on a slab, cut up, cut open, stomach contents sent off for analysis, while she listened to birdsong, warmed by waves of blinding sunlight.

What am I going to do? Stop it. *Stop it.* She stood for a moment in the blurred day, waiting for everything to come into sharper focus.

She'd had a message on her phone: "Morning, this is Morris Louche at Collard Gradden." Her ears popped. "We were just wondering if you knew where Louise is. She hasn't turned up for work today. If you wouldn't mind getting back to us on…"

Finally she knew what to do. *Thank you, Lord.* She clicked out of the Chapel, shutting the door behind her and locking it with her spare key. She needed to get herself in order. And she needed to get her family in order. What was it Alistair had always called it? "Moral rearmament"? Yes, that was it.

There couldn't be many more last days left.

Am I...? One knee throbbed. That side's shoulder too. Though the knee felt as if it was swelling up. Other than that she just had tiny abrasions to the heels of her hands.

Worse by far was the unpleasant dampness between her legs.

She sat on her bottom on the cobblestones by a chained gate with flaky blue paint.

Her hands shook uncontrollably. She clutched her phone as she called James.

Great. Now other people decided to show up. A man in overalls walked by holding a clipboard. Then a woman pushed a bicycle the other way.

James arrived within minutes. He ran from the direction of the nightclub with his eyes pinned on her. She loved him with every cell of her body. Her heart cleaved to his.

She climbed to her feet.

He reached her, threw his arms around her. "Baby..." His chest heaved inside his black sweatshirt. She felt his breath on her neck.

She turned her mouth to his ear. "I'm sorry."

He stepped back, studied her. "Sorry?" She saw the crease at the corners of his eyes. "Are you okay?"

They heard the warning beep of a reversing vehicle and an articulated lorry rolled past and past. The driver's arm stuck out of the cab window. He glanced at them as he checked his side mirror.

"I'm…" While her trembling hadn't stopped, it had died down. "I'm all right. But the bastard took all our money. Every last bit of it." She kept her mouth and eyes clamped shut for a moment, held her breath, otherwise she would have burst into tears. "I'm so sorry."

"Lou…" He held her shoulders.

"Ow."

"Oops." He took her hands, then just her fingers. "Listen, I don't care about the money. All I care about is you." He looked down, up. "What did he do to you?"

"Apart from knock me down, nothing. He just took my handbag. That's all he wanted." The wet fabric of the crotch of her trousers clung to her coldly as she placed one leg in front of the other. "But I just…" A rising shiver. "I was so scared."

He nodded. "We'll get you cleaned up, my love, don't worry. But we need to call the police."

She grasped his arm. "Police? No, it's too late for that. You told me that, remember? And if it was too late then, it's far too bloody late now."

He held his hands up. "Okay, okay."

"Anyway, what could I tell them? Other than it was someone tall, wearing a hoodie. I mean, at first I thought it was Nick."

"Nick?"

"Yes, to begin with. That's why I was so scared." The ripple of another shiver. "Well, he wasn't quite as tall as Nick but then this guy wore flat trainers rather than those platform-style boots Nick goes in for." She leaned against the wall. "Anyway, I'm okay. You go back to work."

"Work?" His eyebrows bunched. "No way. I'm not letting you out of my sight." He puffed his cheeks out. "But if we're not going to the police, there's only one other person we can turn to."

She stiffened. "James, no. We can start work as soon as we get there."

"Lou, we'll need money for accommodation if nothing else. He said to go to him if we need help. Now we do."

James dipped his head, not his eyes.

She stared into them. "You just can't leave it alone, can you?"

"I just want to talk to him, once, before we go." He patted her shoulder—her good one. "We'll go and get you cleaned up and then I'll go and see Nick."

"We."

"What?"

"*We'll* go and see Nick."

He shook his head. "No, baby, I'm not taking you. Not after what you've just been through."

"But, James, you're not letting me out of your sight, remember?" She started walking, in the direction of the high street.

"Lou…" He was trying to keep up, checking his phone at the same time. "Shit."

"What?"

"Mum just tried to call me."

Louise got hers out. "Yeah, me too. Damn, and Morris… I forgot about him." She almost tripped as she forgot which foot to move next. "Hey, you don't think Mum's on to us, do you?"

"I hope not. We still have to go back home to get our bags and passports." She looked at him. He looked at her. "We may end up eligible for Nick's fan club after all."

He smiled at her.

She shuddered.

CHAPTER 20

It was the sort of day Colin always thought of as a fried-egg
day. A yolky sun peeped out from behind an albumen of
cloud. But bright sunshine one minute could be dark
shadow the next; each heightened the intensity, or the
dullness, of the other.

He got out of his MG on the edge of a car-park backed by a
three-story brick building with huge windows. Like an outsized
house, it had matching gaudy yellow window frames, door
frames, gutters and downpipes. Neighboring buildings were
similarly tricked out in primary colors. The entire business park
looked as if it had been designed by some of the more able
attendees of the local day-care nursery.

Yet he had his workface on—serious, conscientious,
depressed.

Late as usual, he locked his car. He'd no sooner picked up
the rotten-egg smell of a catalytic converter on the rifling,
whiffling wind than a hand clapped him on the shoulder.

Whirling around, he saw that the arm belonged to Mrs. Glavier who wore a rather crumpled sage skirt suit.

He lifted his chin to say something but, unsure whether to be rude or polite, ended up gulping instead.

"Sorry," she said. "I didn't mean to startle you."

He smiled thinly, because the skin of his face smarted and prickled. What if James saw them together?

"I know you're just going into work." She cast a glance up at his company's Lego-like building as if for inspiration. "But about that day you came round—"

"Please, there's really nothing to discuss." Her unwelcome overtures then had been bad enough. What this time? Had she graduated to stalking?

"I just wanted to say how sorry I am." She got it in quickly— presumably because she knew he would allow her to go on after that. "For the state I was in. I definitely wasn't myself that day. I hope you understand."

"Of course."

So that was all she wanted. He even ventured a proper, fulsome smile.

"Though that isn't why I came to see you."

His smile slackened instantly. "It isn't?"

"No. I wanted to talk to you about James and Louise."

"Oh." Gears churned in his head.

"You wouldn't happen to know where they are, would you?"

Colin breathed deeply and stretched his neck on one side to try and get rid of the tightness within that felt like pressure from without, as if he were operating at more than one atmosphere. The Glaviers had that effect on him. "Well, James is on the early shift today. He should be in there."

"They said James was here but left. It looks like they've both gone off somewhere."

"I'm afraid I wouldn't know anything about that." He hadn't had anything to do with the twins since he'd seen how they spent their leisure time.

She turned to go.

He breathed easier already.

Until she turned back. "Listen, I know I'm probably overstepping the mark here but a mother cares, you know, and only ever wants the best for her child. I know Louise can be a bit difficult at times but... maybe you shouldn't be so easily discouraged." She smiled.

Unbelievable. Mrs. Glavier, the mother of the most depraved family he had ever come across, had now turned matchmaker.

Vowels and consonants stuck in his throat like a clutch of lettered striking hammers jamming a typewriter.

"Oh, no need to be embarrassed." The woman who had once made an incredibly clumsy pass at him placed a hand on the sleeve of his pea coat with a gesture that, to his mind, was an incestuous mix of motherly and proprietorial. "You know we'd love to have you in the family."

He withdrew his arm with a robot-like gaucheness before rocking back a step. The ghoulish Glaviers had demonstrated their degeneracy, again.

Maybe she hoped to limit the family disgrace.

He put his hand up to block any further advances. "I think we both know where Louise's heart lies."

Mrs. Glavier stared at him, and something like the half-scallop of a question mark appeared on her brow as the light changed.

Valerie felt as if she and everyone else, everything, the whole business estate, had entered a tunnel. The development had just had most of the color sucked out of it. Even the guttering above them wore its yellowness dully.

She put a hand to her cheek. "What do you mean?"

"You *know* what I mean."

"I do?" Her stomach flimflammed. Did she imagine it or did an intimation lurk just out of reach?

Colin splayed his fingers and seemed to twist one way even as he turned the other. His response came out all in a rush: "Well, he's the one sleeping with her."

"Who?" The closer she got to the truth, the more she got a back-draft of the feeling she got when haunted by nameless terrors in turbid nightmares.

"James, of course."

"James?" She leaned forward and laughed. James and his sister had crept into one another's beds as children and still did, occasionally, in the mornings. "Well, yes. They sometimes share the same bed. They're twins." *But he doesn't* sleep *with—*

Suddenly, connections sprang up between things that had once seemed unrelated: James and Louise's inexhaustible capacity for togetherness, their lack of interest in anyone else, the clothes belonging to one twin turning up in the other twin's room—which brought her back to the bed-sharing. Did they spend whole nights together, locked in each other's arms in the womblike dark?

A mental landslide forced her in a direction she didn't want to go, towards a conclusion she didn't want to make. What Colin claimed fit all the facts. She couldn't just dismiss it. Yet, if true, it would be an abomination. It would go against everything that she and Alistair had stood for. "You're not telling me that—that—"

Colin nodded, slowly, emphatically.

She had to lock her knees just to remain upright as a shudder passed through her like food through a snake swallowing something bigger than itself.

"This is the end—the end of everything," she got out between sob-shakes.

"But I thought you knew."

"Knew? Of course I didn't know."

"I don't understand. Last time we met...you didn't seem to mind. The "love-birds," remember?"

"Do you honestly think I'd talk about a son and daughter in those terms? What kind of person do you think I am?"

Two women looked round as they entered the neighboring building and she didn't even care. It was as if important functions, her finer feelings—everything—shut down, one by one, as the truth and its toxins penetrated every part of her being.

Colin clutched the back of his neck. "Oh, God. It must have been a misunderstanding. I'm sorry. And I'm really sorry you had to find out this way. Hopefully things can all be all right."

"All right? How can things ever be all right after this?"

The estate came out of its tunnel, but she didn't. Her world would always be in shadow now and proportionately colder. She could feel it in her very marrow as she turned around to her Peugeot, stepped into the foot space on the driver's side and ducked under the roof.

———

The buzzer sounded and Alistair reached across his desk to press the answer button. "Yes, Miss Querty?"

"It's your wife on the line, Mr. Glavier."

"My wife?" Alistair cleared his throat. He and Valerie still hadn't had a proper conversation yet. Maybe she'd come round at last. "Thank you, Miss Querty. Put her through." He picked up the receiver. This wasn't a call he wanted to take on speakerphone. "Valerie… Hello."

"I've just learnt the truth."

His head jerked. "Truth? About what?"

"Our "family."" He could hear the quotation marks.

He hunched over the phone. "Valerie, what do you mean?"

"Nothing matters any more. It's all fallen apart. So that's why I'm going to leave, with Harriet and Louise."

Something wrenched inside him. "Leave? What are you talking about? And in any case, we have three children."

"James can stay with you. That's the only way we can do this now."

What had sat inside him like solidifying cement turned out to be just the crust that had formed over a still-molten core. Everything returned to a fluid, unsettled, state. "Valerie, listen. You can't—"

"I can and I will."

He placed the thumb and middle finger of one hand to each temple, and squeezed. "What's happened?"

"Maybe you were too busy to notice. Maybe we all were. But they need separating, Alistair. Believe me; this will be better for everyone."

She hung up. He quit his office, left his young client sitting in the waiting room and walked out into the street. What was Valerie talking about? Leaving James, taking Harriet and Louise? It didn't make sense.

By the time he was in his car, thinking about it had dislodged something significant. He just couldn't work out what. It was as if he saw the shadow of something, not the actual article.

Then his brain made its own connections, between Valerie's decision to leave, her insistence that James and Louise needed

231

separating, her broken spirit, and lit up like a circuit board. It was as if he heard before he heard, knew before he knew, the truth about the twins. A lighthouse-like sweep of insight sharply delineated their real relations.

His hand reached for the ignition.

No wonder Valerie had sounded the way she had, as if agitated right down to molecular level. All the additional vibration caused him to heat up, burn up, with the stain to his — the family—name. He gunned the engine.

The fact he'd nearly noticed and hadn't merely gave his foot an extra impetus.

———————

Louise experienced turbulence in the pit of her stomach as she and her brother left their humdrum lives far behind.

Only the claustrophobically close man-made skyline above them and the lone man in front's fat red neck and boiled-looking head spoiled the illusion. Driven at street level rather than piloted at cloud height, a black cab took them to Nick's address.

James' phone rang.

"Yes?" he said. "No. What?" His face turned the pallor of skimmed milk. "Christ in hell. They'll kill us." He ran his sleeve across his forehead. "Thanks, Colin. Bye."

"What was that about?" She stuck her thumb in the waistband of the black trousers they'd bought from Primark with what he had in his wallet, and stretched it a bit.

"They know, Lou. They know, about us." He panted. "Or Mum does. Colin told her. And she'll tell Dad."

"What?" She'd heard each sentence, yet they reached her as if from far off.

It wasn't just the exact chain of events she struggled with or the mysteries contained within it—such as how Colin came to be talking to Mum—but the very notion that she and James had been found out. They'd courted disaster so many times and yet had still got away with it. Surely this would all turn out to have been a monstrous misunderstanding.

Then her insides churned and her stomach started consuming itself. Colin knew about them. Apart from Nick, he was the only one who did. If he'd spoken to Mum, he could well have dropped them in it.

She still had the shock barrier to break through. It only really hit her now: *Mum and Dad know I have sex with my brother.*

It felt as if someone had given her pancreas a squeeze.

James had got his breathing under control. His hand found hers. "You see, we're doing the right thing. If Nick says we have to do it, then we have to do it."

Her heart boomed in her ears.

CHAPTER 21

Lungs heaving, James led the way up stairs and across a landing in a tenement building backing onto a canal.

Each story up, a little more dusty daylight penetrated the only window. Successive windows provided the same view of still, black waters and a hotchpotch of housing—just a little more wide-angled each time.

Something swam around and around in his stomach when they reached the floor they wanted and flipped when he saw the door. They'd definitely got the right one. The stenciled digits on the aluminum letter-box matched the number on the plain printed business card in his hand.

No bell, so he rapped the letter-box.

His heart pumped.

He glanced at his sister as locks turned, the security chain rattled.

A dark-haired woman opened the door. "Yes?"

She had on black leggings and a grey jersey top. In her hand she held a banana, old and leopard-skin spotted, splayed and eaten, down to the middle. The smell of stewed cabbage reached out into the hallway from the kitchen beyond.

James stepped back, level with Louise. "Hi. We're looking for Nick."

Nick's wife, girlfriend, flat mate, whatever she was, stared first at his sister, then him. "Try Satan's Fan Club."

"You know about it too?" His lungs inflated, as if with helium, given the pitch of his voice. "Nick invited us to join."

"Join?" Eye-liner sharpened the woman's gaze. Half akimbo now, she took another bite of the banana.

"Who is it, Hels?" another woman called.

Hels... Not the angel from Colin's party? *Yes.* It was her. Even studying the woman properly, he would never have recognized her as the dark-haired, gum-chewing consort of Nick's that had accosted him at the party if it hadn't been for the mention of her name. And it wasn't just the clothes. She looked older than he remembered. Lines etched her forehead and puffy skin darkened the area underneath each eye. Then again, she wore a lot less make-up, it was daytime and none of them were inebriated.

"Come and see, Cyn."

They were joined by the elfin angel, today without wings. She wore skinny jeans and a pink top.

James smiled. "We're here to see Nick."

"He invited them to join Satan's Fan Club," said Hels. "And I was just about to explain to them that—"

"That's where he's gone, yes." Cyn turned to him and his sister. "We can tell you how to get there if you like."

James glanced at Louise. "Please, yes."

"I will say this for him..." Hels ducked behind the door. They heard, "He looks good in a suit." She reappeared minus the banana skin.

Cyn giggled as she stooped to pick up the pen and notepad next to the phone on the floor and passed them to him. "What's your mobile number?"

James wrote his number down, handed the pen and pad back.

"Right, we have to do this cloak-and-dagger," said Cyn.

James nodded. "Okay."

"Head for the tube station and await further instructions. But hurry."

He and his sister scuttled back across the landing, round the post at the end of it and down the stairs.

Their steps rang out like gunshots.

"Louise?" Harriet watched as Mummy stood in the hallway and called up the staircase. "James?"

"They'll be at work, Mummy."

"No, they've taken the day off, darling." Mummy dashed up the stairs.

Harriet scuttled after her. "Is that why Daddy said I didn't have to go to school?" They turned, right, up the corridor. "So we can be a proper family again?"

Swept along by the urgency and secrecy, Harriet paced Louise's room as Mummy opened drawers, peered under the bed, lifted pillows. "Is it?"

Mummy slid the garments in the wardrobe from one end of the rail to the other.

"It's because we're all going on holiday."

Mummy got on her knees and rummaged through shoes and bags and boxes. "Well, you, me and Louise." She pulled out a lumpy holdall. "See, Louise has packed already."

"Wow, Mummy, where?"

"I'll let you know on the way."

"What about school?"

"We can see about that later, darling. Maybe there'll even be a school where we're going."

Mummy lugged the bag round into James' room.

She strode over to the half-closed curtains. One side bulged just above the window seat.

She reached behind it and raised a bulky rucksack. "Look at that. James packed too."

Carrying both bags down to the kitchen, she placed Louise's holdall on the table and, unbolting the cellar door, dropped James' red rucksack into darkness.

Harriet stepped back, and bumped into one of the kitchen chairs. The grating scrape from the floor caused a funny little quiver inside her ears. "Mummy! Why did you do that?"

"James won't be needing it. He's staying here with Daddy. This is a girls-only holiday. So I want you to go upstairs and pack everything you can't do without. We're leaving as soon as I get back."

On, out, back up the hallway.

Harriet had to break into a trot just to keep up. "Where are you going?"

Mummy paused with her hand on the frame of the front door. "To look for your sister. But if she or James comes home, I want you to call me on my mobile straight away. And don't tell anyone anything. It's a surprise. Okay, darling?"

"Yes, Mummy."

"Good girl. See you very soon." She blew a kiss.

Harriet blew one back.

She turned and ran up the stairs, wondering where in the whole of England they could be going.

———————

James lurched next to his sister amidst ghost-train shrieks and howls. Bodily stimulants coursed through his veins just as their carriage ran through the endless tunnel in unnatural night.

He had his phone out, ready.

As soon as they came overground, he'd receive the next instruction from Cyn and Hels.

"They're not sending us back home, are they?" said Louise. "We're going that way."

"No, they can't be," he said. "Why would they do that?"

———————

He rustles through the grass. It's long and tugs at his feet.

Leaning over the explosion of greenery that's the border, he peers in at the window, just in time to see—close to—the hobbity figure enter.

She's changed out of her school uniform and is wearing jeans and a Hello Kitty T-shirt.

She perches on the sofa, at right angles to him, picks up a pair of dolls and attempts to force them head first into an already stuffed floral-pattern rucksack.

His breath mists the window. He leaps aside, just in time, as she gets up and walks towards him.

Peeping back in, he sees her swerve out of the room.

He plunges down the side of the building.

———————

Up from the bottomless pit of night, the Underworld, the mechanized bowels of London, James blinked in the super-abounding light. The redbrick residential street they walked on was a sea of brightness fringed with dark foreshortened crescents, oblongs and rhombi, all in perfect alignment—except when a gust of wind shook things up a bit.

They reached a junction and waited.

James' phone gave its aural wink. He read the message and showed it to Louise: "Left."

They turned onto a tree-lined avenue.

Sting.

The next text read, "Pass the tall buildings."

He showed it to Louise.

Adrenalin gushed round his system.

Sting.

"Then the flatter building."

He picked up the pace.

His sister had to break into a jog just to keep up.

Sting.

"Now stop."

He halted as directed.

Louise whirled this way and that. "I don't see him."

"We're here," James texted. "Where is he?"

Sting.

"See the big building with the security gates?"

He held up the phone for Louise to read. The text described exactly what they could see. Beyond high black railings, and the kind of raisable red-and-white barriers one normally encountered at railway crossings, towered a gatehouse. It looked like a modest castle, complete with a pair of turrets and a wooden door large enough for a giant.

"Yes," he typed.

Sting.

239

"He's in there."

"Doing"—even with predictive text, he couldn't tap fast enough—"what?"

Sting.

He wasn't quite sure what to make of the answer, so he showed his sister.

"Time," read the text.

He stepped back, and pulled her with him when—between the railings—he made out "HM Prison" on a sign.

"Can't be right," she said. "We'd have heard. Call them."

James rang the number.

"Yes?" It was Hels.

He turned up the volume and Louise leaned her head against his. "What do you mean?"

"Oh, that was Cyn." A laugh in the background. "She will have her little joke. But, yes, that's where he is."

"You said he was at Satan's Fan Club." He could hear the whine in his voice even if she couldn't.

"He is. In a way. Satan's Fan Club is Nick's name for prison. And that's where he's gone. He was sent down in late February."

James' thoughts swerved like a shoal of fish. "For the murders?"

"Murders?"

James watched Louise's eyebrows arch.

"Yeah, all those women."

"Well, the police did question him about one of them, but only 'cause he knew her."

James tried to get the dates to fit. His mind virtually ate itself in the attempt because there'd definitely been murders since then.

"What exactly is Nick in prison for?" he said, flatly.

Hels cleared her throat. "Drug-dealing. He gives the impression of caring when really he doesn't give a shit." She sniffed. ""My chemical dependents," he calls them. And they're the lucky ones. Because he doesn't like his "offers" being turned down. He gets his revenge in other ways."

Louise's chin dropped.

"See, if he can't screw up your body he'll screw with your mind. And you don't see it coming. In just a few minutes of talking to you he finds out things about you you probably don't even know about yourself."

Louise's chin now dug into her chest.

"In that sense he really is the Devil. 'Cause he knows how to say just the right thing. He can make black seem like white and white black. He can fuck you up for life with a mere turn of phrase." Hels' voice dropped, slowed. "And he always chooses those who are innocent but who, for one reason or another, are open to evil. They come from good backgrounds a lot of them." A sigh. "Though, as everybody knows, they're always the first to fall."

James lowered the phone.

His sister strode off.

"Louise," he called. "Louise."

He ran after her.

———

"What will the Church, and Lodge, think?" said Godfrey. Alistair bounded onto the front doorstep and reached into his trouser pocket for his bunch of keys. "It's all right. I know. Your wife's going to take Louise and Harriet and leave you with James." Godfrey clicked his tongue. "I wonder how that'll work out."

Alistair's hands shook—so much so that he struggled to get his key in the lock. "How do you know all this?" He hadn't intended to get drawn in. "Were you watching, listening in? To me or to her?"

"I told you, everything is transparent to me." Alistair got the door open. Something small and plastic bounced on and skittered across tiles. He ran up the hallway to the kitchen, where Harriet crouched to pick a carton top up off the floor. "Still, it's good this has happened, in a way. It means I'll be doing you a favor."

Harriet stood up and spun around, smiling. "Daddy." She glided towards him.

Alistair put a forefinger up and she stopped. "Wait, what do you mean? Godfrey? Godfrey!"

He studied his phone.

The call had ended.

His hand jerked up to the back of his head. "Have you seen your mother?"

Harriet nodded.

"Where is she?"

"Looking for Louise."

He set his mobile down on the table, beside Harriet's rucksack and what looked like Louise's holdall, both full. "Going somewhere?"

Harriet grinned. "Yes, Mummy's taking me on holiday."

"No, she's not." His soul seethed, roiled. "I want you to go upstairs and unpack."

"Oh, Daddy!"

"Now, Harriet."

Tap-tap-tapping the screen of the phone they'd bought her for her birthday, she placed one foot in front of the other and twisted left and right.

"What are you doing?" he said.

"Texting Mummy."

"What about?"

"You."

"Give it to me." He held out his hand. "I'll look after it."

She handed it over and he dropped it in his pocket.

"Right." He pointed at the ceiling. "You need to hurry up and unpack."

She galumphed around the table. "But if I'm not going anywhere, why do I need to hurry?"

"Harriet—"

His mobile rang.

She leaned over it.

He snatched it up. "Yes?"

"Ah, there you are." Rich tones enveloped him. "Listen, I'm glad I caught you."

"Hello, Deverick."

Harriet lolloped over to the kitchen table and flopped down at it.

"I wanted to give you advance warning of something," said the Detective Chief Superintendent.

"Oh?"

"Don't worry, I've asked my people to be sensitive on this one because it'd be a shame if the Doomsday Church got adverse publicity as a result of it. But they'd like to talk to James."

What—? His mind swallowed itself, spat itself out. "You're taking James in for questioning?"

Harriet looked up.

"He'd be helping us with inquiries."

"Louise too?"

"No, just James at this stage."

"Why?"

"Well, Riika was an attractive girl. They lived in the same house. It's possible James may be able to tell us something."

Only about me and Riika…

"I just wanted to give you a heads-up, so that it doesn't come out of the blue and worry you unduly."

But he'll ruin me, to save himself.

"Alistair?"

"Yes, thanks for letting me know."

"No problem. See you at the next Lodge meeting."

"Yes, hope so. Bye."

"Oh, one other thing. That Godfrey chap you asked me about… There's no trace of him. I don't know who he is but that's not his real name, that's for certain." A nasal sigh. "Be careful, Alistair. Let me know if you want to take this further."

"I will. Just got a lot going on at the moment."

Valerie leaving… James being taken in for questioning… James and his sister…

"Thank you, Deverick."

———————

Louise chewed the inside of her cheeks.

Just his Nick-name for prison…

She clamped down hard on one side to offset her raging soul-ache.

All our theories, Paranoid Central…

She and James sat on a hexagonal roundabout on a patch of Tarmac to one side of a medium-sized park. Her brother held on to the handles of the adjacent section with white knuckles as if they were rotating really fast, when they weren't even moving.

He peered past the see-saw, slide, swings and hobbyhorses on springs. "They were playing with us."

She cleared her throat. "He was. Because if he didn't commit the last few, he didn't commit any of them." She shifted her weight from one buttock to the other as a thought blopped to the surface of her mind. "Which means that The Fiend is still out there. And if Nick's not the killer, who is?"

Her brother shrugged. "How can we know now? It's nothing to do with us anymore."

Something tugged at her. "We can't have imagined it all, can we?" Like a child pulling her sleeve, it wouldn't let go.

No, we didn't.

"James, James, listen, whoever it is has still been getting closer and closer, haven't they? Your map. The signs…"

"Signs?"

"Riika's death, the trespasser, the planted evidence… It's always been centered on our family. We just got the wrong person, that's all. Everything else still stands. Whoever it is has had our house in his sights from the start."

James sat up. "Yes. But who…?"

She sighed. "I don't know. But maybe we're not the ones in danger. Maybe someone else is."

Her brother's eyes flicked this way and that. "Yes…"

A gust of wind lifted the branches of the copse at the center of the park and those of the trees dotted in a horseshoe around half of the park. Glossy green leaves went frilly as they turned over, showed their paler under parts, in a Mexican wave.

Children's shouts yanked Louise's attention behind them. She couldn't quite see. A few moments later, multiple shod feet scraped the Tarmac. It sounded like an army marching in step. Yet all that came into view were two boys wearing football boots.

They veered off for a kick-about.

Next came a little girl with blonde hair and glasses, who hitched herself into one of the swings just as the sun made one of its fitful appearances.

Louise's arms and legs goose-fleshed. "Oh, God…"

Completely oblivious, with glasses twinkling in the temporary sunshine and legs alternately out straight and tucked under her seat, the girl swung backwards and forwards, backwards and forwards, a little higher each time.

James leaned over. "What? What is it?"

Louise swallowed pure emotion. "Harriet. We forgot about Harriet." She checked her watch. Ten to three? Where had the day gone? Harriet would be arriving home soon, if she hadn't already. "She might be in danger."

James clutched her forearm. "We'd better go."

"Yes, quick." She staggered to her feet, exactly as if they'd been spinning, spinning.

As clouds pitched the whole park into shadow, they abandoned the path and cut across the grass towards the nearest exit, both breaking into a run.

As the gate jounced closer, Louise pictured Harriet with her bottled eyes lowered, playing on the floor with her dolls, oblivious to the peril she might be in.

Maybe she and James had both grown up a little today. They had gone from contemplating killing Mum and Dad to wanting to protect their little sister. There was still time to do the right thing, just.

Disorientated, she scanned the built-up skyline for a landmark. She couldn't see one. "What park is this?" she panted.

"There's a board there," James said, through labored breaths. "I can't quite make it out. Hang on. It looks like… Amberly Park."

"That was one of the earliest murder sites, wasn't it?"

"Yes."

Louise glanced back at the copse and shivered. *Hold on, Harriet, we're coming.*

CHAPTER 22

"It's me," said Godfrey.

"I know it's you." Alistair folded into one of the kitchen chairs. "What do you want?"

"You've been looking for me."

"Yes."

"That was foolish."

Alistair's insides thrashed. Although he still had the downstairs to himself and although he'd always found it amusing when he'd heard other people do it, he lowered his voice to shout. "Who the hell do you think you are?"

"I've been trying to tell you that this whole time. You just haven't been listening."

Alistair sat up. "What do you mean?"

"Haven't you noticed when you hear from me?"

Alistair's head felt as heavy as cement. "When there's…"

"Yes?"

But I would have noticed. "When there's a murder, or…"

"Yes?"

His heart thumped. "When there's going to be."

"Yes."

Alistair gripped the table. "It's… It's you?"

"It's good to finally have your full attention."

"You're not serious?"

"You think?"

It's him. It's really him.

"Godfrey, this has to… You have to… You've got to stop."

"No, Alistair. It's far too late for that."

"What do you mean?"

"It's time we met face to face."

Alistair shook his head. "No, I don't think that's a good idea."

"Come outside."

Alistair spun in his seat and stared at, not even wanting to see through, the net curtain. "Yes, come on."

"No."

"Come outside. Or I'll come in…"

Alistair shot to his feet. "No. No, you're not coming in. I won't let you hurt them. I'll come outside. Just give me a minute…"

He reeled away from the table. Putting his phone away, he lurched out into the hallway. At the foot of the staircase, he whisper-shouted "Harriet."

Footsteps pounded closer. Suddenly she skipped, with flowing floaty movements, down the stairs. "Yes, Daddy?"

He took her hand and led her back up the hallway. "I need you to do something and I don't want you to ask me any questions."

"What, Daddy?"

They stopped in the kitchen. "I want you to hide for me."

"Hide? Why? Is it a game?"

"No, a precaution."

"But why, Daddy?"

"Harriet…" With his back to the window, Alistair added in a whisper, "He's here."

Harriet whirled around. "Who, Daddy?"

"The man."

Now she whispered too. "What man?"

"The bad man."

Harriet opened her mouth to speak but he held his hand up. "There isn't time to discuss it. I want you to hide." He opened the cellar door. "Don't make a sound until I tell you it's okay to come out, all right?"

Stone steps greyed into nothing. She started disappearing from the feet up. "There's a torch down there. On the shelf. Turn it on if you get scared. Just don't point it at the door, okay?"

She ran back up, clutched his arm. "Daddy…"

"Yes?"

"Take care."

He had to swallow in order to be able to reply. "You too, sweetheart. But I'm going to take the key so you're perfectly safe, okay?"

She nodded.

He waited until she grabbed the torch, then he shut the door, locked it and dropped the key in his trouser pocket.

Breathing in through his nose and out through his mouth, he turned, put his head down, strode towards the back door and stepped out into the yellowy light.

———

Louise caught a glimpse of gnomelike fishermen down by the canal. She willed the bus to go faster.

She and James sat on the top deck just in front of the narrow stairwell, right above the driver.

She rested her temple against the side window. The pane of glass vibrated, occasionally juddered, yet couldn't shake thoughts of Harriet out of her head.

Please, be safe.

They'd neglected her for over a year. Even on the odd occasion when they had bothered to speak to her, they'd been horrible to her.

Sorry, sis.

Their souls were as sullied as city snow, but her they could save, if only they could get home in time.

The driver slowed to pick up more passengers.

No! This is an emergency.

Valerie closed the front door behind her. She scuttled up the hallway to the kitchen, opened the cupboard door, got the ironing board out, clattered around with it and eventually got it set up. Fetching the iron, she plugged it in and placed it on the board.

She ran back out, trotted up the stairs, crossed the balcony of the landing, dived down the tunnel of the corridor and turned into her room. She dragged an empty case from the top of the wardrobe, threw it on the bed and opened it up.

A tink from downstairs.

She turned.

"Harriet?"

Louise sat up as the bus finally took them through more familiar territory. She spotted the distant arch of Wembley

Stadium. Nearer to, she made out the roller-coaster ride of the flyover. The violet neon cross that stood outside the White Chapel shuddered upside-down in a puddle as they roared past.

Their stop approached. James dinged the bell. They got up and turned down the stairwell.

The bus braked hard, suspending them in zero gravity half-way down.

Just as quickly released, they bang-bang-banged down the stairs and dashed out through sliding-back doors—off a bus the color of blood, past a blood-red post-box.

———————

A movement of air at his back. The door he's come through ticks and clicks.

With the lethal lineality of the knife out before him, he pushes on, past the kitchen table and the ironing board, towards the pointed archway.

Out, down the cream-carpeted hallway and round and up the wide sumptuous staircase, between oak banisters and framed charcoals and lithographs by Odilon Redon on the other.

The top of the stairs... Now which way? Right? Left?

Round to the right, down a crooked corridor, into a bedroom strewn with clothes and shoes.

He takes a step back and, beneath the carpet, a floorboard groans.

"Harriet? Is that you?"

He freezes, clutching the knife.

On the same floor but the other side of the building, the female voice continues: "Harriet, I hope you've finished packing? I'll be checking."

He lifts his foot and the floorboard protests.

Out, quickly, and back the same way. Across the landing and on up another long windowless corridor.

The door to the left hangs open, revealing a much larger bedroom with a burgundy bedspread and white curtains. A Bible rests on a cabinet to the right-hand side of the bed.

Inhaling her scent first (jasmine with orange notes), he spots her, side on, pressing clothes into a suitcase.

When she turns her head and sees him, he charges.

Her mouth opens to cry out but one slice and she's spluttering bubbles of blood.

Her body eats the knife, again and again. Mouths open all over her, vomiting vibrant red.

CHAPTER 23

Louise and James sprinted up the garden path to The End House.

She crashed through the front door ahead of him. "Harriet?"

Layers and layers of silence.

Where is she?

As James ran past her, up the stairs, Louise poked her head around the lounge door, just to make sure.

No, so she pushed on towards the kitchen.

"Harriet," shouted her brother from the landing.

His footsteps crossed hers, on the floor above.

She stuck her head through the archway. "Harriet?"

Again, nothing.

Just about to leave, to resume the search elsewhere, she noticed her sister's Cath Kidston rucksack, filled to twice its normal size, on the kitchen table.

"She's not in her room," came James' voice. "Any luck down there?"

Louise scuttled out and round and up the stairs. "She must be here somewhere."

Find Harriet. Find Harriet. She couldn't think of anything else.

She dashed into Mum's room, tripped and fell in something wet. The skin of it had a dark sheen that had started to turn sticky.

Just beyond her feet, an adult lay in a heap on the floor. Crimson-lined wounds crisscrossed the trunk.

Looking closer, she saw Mum's clothes, Mum's face.

Using the bed, Louise clambered to her feet. Gloops of blood dripped from her hands and knees. "Oh, Christ... Oh, Christ..." She wiped her hands on the bedspread, shaking with and half-blinded by sobs. "James, James..."

"Harriet isn't..." He swung around the doorway, stopped. "Fuck."

Gripped by wrenching convulsions that started in her stomach and pushed up, up, up, she ran past him, back down the corridor. Bending, bending, she got as far as the landing before she had to double up completely. Grasping the balustrade, she splattered the contents of her stomach over the carpet.

The smell that hit her was enough to send her off again, dry-heaving this time, in between sobs bigger than she was.

So this was what life boiled down to, what it consisted of at the outer margin: blood, vomit, tears.

James ran to her. Patted her back.

She coughed and wiped her mouth.

Her stomach felt scoured out.

Creak.

It came from the attic.

Her empty stomach tightened as they clung to each other. *The killer.*

"He's still in the house," she whispered. "What do we do?"

"We've got him cornered."

She seized James' arm, holding him back. "No. The police…"

"What, Mace?" A fleer, then flinty-faced again. "Louise, he might have Harriet up there. There isn't time."

"Oh, God." A sharp shooting pain like a stab between the ribs.

Harriet.

She crept up the corridor after her brother. Hugging the wall, they climbed the attic stairs.

Riika's door was ajar.

James kicked it and it knocked against the inside wall.

The killer must have long since fled because all they saw was Dad.

Tectonic plates of muscle moved and collided under the skin of his face as he stared, out of his mind, at intangible horrors.

He sat on the edge of the bed, hugging a pillow. He had it up to his nose, inhaling it. "I can't smell her anymore."

"What the hell happened?" said James.

"I don't know. I went out looking for him and when I came back I found… that." He still hadn't looked up. "He's taken everything."

"Who, Dad?" James bent towards him. "Dad, who?"

Their father had his mobile in his hand. He put it up to his ear.

"You calling the police?" she said.

Dad put his other hand over the phone for a moment. "I'm talking to *him*."

She swallowed. "The killer?"

"What?" from James.

"Yes," said Dad.

James snatched the phone from him. "Listen, you…" He looked at it and held it up. "Dad, there's no one there."

"He must have hung up."

"Well, what did he say?"

"He said he's coming back to finish the job."

"Oh, Christ," said Louise. A fluttering started deep within her. "Dad, where's Harriet?"

"Safe. For now."

Louise blew a strand of hair out of her face. "What do you mean? Where is she?"

"I can't tell you. He'll hear."

Her insides churned. "What? You mean he's back, now?"

She twisted from the waist and strained, listening.

James did too, but only for a moment.

"Look out," he cried, yanking her back by the elbow.

Something swished and she turned to see their father holding a knife with a long, wide blade stained vermillion.

"Dad," she said. "Is that… You shouldn't have picked that up."

The knife swooshed again. They both leapt back.

"It's him," cried James.

Her heart thrashed like a landed fish. Things had no bottom. The poles of her mind flipped. All the time she'd believed some cheap-suited Devil was the murderer, the real evil lay much closer to home.

Oh, God. Dad was the serial killer who made wry-necked women scurry from streetlamp to streetlamp in big, gagged, night. The entire time she and James had been rebelling against their parents—rejecting Christianity, embracing Satanism; undergoing a complete morality inversion—The Fiend had been their father.

"Dad, why?" She clapped her hand over her mouth. "All those women…"

"Because of her." Dad spoke but another voice, deep and rough, tore out of him. He pointed back at the bed, or the pillow that he'd tossed on it. "A woman like that makes one question everything, doubt everything."

"But why Mum?" she said.

Had Mum known, subconsciously? Was that why she was always scared?

"Because she was going to leave." The same sandpapery voice as he stared at them with obsidian eyes. "And do you know why?"

"She was?" said James.

"Because of you." The man who used to be Dad thrust the knife in their direction. "It's all your fault."

They squeezed through the doorway.

He came after them, out onto the landing.

His heavy automaton-like movements reminded her of something, and then she remembered what—James in his sleepwalking state.

The father-stranger looked from her with her boyishly short hair to James with his hair gradually working its way back through the decades, then back and forth between them. His eyebrows merged into one. Normally only visible viewed from a certain angle, the slight astigmatism had developed into a pronounced squint. He stared with eyes askew as if he had a piece of buckshot lodged in his brain. "You've offended God and man." Her throat closed up inside. "Oh, yes, I've heard all about it… Your stinking foulness. Your abominations."

"Ours?" said James.

"And now you've unleashed the fiends of Hell." The man who'd taken over their father charged with the knife.

She and James dropped three, four steps at a time down the narrow staircase. Their elbows and knees knocked walls. Pulses of pain from her bad knee got lost in the hurly-burly.

They crashed into the wall at the bottom and sprang, in a different plane, at right angles, up the corridor.

The knife clanged as it struck the wall.

They ran past their rooms, with another set of footsteps right behind theirs.

When they reached the lower landing, James stopped and turned. His eyes narrowed and his brows contracted. "If Mum was going to leave, it wouldn't be because of us, it would be because of you. Our only crime is a surfeit of love."

Louise paused at the top of the stairs.

James, no, you can't argue with a madman.

By now, Mad-Dad's eyeballs swiveled independently. "It's a match made in Hell. And the only way to deal with something shameful is to extirpate it."

She could tell from the glimpse she caught of the concentrated look in James' eyes that his meters were all in the red. "Maybe you should look to yourself first then."

"You little…" Dad—for even if it didn't sound like him, it was still their father, or a hived-off part of him—raised the knife.

James grabbed his wrist. They tussled.

A hard knot in Louise's chest got drawn tighter still.

Finally her brother slammed the hand gripping the knife into the balustrade.

The knife fell, *thunging* into the hallway below, piercing the carpet and burrowing itself in the floorboards.

When Dad came for him again, James punched the older man in the face.

Dad got in a low, southpaw blow.

Her brother hugged his belly. "Hey, aren't you supposed to turn the other cheek or something?"

"Oh, no, you…"

"Get…"

Choked gutturals resounded in the lateral enclosure of the landing as, clasped in combat, they reeled this way and that.

Dad had one hand round James' neck. He wound a hank of hair around his fingers and knocked her brother's head against the balustrade. James went down, clutching his brow.

Louise's heart pummeled at the wall of her chest. She lunged at Dad.

He caught her and, using her momentum against her, swung her around. His eyes looked as unnatural as boiled sweets. Like a conglomeration of fish scales, his crinkly lips appeared dissociated from the rest of him. He was the only thing she could see clearly. Everything else blurred dizzily past. *Ow.* A shock of pain like an electric current shot up her arm as she crashed into the edge of the wall.

Dad got hold of James and pushed his head in the mess she'd made, rubbing his face in it.

"The dog returns to its own vomit," he shouted, in the other man's voice. "Come on, eat up. There's a good doggie."

Grasping one of the carved helices of the balustrade's uprights, James coughed. Sick coated his nose and cheeks. It dripped from his lips. Louise still had its acrid taste on her own tongue.

She rushed at Dad again. Falling off the precipice of his mind had endowed him with a superhuman strength.

He grabbed her and shoved her backwards, hard.

For a moment her feet kept up with her. She took another step and there wasn't anything there. She tipped backwards, found herself going over—into nothing.

She reached for the smooth carved post at the head of the banisters but it went by too fast. The cream-carpeted stairs whammed into her. Because of her unstoppable momentum, the brown banisters went over and the matte white ceiling went round as she rolled—eventually ending up flat on her back at the foot of the stairs feeling as if the world was still revolving, revolving, revolving, just no longer knocking into her.

Her head felt headache-heavy. Seashell-like waves crashed in her ears and her vision grew grainy, as if filling with black sand.

"Louise… Louise…"

Slowly becoming aware of James' voice, she lifted her head in an effort to reassure him she was all right, only to see him being dragged backwards, by the neck, down the staircase. His heels thumped from one stair to another.

"Come on, Adam," said Mad-Dad. "Time for your punishment, for touching your sister."

She gathered her limbs together. She'd sat up and was about to try to stand when Dad came level with her hand. She didn't even have time to react when his foot shot out and crunched down on her fingers. The pain screamed through her. She fell back, clasping her hand.

A laugh. "I'll deal with you later… Eve."

Through a film of tears, she watched James get hauled away kicking and cursing.

As soon as she saw Dad tug the knife free, she got up and staggered after them.

She entered the kitchen just in time to see Dad slam James' head into the kitchen table. Yanking him back up by his hair, he pushed him down into one of the four chairs.

Before she could do anything, Dad placed James' forefinger on the edge of the table and brought the blade down.

James screamed.

Blood poured from where his finger had been.

She ran to the cooker, whipped a Clovelly tea towel off the oven handle rail and wrapped it round and round his hand.

She could hear the microwave. Dad hunched over it.

He's cooking—now?

He peered in through the door at the plate going round and round.

Ping.

Dad took the plate out and placed it in front of James.

If there had been anything left in her stomach, Louise would have thrown up again when she saw the steaming, shrunken finger with its shriveled nail.

Dad pushed her out of the way and dragged James out of the chair, over to the side of the sink.

He took the lid off the food processor, flicked the switch, got James' other hand and pushed it down inside, towards the whirring blades.

"No," she screamed, lunging at him.

Dad sliced the air with the knife and she leapt back.

James' hand sank lower and lower. The food processor churned, hungrily.

The envelope of Louise's emotions expanded and kept on expanding, until soon it was bigger than she was. Shape-shifting emotions took fire-drakish form. Spotting the iron on the ironing board, she seized it. Still plugged into the wall, it came away with a yank and a fizz and a flash. She'd been going to hit Dad with it but, feeling the waves of heat emanating from its flat surface, she raised it to the top of his back and pressed down hard. It burnt through his shirt and, in no time at all, into his skin. The bacony smell of burning flesh filled the room.

Dad screamed, in his own voice. His eyes bulged and slid. The knife clattered to the tiles. Trying in vain to reach the bubbling patch of skin, his hands clawed at his back.

Released, James got hold of one of Dad's arms. Louise helped him force the hand down into the food processor.

Footsteps shuffled out of synch with hers or James' or Dad's. *Under the floor?*

"No," shouted the old Dad. "No!"

———————

Having just run up most of the stone steps to try to peer through the crack of light under the door, without any success, Harriet ran back down them.

While the strange man had been out there, she'd huddled in dusty darkness, hardly daring to breathe, let alone move or make a sound. But when she'd heard Daddy screaming, she hadn't been able to stand it.

What are they doing to him?

Shining the plastic torch this way and that, she looked for something to break the door down with. But apart from an empty wine rack and a thick brown paper sack of potatoes, the cellar mostly contained cobwebs.

James' red rucksack, caught in a sweep of the beam, provided the only splash of color.

Pouncing on it, she tipped it up and shook the contents out on the grey stone floor. T-shirts, boxer shorts and socks piled up along with a pair of jeans, a pair of trainers, a passport, book, phone charger, electric toothbrush and charger, a crumpled piece of notepaper and a knotted freezer bag containing a bit of light blue material with at least one tassel attached.

She couldn't see anything to use to open the door, either to knock it down or force it open, but she'd seen the color of that piece of fabric before, and not on James. What were those stains? It looked like... *Riika's scarf.*

Quickly smoothing the piece of paper out on the floor, she pointed the torch at it.

She stared at a Hangman-type drawing with two figures, one labelled "Dad", the other "Mum".

"No!" screamed Daddy from above.

Harriet jumped up, raced up the steps and barged into the door. It gave but didn't open.

Daddy screamed again.

She banged and banged, in between heavy, racking sobs. "Stop!" The door rattled on its hinges. "Let him go!" Her tears stung her eyes. "Daddy! Daddy!"

Louise felt Dad's whole body convulse as the blades bit and chewed, felt, through him, the ratchety resistance of bone. The blades dug in. The motor whined. Thin gouts of smoke poured out. The niff of burnt electrics made her nostrils twitch.

They freed Dad's hand and fed it back in. Blood spurted up the net curtain.

He yelled incomprehensibly.

"Daddy!"

Harriet.

Louise switched the food processor off.

"Daddy!"

A thud.

Where the hell's it coming from?

"Daddy!"

The cellar door shook.

Louise lurched towards it.

"Lou, look out," cried James.

Dad had picked up the knife and came for her with eyes like burnt-out fuses.

She retreated.

Dad shuffled closer faster.

With his good hand, James scrabbled about in a drawer and pulled out a screwdriver.

He stole up behind Dad and drove it into his ear. It went in easily, with a click.

Dad's eyes widened. Slipping from his fingers, the knife clanged to the tiles.

But still he didn't go down. He had his hands out before him, ready to tear her eyes out, strangle her, do whatever harm he could.

The backs of her wedge-heeled shoes clacked against the skirting board.

Oh, God.

Behind him, James bent down, reared up.

When he raised his hand, it had the knife in it. It blurred as he brought it down.

Twisting as he went, Dad sagged to the tiles.

James placed a foot on Dad's back.

The wound made a sucking sound as he pulled the knife out.

Louise ran to the cellar door. She tried the handle but the door wouldn't budge and the key was missing.

Sobbing echoed on the other side.

Still holding the knife, James stepped over and used the blade to prise the door open.

The lock gave with a snap and a clatter and Harriet fell out.

The dividing line between light and darkness had never looked so stark as when Harriet tumbled over it. She got up and her ponytail jerked as her head twitched this way and that. She peered out through the oily smears blurring the lenses of her glasses with eyes that looked as if they'd been inflated several psi.

She looked at James' giant red tea-towel hand, their blood-splattered clothes and blood-speckled faces, and screamed. She looked at blood-roses blooming on the white net curtain, and screamed. She looked at the knife in James' hand, dripping with blood, and screamed. She looked at dead Dad with his gauged hand, his hanging-off fingers, his burnt back, the knife wound, the screwdriver sticking out of his ear, and screamed.

Louise stretched a hand out. "Harriet, Harriet, listen…" Her sister darted out of the kitchen and a moment later footsteps pounded up the stairs. "No, Harriet, come back. There's…"

A second's silence, then wave upon wave of screams from Mum's room.

Too late.

CHAPTER 24

Louise's tearing breathing and hammering heart had yet to catch up with her. Her cheeks burned up. Her brother's looked as if they'd been branded.

Why had it gone quiet upstairs?

They stumbled out into the hallway.

"Harriet," called Louise.

A flurry of stomps gathered pace towards them, till Harriet flew down the stairs.

Arms outstretched as if he'd been nailed there, James stood with his back to the front door.

Louise made a lunge for a handful of Hello Kitty T-shirt.

Harriet dodged out of reach with fly-quick movements.

They set off up the hallway after her.

In the kitchen, the back door hung wide open.

James got there first. Louise shadowed him out.

A swipe of wind caused her to lower her gaze for a moment.

She looked up and saw their sister, half turned away, at the bottom of the back garden.

Moss fringed the patio's paving stones and thick tufts of grass poked up between them. Bindweed had threaded itself through the borders. Keeping a coffin's length behind her brother, dragging her feet through shaggy grass, Louise moved as if without needing to lift her feet, glided, like a ghost. Amid the rain-like sound of the trees' leaves and the ratchety chatter of magpies, she passed the cherry tree that sported blossom once again, down to where Verge had died and where Harriet stood, with head inclined.

Louise no sooner reached out to her than red-rimmed eyes blazed around at them.

The waving of the trees sounded almost sea-like.

Louise lowered her hand.

A pulse throbbed inside her head, which she'd heard sometimes at night, on placing her ear on the pillow, yet never during the day before.

"You killed them," said Harriet, with a voice like a cracked bell. "You murdered Mummy and Daddy."

Louise shook her head. "No, darling, we didn't. Daddy killed Mummy."

"You killed Daddy."

"Well, Daddy was... Daddy was a bad man." Louise glanced at James, who nodded.

"No, Daddy was good. Everyone knows he was."

"Daddy was bad, sweetheart."

"No, that's you. Look. I read the note." She unfolded a piece of paper and held it out. "You wanted Mummy and Daddy dead." The flapping piece of paper showed James' crude depiction of their parents' execution. "See? You were going to kill them all along, with the man's help."

"Which man?"

"The man who was here."

Louise rubbed her knee. "What man?"

"The bad man, your friend."

God, she even knows about Nick.

"Harriet, he wasn't here. He never was."

"I heard him."

"That was Daddy you heard."

"Daddy doesn't talk like that. He had the voice of the Devil."

"Harriet, the only Devil is Dad," said James.

She turned to him. "And you killed all those women."

"No, Harriet," he said. "You've got it all wrong."

"Well, then why does Daddy's policeman friend want to talk to you about it?"

"Me?" Her brother's voice went all scratchy. "Why me?"

"And I've got the evidence." She held up the freezer bag containing the fragment from Riika's pashmina. "This was buried at the bottom of your rucksack."

"Oh, look, mini Miss Marple's solved the case." He laughed, harshly, as he bent forwards and raised a hand to his temple. The hand never got there. It made a jerky motion like jammed, juddering clockwork before veering off again. "Listen, I'm not being fitted up for what Dad did by one of his cronies."

Harriet pointed at them. "You're bad and you're evil."

"Oh, this is ridiculous," he said.

Hearing the mournful wail of a siren in the distance, Louise swung her head round, perpendicular to the source.

Instead of passing, it got steadily louder, nearer.

She turned back to Harriet, whose glasses glinted in one of the few stray beams of sunshine occasionally reaching them down here.

James was already looking at her. "You didn't?"

Harriet blinked and slowly backed away on pale thin legs, ending up just in front of the compost heap, knee-deep in nettles. In her hand—as Louise only now noticed—she clutched Mum's mobile.

Several sirens could now be heard, first on one side, then the other, until soon it seemed as if all the sirens in the city converged on them.

The nearest bings and bongs and whoops were just streets away.

"Harriet, quick." Louise stepped forward and stretched a hand out.

Witnessing the hair-trigger twitch of a Bambi leg, she desisted, and her arm flopped to her side.

She looked at James and he looked at her.

If they didn't run soon, all the machinery of the state—the police, the courts, the press—would be brought to bear on them.

She stepped over to him and wrapped her arms around his shoulders. He wrapped his around hers.

"She's right," Louise whispered. "We were going to do it, remember? We killed Dad and we were going to kill Mum too. We're guilty in thought if not in action."

"Hey, we only killed him." James held his tea-towel-wrapped hand up. "And even then in self-defense."

"With a little torture thrown in." She shook her head.

He lowered his voice. "But if our own sister won't believe us, how can we expect anyone else to?"

"We have to take that chance. If she won't come with us, we have to stay." She kneaded her brow. "And all those women... It's our fault. We should have been paying attention."

Her brother spread the fingers of his good hand. "My prints are on the knife that killed them. And Deverick won't want to believe, or everyone else to believe, that he could have been friends with a killer."

"I know. My prints are on the iron. I'm drenched in Mum's blood. But whatever happens, we owe it to her"—glancing in Harriet's direction—"to stay."

James' hand came up. Louise let her gaze drop. He rested it on her shoulder. "It's all going to come out. Everything. You know that, right?"

She looked up. "Yes."

"And the disgust reflex will kick in. They'll want us to be guilty. We'll look guilty, simply because of…"

He was right, of course. The stronger their kind of love—and theirs was adamantine—the more it would be reviled. The moral majority would take great pleasure in crushing it.

Steeped in sin.

That was the sort of phrase they'd use.

Steeped in it.

All it would probably take to separate her and her brother would be a few well-placed distortions.

Louise pointed at Harriet. "James, we're all she's got."

He nodded, slowly.

She knew he would do it for her if not for their sister.

They tilted their heads sideways, opposite ways, and—an interminable second later—she tasted his mouth.

For the last time?

Her tongue rooted around his.

"Eurgh," from Harriet.

Afterwards, a filament of saliva dangling between their faces broke.

James failed to wipe the spittle from his chin, so Louise did it for him.

"Meet me at the gates of Hell?" he said.

She didn't attempt anything so ambitious as a smile but wanted to tell him how much she loved him.

An ache of a pause.

She managed a nod.

Suddenly, he threw an arm up over his eyes.

When he removed it, she saw his smiling, crying face and somewhere inside she hemorrhaged, hemorrhaged.

The scream of sirens on the close—then vehicles screeched to a halt just the other side of the house.

Doors opened and slammed. Men and women shouted. Footsteps crunched. Someone pounded on the front door as the sirens went off one by one with a dying whine.

"You're a good girl, Harriet." Even though her heart felt as if it dangled at the end of a plumb-line descending to the very center of the Earth, Louise tried to sound vital-voiced. "You did the right thing and this is the only way we can try and make things up to you now. It probably won't seem a lot but, one day, when you love someone and can't bear to be apart from them even for a single second, you'll realize just how much we love you."

Taking one of James' hands, she squeezed it.

Their transport to Satan's Fan Club had finally arrived.

ABOUT THE AUTHOR

Mark Kirkbride lives in England. He is the author of *The Plot Against Heaven, Game Changers of the Apocalypse* and *Satan's Fan Club. Game Changers of the Apocalypse* was a semi-finalist in the Kindle Book Awards. His stories have appeared in *Under the Bed, Sci Phi Journal, Disclaimer Magazine, Flash Fiction Magazine, Titanic Terastructures* and *So It Goes: The Literary Journal of the Kurt Vonnegut Memorial Library.*

https://markkirkbride.com/

Curious about other Crossroad Press books? Stop by our website: http://crossroadpress.com
We offer quality writing
in digital, audio, and print formats.

Subscribe to our newsletter on the website homepage and receive a free eBook.